The Legend of James Jack

Zachary Jamison Allen

Allen Historical Press

This is a work of historical fiction. While it is based on historical events and figures, certain characters, events, and dialogue have been fictionalized for dramatic purposes. Any resemblance to actual persons, living or dead, beyond those explicitly based on historical figures, is purely coincidental.

The Legend of James Jack

ISBN: 9798218991661

Book Cover by ozonostudio

Printed in the United States of America

For permissions or inquiries, visit:
www.thelegendofjamesjack.com

Contents

To my mother for always encouraging my passions, to my father for his unwavering faith, to my wife for her steadfast love, to my sister for her loyal friendship, to my grandmother for sharing with me our heritage, and in memory of my grandfather, whose quiet strength supports me daily, I dedicate this book.

"That the Presbyterian ministers south of the Yadkin had been true patriots, no man in the country, or in the British army, pretended to deny. Their names were not unknown in the camp; and the pulpits of the seven churches poured forth the highest intellectual efforts in discussing the rights of man, and sustaining the sinking spirits of the distressed country..."

William Henry Foote, 1846

"The first voice raised in America to dissolve all connection with Great Britain came, not from the Puritians of New England, not from the Dutch of New York; not from the planters of Virginia; but from the Scotch Presbyterians of Mecklenburg County, North Carolina."

William Warren Sweet, 1936

Prologue
Concord, Massachusetts
April 19th, 1775

The morning mist clung to the dewy grass of the fields in Concord as the sun crested over the horizon, bathing everything in a golden glow.

Colonel John Parker coughed, speckling his handkerchief with blood, and steadied himself against a nearby oak tree. His militia of farmers and merchants stood at ragged attention before him, pitchforks and muskets in hand, their jaws set in determination. They looked onward with fearful resolve as the might of the British legion organized before them.

Parker straightened, squaring his shoulders against the pain in his chest. He would not show weakness now. Now was the moment for impossible courage.

"It's but a few hundred lobsterbacks," he said, forcing a grin. "Nothing we can't handle."

A nervous chuckle rippled through the ranks. Parker glanced over at William Diamond, the drummer boy who had followed them from Boston. Only twenty, but with a judicious soul, Diamond gave him a solemn nod.

Parker cleared his throat and spat, the bloody phlegm staining the grass. "We stand here today to defend our homes and our families." Parker took a large breath. "Though they seek to march on Boston, by God's defense, they shall not pass!"

A ragged cheer rose. Parker forced down any cough that came up through his diseased throat, determined to do nothing that would give pause to his men's courage.

Diamond raised his drumsticks and rapped out a sharp beat, the sound echoing across the field. The militia straightened, gripping their weapons tight.

Parker rested a hand on the hilt of his sword and gazed north, away from Boston, waiting. The lobsterbacks would come from the hill, and when they did, he and his men would be ready.

Across the field, a column of scarlet emerged from the trees, marching in crisp formation. At their head rode a British officer on a white stallion, surveying the scene with a disdainful eye. Colonel John Pitcairn. A portrait of military dignity and might.

Parker gripped his sword hilt tighter, yearning to greet his opponent with calm fury.

Behind Pitcairn stood hundreds of regulars, bayonets fixed to their Brown Bess muskets. Trained soldiers of the empire, all hardened by combat. In response to this scene, Parker glanced over his shoulder at the motley collection of farmers and tradesmen who made up his force. Most had never seen battle. At least three times as many British soldiers faced the Massachusetts militia, and no reinforcements were coming to save them. The odds could not have been bleaker.

Yet still his men stood firm, awaiting his order. Pride swelled in Parker's tuberculosis-ravaged chest, and the dying citizen-soldier turned away from the advancing enemy to speak to his men.

Parker raised his sword and called out, "Steady, men! Hold your fire!" His voice rang out, clear and strong. "Let them make the first move. Stand fast!"

A defiant shout rose from the militia. Parker watched Pitcairn closely, waiting. Parker's draws of breath harshly combined morning dew and blood.

Pitcairn raised a hand, halting his troops. An uneasy silence fell over the field as the two commanders stared each other down.

Parker's heart pounded in his chest. His fingers curled and uncurled around his sword hilt, slick with sweat. He struggled to keep his breathing steady, refusing to give Pitcairn the satisfaction of seeing him waver.

"Disperse, you damned rebels!" Pitcairn's voice boomed at last. He sat straight-backed on his horse, like the most refined portraits in a grand country home. "Lay down your arms and return to your homes, or you shall all hang as traitors!"

A low, angry murmur ran through the militia ranks. Parker clenched his jaw.

"We have committed no treason!" he shouted back. "We desire only to defend our rights as free Englishmen. 'Tis you who have betrayed the spirit of our laws and liberties, not us!"

Pitcairn's lips curled in a sneer.

A hush fell over the field. The lobsterbacks shifted uneasily but held their positions. All eyes followed Pitcairn, awaiting his response.

Time seemed to slow. The silence stretched on, fragile as spun glass, ready to shatter at a moment's notice. Parker's heart thudded in his chest. His fingers were numb around the hilt of his sword as the fate of nations balanced upon the joining of shaky hands and case-hardened steel.

Then, a sharp crack split the air. A puff of white and gray smoke rose into the distraught heavens above.

Chaos erupted as men on both sides fixed their rifles. Muskets roared up and down the line, volley after volley, until thick smoke completely obscured the field.

For a single moment in time, Parker stared in disbelief at the rapidly collapsing chaos and misery that now surrounded him.

Parker drew his sword and raised it high, shouting, "To arms, men! For liberty and freedom!"

A ragged cheer went up from the militia. Parker grinned fiercely through the blood in his mouth.

Additional ill-placed, red-hot rounds blazed through the early New England air, piercing the boyish flesh of volunteers.

The quick blood flow of young men, screaming cries of a terribly wounded animal, had paid the price of courage. The bodies of the volunteers collapsed lifelessly into the grass, still firm from the night's indifferent frost.

The lobsterbacks were now advancing, bayonets fixed. Parker's stomach churned at the carnage, but he steeled himself and plunged into the fray, slashing and parrying with his sword. "Hold the line!" he roared. "For God's sake, hold!"

The enemy flanked them. Pushed back, step by step, towards the sheltering trees. Parker hacked and stabbed like a man possessed, but for every redcoat that fell, two more of his own joined the mosaic of mutilated corpses littered in the field.

All the while the gunfire was deafening. Parker's lungs burned as he sucked in black smoke and the acrid tang of blood. His limbs felt leaden, each step harder than the last. Finally, with the last provision of strength left in his pathetic mortal vessel, Parker yelled to his surviving compatriots, "Fall back! Retreat!"

The remaining men did not need to be told twice. They turned and fled as the British cheered in triumph, leaving behind their dead and dying. And Parker, watching the lobsterbacks over the sights of his musket, swore a silent oath of vengeance.

The Battle of Concord was over. The British would fail to subjugate the proud Bostonians upon which they marched, but it did not matter. The shots of revolution had been fired, and there was none who could undo them.

Chapter 1: Among These Hills
Mecklenburg County, North Carolina
May 19th, 1775

The fading light painted the treetops gold as a lone rider's horse carved a steady rhythm through the tangled wilderness of colonial North Carolina. Nestled among timeworn pine, oak, and sycamore trees, the scarcely populated community of Charlotte stood as a fledgling outpost in an enduring frontier. As Henry Miller, the young express rider from Boston, raced his steed down the desolate winds of the Great Wagon Road, the evening breeze of Mecklenburg County seemed to propel him further into her fold.

Henry had ridden from Boston, his steed weary from an eight-hundred-mile journey, but there was no time for rest. Henry bore upon his soul the heavy burden of his announcement: that on the sacred fields of Concord and Lexington, the British had bled America's sons. With each beat of his heart and each stride of his horse, the determined Bostonian rode for the final stop on his long voyage.

For it was in this frontier wilderness that the ever-weakened Wagon Road ceased. Indeed, "Old Mecklenburg" was the end of the trail.

As he traveled along the dirt path, Henry weaved through the dense foliage and out-stretched branches. After several minutes of traversing across the rugged terrain, Henry came across a single cabin on the side of the road. Weather and wear had aged its wooden walls. Next to the home, a small garden thrived under the care of an elderly man whose back appeared bent from years of labor.

"Excuse me, sir!" Henry called out, his voice cracking from the sudden break in his day of unspoken journeying.

The old man turned from his cabbage shoots and towards the unfamiliar visitor. His whisps of white hair glistened like ice under a bright sun, and his dark brown eyes matched those of the steed he now surveyed. Centered between his eyes, full of curiousity, was the man's bulbous red nose, which appeared to wince as the aroma of fresh vegetables gave way to an unbathed traveler.

At last, the elderly gardner offered his response.

"Ah, good evening to you, youngin. The name is Tom Jamison and this humble abode is my own. What brings you to Mecklenburg?"

"Sir, I am Henry Miller," replied the young rider, dismounting his horse with practiced ease. "I've come all the way from Boston, delivering urgent news to all towns along the route."

"Your journey's been long, young Henry," Tom replied quickly. "What can I do for you?"

"I must deliver this message, which I have been sent to share with your townsfolk. Pray tell Master Jamison, where might I find the town square?"

"Town square?" Tom chuckled, rubbing his chin thoughtfully. "Well, now we don't have a proper one, as such. But what we do have is Pat Jack's Tavern." A wry smile played upon his lips as he continued, "Mind you, given the hour, I reckon most of 'em will be in high spirits already, if you catch my drift."

Nodding in understanding, Henry mounted his horse again, determination burning anew within him.

"Would you be so kind as to direct me to this tavern?" Henry asked the helpful guide.

"You will carry on down Trade Street," Tom instructed, his voice tinged with the warmth of a seasoned storyteller. "There'll be a two-story wooden structure that stands tall and proud, its sign painted with the brightest yellow hues you ever saw. A gathering of merry souls will make their presence known, and I reckon you won't have any trouble finding it."

"Much obliged, sir," Henry replied, gratefully nodding as he tipped his tricorn hat. Henry's steed snorted beneath him, and the steady fanfare of hooves upon dirt resumed.

As Henry ventured forth, his surroundings seemed to burst into life, each subtle detail coming to life like an artist's brushstroke on canvas. The road was stretched before him, made smooth by countless hooves and footsteps, while the trees swayed gently overhead, their leaves whispering secrets to one another in the breeze.

Henry's thoughts teemed with anticipation, his heart pounded like a battle drum in his chest. As he rode further down the withering Great Wagon Road, the surrounding landscape grew more populous. To his left, a wood and stone church, no larger than a smokehouse, stood as a testament to the settlers' faith—a plain and unassuming Presbyterian "meeting house," as they were called. It bore no ostentatious embellishments, save for its wooden cross and the lasting imprints of the men who knelt before it.

The homes he passed were modest in their construction—small wooden dwellings with varying degrees of refinement. Some boasted stone chimneys and porches that hinted at a touch of prosperity, while others remained plain. Pens dotted the landscape, filled with livestock: pigs rooting for sustenance, chickens pecking at the earth, and horses grazing lazily as the day drew near.

Henry's eyes then fell upon a tall wooden building that stirred memories of Boston. This building, resembling a silo, was unmistakably a magazine for storing guns, powder, and other weapons. Its presence cut through the idyllic setting, a stark reminder of the war to come.

At last the tavern came into view, illuminated by the warm glow of candlelight that spilled out onto the street like honey. The two-story wooden structure beckoned weary travelers and jovial townsfolk alike, its brightly painted sign swaying gently in the breeze.

"PAT JACK'S TAVERN"

A chorus of laughter and animated conversation emanated from within, inviting all who approached to join in the camaraderie.

Henry dismounted his horse, feeling the weight of his task settle firmly upon his shoulders. He breathed in deeply, taking in the scents of tobacco smoke, ale, and the promise of a hearty meal that wafted from the open windows of Pat Jack's Tavern. As he climbed the creaking steps and opened the door, a flood of sound overwhelmed his senses, rivaling even the choirs of Heaven.

Above the joyous strains of a fiddler playing a lively reel and the sound of women laughing, members of this great extended family occupied every inch of floor space in the dimly lit tavern. Men sat across from one another, rolling dice and holding decks of cards, while others filled their cigars with powder and passed a candle around the table to light them. As Henry awkwardly tried to shift towards the center of the crowd, a portly man raised his tankard in greeting.

"Evenin', stranger! You must try Margaret's pot pie! Madam found her way to some fine chicken!"

"G'Evening," Henry briefly replied. His focus turned away from the man and toward seeking a means to announce his news. Henry returned to the jolly greeter. "I come from Boston, and I have news to share with your townsfolk."

The man washed down his mouthful of chicken with some ale before speaking with a smile so large it appeared as if his mustache was performing a jig, "Ah, then ye best make it known!" the man declared. "We're all ears 'round here." The portly man rose from his barrel seat and, with the clamor of a lion, yelled above the cheerful sounds of the tavern, "Folks! We've got ourselves a Boston news-bearer in our presence! Claims he's got something important to share."

The sudden silence caused Henry to blush as all the concerned eyes of the crowded tavern turned to look at him.

"Please, gather 'round," Henry implored, scanning the room for a vantage point to address the assembly. His eyes alighted on an unoccupied table near the center, and with a nod of gratitude to the fiddle player–who paused mid-tune–Henry hoisted himself up, his boots scraping against the hard wooden surface.

"Thank you," Henry began, his voice carrying above the indistinct murmur of conversation that had resumed in his brief hesitation. "My name is Henry Miller, and I come to you from Boston, bearing urgent tidings of events that have transpired there."

"Friends," he continued, his voice having now found its grounding, "approximately one month ago today, the Massachusetts Militia exchanged fire with the forces of the British Army. Many of our brothers died fighting to defend and chase the invaders from Boston."

The clamor of voices and laughter in Pat Jack's Tavern had gone out entirely.

Henry continued, his words weaving a vivid tapestry of the events that had unfolded in faraway Massachusetts. The air grew thick with tension, as if the room held its breath, waiting for the next revelation.

"On the morning of April 19th," he proclaimed, "the British marched on Lexington and Concord. The British attempted to seize our arms, powder, and provisions, but faced resistance."

A hush had now fallen over the tavern, broken only by the crackling fire in the hearth and the creaking of floorboards beneath the weight of ready listeners. Their faces bore the marks of mounting dread, their eyes wide with disbelief and fear.

"That day claimed many lives," Henry continued, his tone somber. "Good men, fathers, sons, and brothers, all fallen to defend their homes and rights."

A murmur rippled through the crowd, a growing tide of anger and indignation that swept away any lingering doubts or hesitations. As one, they turned to face each other, their voices a cacophony of outrage and determination.

Before Henry could continue, one man lunged from his seat, shouting, "Enough!" slamming his fist down upon a table with such force that the tankards rattled and jumped. "Those wretched redcoats have now opened fire on colonists a second time!" The memories of the Boston Massacre stirred in his mind.

"Aye!" yelled another man from across the tavern. Patrons of the tavern now turned away from Henry and inward among themselves to discuss the news with growing passion.

"What news is there from the Congress? Are we at war?" one woman in the tavern asked.

Henry replied, "No, nobody has yet taken such action."

The minds of the tavern then turned towards themselves and their home. "If the British will make war with the rebels in Boston, who will stop them from making war on us?!"

The warm hues of the tavern had turned to gray; its joys now turned to wrath and fear.

"Must we sit idly and wait for slaughter?! No!" yelled one of the many men raised from their table. Red manes complemented by ale-induced red cheeks, the tavern became ablaze with violent calls and guttural discontent.

"God damns the bastard king! He will not spill another era of Scots blood!" cried another as the room erupted into a tempest of fervent assent.

Henry was taken aback by the responses, wondering if the potent presence of ale played any role. For at no other stop along his route, had the fury and rage been as it was in brave Charlotte.

Amidst the uproar, as passionate voices shouted for action and retribution, an imposing figure rose from the sea of Presbyterian patriots. Thomas Polk, an elder statesman whose wisdom and leadership had long guided his people, stood tall - his gray eyes alight with a determination that pierced through the commotion.

"Silence, my friends!" he roared, his voice booming like thunder, instantly capturing the attention of those around him. "Forsake your panicked fever! We must act, but we must act wisely! Let us call forth an emergency meeting of our county militia." Thomas looked over the scattered tavern-goers with a steadying grace and said assuringly, "To determine our course in these dark times."

The tumultuous wave of voices receded, replaced by an undercurrent of whispers as the patrons eagerly agreed to Polk's directive. Henry made eye contact with a man behind the bar counter as the room vacated. James Jack, the handsome and mild-eyed manager of the tavern, had been watching the events unfold with equal parts trepidation and resolve, with his wife Margaret at his side. James smiled gently at Henry and walked from around the counter towards him.

Henry stepped down from the table to meet him.

"Mr. Miller," James began, "I am James Jack, and this is my wife, Margaret. We are honored to welcome you into our home." While still shaking James' hand, James' wife, Margaret, brought Henry's attention away; her curly blonde hair and honey-brown eyes were a pleasant reprieve for the weary traveler.

James resumed, "Please allow us to provide you with lodging for the night. The upper rafters have several vacant rooms, and my wife shall escort you there shortly."

"Thank you kindly," Henry replied, his gratitude mingled with exhaustion.

As this exchange concluded, Thomas Polk strode over to James, his graceful demeanor replaced by an uncensored urgency. "James, we shall need your help at the courthouse," he said, his tone brooking no argument. "You are our keepers of keys - your presence is essential."

James inclined his head in acknowledgment, his mind barely able to process the rapid-moving sequence.

"Lead the way, Mr. Polk," James said resolutely, lifting his head to meet Thomas' commanding gaze. James' voice was an infusion of a bold but anxious servant.

With that, James stepped out into the fading twilight, joining the procession of men who marched purposefully toward the modest wooden county courthouse. The clatter of their boots on the trodden path echoed through the stillness, as the leaves sang with a watchful union over Old Mecklenburg.

Chapter 2: By Candlelight, Our Fury

B eneath a sable sky, James Jack stood steadfast on the steps of the county courthouse, keys glistening in his hand like silver daggers. The night draped around him as if attempting to conceal their bold conspiracy. James watched with quiet intensity as over two dozen men ascended the tattered steps and crossed the threshold into the unassuming, one-story wooden building. Shadows danced with each flicker of their bronze lanterns, each glimpse revealing faces etched with lines of conviction.

"Evening, James," greeted the familiar figures, each extending calloused hands in fellowship. The dignified Alexander clan came forward: their patriarch Abraham, whose gnarled fingers bore the testament of years spent building their family; Adam, Charles, Ezra, John McKnitt, and Hezekiah followed behind him. The soldier-like John Davidson, William Kennon, Neil Morrison, John Phiffer, and Zacheus Wilson followed closely thereafter, each engulfed in a steel of tempered fortitude.

"Good to see you, James," spoke Robert Irwin, a man of gentler material. James' long-time friend clapped him on the shoulder with an air of solidarity. Several other unfamiliar faces emerged from the darkness and proceeded through the courthouse doors.

With a firm nod, James closed the door behind him as he let the silence of the empty hallway surround him. James inhaled a deep breath and began his walk down the short corridor toward the room where Charlotte's elders had gone to convene.

Upon entering, he found a scene that mirrored his own soul's restlessness. The candles that adorned the long table dropped hot wax onto the stained oak wood. In the multiple windows along the walls, more candles burned, their gleam mingling with the faint moonlight that filtered through the panes, creating an uneasy illumination.

"James, I'm glad you could join us," said Abraham Alexander, seated at the head of the table. Abraham's handsome blue coat stood in stark contrast to his weathered frame of nearly eight decades. For generations, Abraham had led the Alexander clan and, by extension, a large number of wandering Scots-Irish to their promised land here in the desolate Carolina wilderness.

James replied, "Thank you, sir," and with a respectful nod, went to take his seat.

The remaining militia members were on their feet, pacing around the room like caged lions. Legions of concerned and anxious voices piled atop one another until Abraham Alexander summoned his familiar call.

"Enough!" he shouted. "Take your seats, gentlemen."

His command sliced through the discord, and the room settled into silence as the men found their places around the table. Thomas Polk found his seat next to James. James turned to his left to hear Abraham beside him say: "Let us begin with a prayer."

As one, the men bowed their heads, their bodies struggling to stay still upon command. James closed his eyes, his heart pounding as he listened to the words that flowed from Abraham's lips.

"Dearest God, Father of the covenant, and sculptor of mankind, we beseech Thee to guide us in righteousness and inform our decisions as we seek to resolve ourselves from oppressors and tyrants. Grant us Your wisdom, O Lord. Be our compass and our guide, our shield and tower. Amen."

"Brethren," Abraham began, his voice firm and focused, "the violence in Massachusetts marks the second time British hands have spilled the blood of our brothers. We cannot stand idly by while our fellow colonists suffer under the yoke of oppression. We must take action."

As the gravity of Abraham's words settled upon the gathering, William Kennon rose from his seat, his face contorted with indignation. "Aye, we must take action," he declared. "The men of Concord are dead because they stood in between the Army of King George and a stockpile of weapons which they collected." He paused, momentarily frightened by the truths his tongue produced.

"The British authorities already look upon us backcountry citizens with skepticism and disdain—what should happen if they come for our arms and munitions?" Fear had now overtaken William's message. His voice quivered at the delivery.

"Aye!" The chorus of agreement came from the other men, with their simmering outrage fueling a fire that could no longer be contained. "We will not tolerate this!"

Abraham's eyes swept the room, capturing each man's gaze as if to solidify their collective conviction.

James Jack listened intently as each man gave his peace. The rising heat in his heart confirmed what everyone present already knew—this would not be an easy fire to extinguish. He listened as Zacheus Wilson rose to speak, his voice tinged with bitterness and determination.

"Let us not forget," Zacheus began, "the king's blatant disregard for our Presbyterian faith." For this remark, the militia members all murmured in agreement. Zacheus continued, "The Parliament's Vestry and Marriage Acts imposed fines on our ministers who dared to marry outside the Church of England!"

Without waiting for the echoes of Zacheus's words to fade, Neil Morrison stood, his eyes ablaze with frustration. "And let us also not forget," he thundered, "the king's revocation of our college's charter! He damns all who seek to escape the chains of ignorance!" The outrage in Neil's voice was contagious, now spreading like wildfire throughout the assembled men.

James could feel the room's fervor intensifying, the air growing thick with tension. As he looked around, he saw their rage strengthening. What had begun as a condemnation of violence in faraway Massachusetts had now become personal.

"Enough is enough!" cried another Ezra Alexander, pounding his fist upon the table. The others joined in, their voices rising in a chorus of defiance.

"Indeed!" echoed another, this time, John Davidson. "We will not be silenced! We will not bow to tyranny!"

"Freedom or death!" shouted John Phiffer, his voice tremulous with emotion.

Their fury had become beyond restraint. The large and heavy nails of each floorboard seemed to splinter and crack beneath the pressure of the rebellious rogues. Candles burned with ferocity into the dead of night.

It was then that Thomas Polk, who had previously remained silent, rose from his seat to the right of James; his voice powerful like the blast of a cannon as he declared, "If the king and his bloody redcoats want to silence our sermons, muffle our movements, and water our fields with innocent blood - then may he try to bleed us as freemen, no longer cattle to slaughter!"

His words struck like a lightning bolt, galvanizing the men into a torrent of applause, their hearts aflame with the fire of rebellion. James joined the cheers with something in between a gasp and a laugh as their collective wave of bold protestations grew greater by the minute.

"Brothers!" cried Charles Alexander amidst the uproar, his voice rising above the din. "We are not Englishmen but heirs to centuries of rebellion, ostracization, adaptation, and survival! From the king's war in Scotland to our bloody settlements in Ireland to our banishments in New England," Charles paused, his black hair wildly aside. "Have we not all followed in the steps of men like Alexander Craighead?!"

Alexander Craighead, the decades-deceased forefather and early settler of Mecklenburg, still served as his flock's spiritual guide. His ghost remained to haunt those opposed to his fervor and cause.

"Men," Charles' brother Hezekiah continued, his eyes inflamed with principle, "We have nowhere left to go - our stand happens here on this soil, or it happens nowhere!"

The tide of their fervor swept James away, his heart pounding as if it wanted to escape his chest and join the chorus echoing through the hallowed halls.

Abraham Alexander's resounding voice silenced the room amidst the babel of expressions. The elder Alexander unfurled a blank piece of parchment and brandished an ink quilt, his hands careful not to spoil the precious script. "Gentleman of the militia," he began, addressing them all with solemnity, "the time is now to place our grievances to pen, and to declare ourselves..." He paused, allowing the consequence of the moment to settle onto each man's consciousness.

The air hung thick with anticipation, a tangible tension that begged release. Then, Thomas Polk, emboldened by the passion that stirred within him, lunged from his seat to finish Abraham's remark: "Independent of that pig King George, his legion of dandy prats, and all authority henceforth!"

James Jack's heart hammered in his chest as a grand smile shot across his face in amusement and amazement at this unstoppable spell of united courage.

The shouts of "aye" swept through the room like a wildfire, lifting the spirits of all present. James rejoiced in the energy vibrating around him as the men clapped and laughed, their voices one in a symphony of defiance. "Independent!" hollered Robert Irwin, his cheeks now completely red from laughter and jubilation.

"Write! Write Abraham!" cried Neil Morrison, his voice floating through the single chamber. "Let this whole earth be witness to our resolve!"

Abraham Alexander nodded gravely, his eyes alight with purpose as he took up his quill and dipped it in ink. The men rose from their seats, now coming to the head of the table to crowd around James, Thomas, and Abraham; each of the militia's men was eager to contribute to this monumental task.

"Begin with our grievances," suggested John McKnitt Alexander, leaning over Abraham's shoulder, his eyes narrowing in concentration. "I declare that we have suffered long under the English yoke of oppression."

"Indeed," agreed Zacheus Wilson, his brow furrowed. "And make clear our intent: that we will no longer be subject to the whims of some distant monarch, but will instead govern ourselves, united in common cause."

James watched on, hardly able to believe what he saw as Abraham's quill danced across the parchment. With each stroke of ink, the men pushed Mecklenburg into uncharted territory.

"Our declaration must also plead for unity," William Kennon declared, his voice hoarse from the night's fury, "for we cannot stand alone in this struggle. We must join with our fellow colonists and stand together."

"Indeed," agreed Abraham, his hand steady as he continued to write. "We shall make it known that we are prepared to pledge our lives, our fortunes, and our most sacred honor to this noble cause and that we shall not make rest until our conquest is complete."

James looked out the courthouse window into a vast black midnight sky as the last words were set to parchment. Did Charlotte's sleeping women and children know what had been done? Did the whispering trees now share rumors of a great rebellion? Did the people across the vast American continent hear the cries of freedom ringing loudly from the Carolina backcountry? As the wind swept through the four walls of the courthouse, James pondered these questions, as he found himself one among a company of outcasts turned traitors to their empire and king.

As the hours wore on, the candles burned low. Yet despite the late hour, the men of the Mecklenburg Militia showed no signs of fatigue; their passion for freedom seemed to outpace all physical considerations.

At long last, Abraham Alexander placed the quill upon the table as his aged hands gripped the edges of the parchment, handling it as though it was the most precious of treasures. He cleared his throat and read aloud the words born from their mutual cause:

"Resolved, that whoever directly or indirectly abetted, or, form or manner, countenanced the unchartered and dangerous invasion of our rights, as claimed by Great Britain, is an enemy to this country–to America–and to the inherent and inalienable rights of man."

James Jack watched in awed silence as Abraham continued,

"Resolved, 'That we the citizens of Mecklenburg county, do hereby dissolve the political bands which have connected us to the Mother Country, and hereby absolve ourselves from all allegiance to the British Crown, and abjure all political connection, contract, or association, with that nation, who have wantonly trampled on our rights and liberties — and inhumanly shed the innocent blood of American patriots at Lexington."

As one, the men erupted into cheers, their voices a triumphant chorus that echoed throughout the small courthouse. James felt a shiver of exhilaration run down his spine.

"Resolved," Abraham raised his voice to a resounding crescendo, *"That we do hereby declare ourselves a free and independent people, who are, and of right ought to be, a sovereign and self–governing Association, under the control of no power other than that of our God and the General Government of the Congress; to the maintenance of which independence, we solemnly pledge to each other, our mutual cooperation, our lives, our fortunes, and our most sacred honor."*

"Aye!" echoed the men around the table, their voices strong and united. As the rallying cries filled the air, James clenched his fists, his knuckles white with intensity.

Abraham Alexander continued to read from the parchment held firmly in his hand. *"Resolved, that as we now acknowledge the existence and control of no law or legal officer, civil or military, within this country, we do hereby ordain and adopt, as a rule of life, all, each and every of our former laws, wherein, nevertheless, the Crown of Great Britain never can be considered as holding rights, privileges, immunities, or authority therein."*

"Here, here!" cried out John McKnitt Alexander, his strong features set in defiance. The room filled with an agreement as the men rose from their seats, fists clenched with determination. Abraham's voice echoed as he announced the final stanza of the declaration:

"Resolved, That it is also further decreed, that all, each and every military officer in this county, is hereby reinstated to his former command and authority, he acting conformably to these regulations. And that every member present of this delegation shall henceforth be a civil officer, a Justice of the Peace, in the character of a 'Committee-man,' to issue process, hear and determine all matters of controversy, according to said adopted laws, and to preserve peace, and union, and harmony, in said county," Abraham looked up from the parchment, and in a moment stared upon James, who now stood opposite from him across the old wooden table — *"and to use every exertion to spread the love of country and fire of freedom throughout America until a more general and organized government be established in this province."*

The men erupted into cheers, chants, jeers, and cries of celebration. At last, the senior-bodied Abraham rose from his seat and, with a great thud of his beech wood cane, brought the men's attention to focus one last time: "Gentlemen, "he proclaimed powerfully, "this declaration cannot survive if we contain it solely within our frontier borders."

The men stood in silence, every eye fixed on Abraham as he continued, "this declaration must be read before the Congress for acknowledgment of our resolution, aid to our cause, and comradery in the war; we will insist the Congress join us in this great battle for independence!"

The militiamen looked at one another and murmured their agreement, all sharing solemn nods of affirmation. While seated across from his friends, the gentle-natured Robert Irwin and the studious Hezekiah Alexander, James Jack searched his colleagues' faces for reassurance and comfort as they searched his face for the same. The prospect of extending their fiery rhetoric beyond the forested borders of the backcountry posed a sudden and harsh grounding of their spirits.

"Brothers," Abraham declared, "we need a courier to carry this declaration to Philadelphia. A brave soul who will ride with haste." Abraham emphasized: "this courier must evade British detection and keep our conspiracy secret and safe until it may be delivered into the hands of the Congress." He looked around the room, his gaze unwavering, as he asked, "who among you will volunteer for this task?"

Silence had now engulfed the room, broken only by the sound of men retaking their seats in the plain wooden chairs. The silence persisted until, all at once, a chorus of excuses pierced it. "I am far too recognizable," said one man, his voice wavering with apprehension. "If I carry it, seeking regulars will surely apprehend me."

Another man chimed in, his voice laced with regret, "I do not know the road well enough to traverse it."

James looked around at the familiar faces of his fellow countrymen, each offering honest and fair reasons why they could not take on this monumental responsibility. James could understand their reluctance–the journey was fraught with danger, and the consequences of failure would be dire.

"Is there no one among us who will bear this burden?" Abraham implored, his voice tinged with desperation.

The dimly lit room swelled with excuses like a gathering storm threatening to consume all hope. Every voice seemed to echo with a subtle sense of shame. In the early hours of that spring morning, James watched the fire of revolution prepare to die meekly.

Tensions swelled one last time as excuses began to temper on accusations of cowardice until at last, James rose from his seat.

"Enough!" James cried out, his voice crossing through the men now seated. The rumblings ceased abruptly, every eye now fixed on him as he stood alone, the candlelight casting a tall shadow of the youthful husband and father. With genuine reverence, the tavern owner lifted his brown tricorn hat, revealing his dirty blonde hair atop his head, and placed the hat on the table before proclaiming,

"I will carry the declaration to the Congress."

James Jack exchanged glances with his friends and companions, each sitting with mouths partially agape. James breathed in deeply before continuing,

"I am a merchant by trade and know the route. I am indistinct; they will have no reason to stop me."

Cold sobriety replaced the drunken warmth of contagious courage, and for an eternal moment, time seemed to freeze. Each of the militia's men looked upon James, who continued to stand alone. Concern and admiration were etched onto the faces of James' co-conspirators. Then, slowly, emotion flickered in their eyes: relief, gratitude, and an ember of courage reignited by James' bold enlistment.

"May God bless you on your journey, James," Abraham intoned solemnly. "May your courage carry our prayers for victory and freedom."

The room erupted once more into cheers and fervent well-wishes. As James stood tall, he turned to face Mr. Thomas Polk, who stood to meet James at eye level. The gray-eyed statesman placed a hand upon James' shoulder and asked him quietly, "James, are you sure you're ready for this?"

Before James could respond, he turned back to see his many compatriots hurry from across the room to embrace him, each wearing a smile of pride and relief. James stood humbly, unable to do much but smile back at the men.

"James," Abraham's voice re-emerged to finish Thomas' question: "Are you certain you wish to accept this call? The road to Philadelphia is long and untamed, and though you were just a boy when your father, Pat, brought you down the Great Wagon Road, your memory may recall its many hazards. Soldiers, spies, and thieves beset its path." Abraham looked down at the parchment paper, inked with words of treasonous declaration. "Revealing the contents of this declaration, which we crafted here in Mecklenburg, will kill you if those who oppose our cause learn of them."

"James, I must know. Do you accept this mission?"

James met Abraham's searching gaze. James could see the earliest glimpses of the dawn breaking from within the courtroom's walls. With a spirit of courage that James could not place, he cocked his head and spoke before Abraham, his friends, colleagues, and co-conspirators alike:

"I do."

"Then it is done," Abraham declared, taking up his ink quill with a sense of purpose that reverberated throughout the chamber. With deliberate strokes, he added one last section to the Mecklenburg Declaration, sealing their collective fate:

"Resolved — That a copy of these resolutions be transmitted by express to the President of the Continental Congress assembled in Philadelphia, to be laid before that body."

With the declaration complete, the room swelled one final time as the long night came to a close, renewed with purpose and thanksgiving. Each man clasped hands, their voices raised in fervent prayers.

"Godspeed, James Jack!" cried Robert Irwin, his hand gripping James' shoulder firmly. "May the wind be at your back, and Providence guide you on this journey!"

"Take heart, my friend!" chimed Hezekiah Alexander, his eyes alight with hope.

A deafening roar erupted from the assembly, their voices melding into a singular cry of defiance that shattered the dawn's stillness. As the first rays of sunlight pierced the windows, casting golden beams across the worn wooden floor, James felt a surge of courage coursing through his veins.

"Here's to Charlotte!" cried John McKnitt Alexander, raising his tankard in salute. "And here's to her greatest hero, James Jack!"

"James Jack!" echoed the gathered men, their voices melding into an anthem that refused to entertain exhaustion.

The chanting of his name became part of the muted noise, as James watched Abraham roll together the declaration for safekeeping. With a last embrace by his brothers-in-arms, James shuffled through the crowd of patriots to step down the short hallway, and onto the tattered steps of the unassuming one-story wooden courthouse. A peaceful sun crested the horizon, and James looked up into Heaven, courting nothing but a prayer to God, that He remains forever "the help of the helpless."

Chapter 3: Breaking the Covenant

This darkness was different. It was not the wide vastness of a midnight sky over rows of crops, nor the suffocating swallow of a cellar when the door becomes accidentally closed behind you. This darkness appeared fast and then fled rapidly, as if the shadows on the other side of this off-white wagon tarp danced with malice. Unmistakable were the noises. The lullaby of the weary traveler was often the rhythmic creaking of wooden wheels over coarse earth, interrupted only by the occasional clashing of wood against metal rims and the breaking of twigs and branches.

The next clamoring of noise was deeply familiar and comforting for the young observer, still tucked beneath the beige cover of the wagon's tarp - it was the ever recognizable sound of a father dispelling shadows and constructing remedies. It was impossible for James to distinguish if the warmth he felt against his skin came from the wool blanket in his bed, or the dry canvas of the wagon which carried him as a child. Nor was it possible for James to place if he laid between the guard of familiar walls or the gaze of uncharted wilderness, for in the presence of his father's assuring voice, the safety of home was inseparable.

In this unknown state of being, James listened with mild interest and regular pacificity as the men of the convoy, led by his father, used nature's strength against it as men of stone pulled a large tree out of their path.

Then, the young James began to float, and the feeble boy drifted not around but through the lengths of the wagon's tarp, now damp and bitterly cold to the touch.

James was kneeling in the mud, and laid before him was an absence of everything that had brought him to his place of contended comfort. They pulled the tree away and pushed it into the ditch, running parallel to the path.

The father, the mother, the wagon and her parched wings, the voices and the touch—they were gone. The tree was rolled away, and now all that remained was a frigid boy and a devouring forest.

James' body bolted straight up, as he looked down to discover the length of his frame had been without the bed's blanket and its warmth. Next to James laid his wife Margaret, her body wrapped in a warm cocoon, and her chest rising and falling softly in a tranquil rhythm. It was a fleeting moment of peace before the shrill cry of their infant son pierced the morning air.

James stirred, his heart heavy with the burden of unspoken truths. He rose from the bed; the floorboards creaking beneath him as he made his way to the cradle where young Patrick lay, red-faced and wailing.

"Good mornin', my love," came the sleepy murmur of Margaret, her voice interwoven with remnants of dreams. She rolled over, strands of golden hair framing her face like a halo.

"Good mornin'," James replied, attempting to keep his voice steady as he scooped up his infant son. The child's cries softened into whimpers. Margaret's eyes followed James, but she did not inquire about the meeting that had transpired the previous night. Though the question lingered between them, James felt a knot tighten within his chest, for he yearned to share the dangerous journey that lay ahead but could not yet find the courage.

"Everthin' alright?" Margaret asked, her brow furrowed slightly with concern as she gazed upon her husband.

"Aye, all is well," James lied, his eyes betraying a flicker of uncertainty. In truth, the monumental task entrusted to him consumed his thoughts. A burden he would bear alone until it was right to reveal it.

He turned his attention to baby Patrick, whose tiny fists clenched and unclenched as he nestled against his father's chest. James marveled at the featherweight smile that accompanied his soft giggle.

"Rest now, Margaret," James whispered to his wife, who remained comfortable atop their primitive mattress; filled with corn husk and horse hair.

With a nod, she closed her eyes, and James was, for a brief and terrible moment, left alone with his thoughts. Quickly, he turned to embrace his daughter Cynthia, who stood timidly by her mother's bedside. James' heart swelled with love as he bent down and enveloped her tiny form in a warm embrace.

"Good morning, 'blueberry'," James said, ensuring Cynthia heard her nickname laced with affection.

Cynthia giggled, returning the embrace. Her tiny five-year-old arms barely encircled his neck. As he straightened, James retrieved his coat and boots from nearby hooks, and donned them before turning to descend the home's steps.

James turned to see his wife now playing with his daughter atop the bed, while baby Patrick slept contently. His eyes lingered for a while on the peaceful scene before stepping out of their sanctuary.

He descended the staircase, entering the tavern's main room. The contrast between the clamorous revelry of the night before and the hushed stillness that now permeated the space was striking. Shafts of sunlight filtered through the dusty windows, casting white beams across the empty tables and chairs. A sense of tranquility settled over him like a warm shawl, though it did little to quell the turmoil within his soul.

James moved toward the back door, his footsteps muted by the worn wooden planks beneath him. He stepped out into the cool morning air, the earthy scent of freshly turned soil and dew-kissed grass filling his nostrils. Before him laid his humble garden, a labyrinth of corn, beans, cauliflower, and cotton.

Along the edge of the garden stood the chicken coop, its inhabitants clucking softly as they pecked at the ground. With a small wicker basket cradled in the crook of his arm, James walked purposefully towards the coop. As he approached, the chickens scattered, their feathers ruffled with mild annoyance. He could not help but smile at their antics.

"Good mornin', ladies," he murmured softly, the words barely more than a whisper upon the breeze.

He reached into the coop, his hands deftly searching for eggs among the warm straw. He felt the cool smoothness of each one as he carefully cradled them in his palms.

Upon re-entering the tavern, he set the basket of eggs down on the counter with great care. James was desperate for a distraction and an occupation of his hands and mind. He wandered down the hall of the tavern, his footsteps again muted and silent.

James arrived at an attached room, its doorway standing wide open. He hesitated for a moment, then stepped inside.

As James entered the dimly lit room, a faint scent of aged wood and lavender tickled his nostrils. The morning light filtered through the thin curtains, casting a hazy glow upon the figures of his elderly parents, Patrick and Lilas Jack. His mother, Lilas, lay upon the bed, her frail form wrapped in a quilted blanket, while his father sat at an old oak dresser, carefully shaving the stubborn remnants of his gray beard.

"Good mornin' to ye both," James greeted them, his voice gentle and warm as he approached their bedside.

"Ah, good mornin', my lad," Patrick replied, his Irish brogue thick with age. Lilas whispered a soft greeting from the confines of her bed, her eyes distracted and preoccupied.

Patrick paused in his grooming and studied James for a moment, his twinkling eyes taking in his son's disheveled appearance. With a sly grin, he remarked, "ye look like ye've been dragged backwards through the hedge, James. Did ye wrestle with the chickens this morn?"

James chuckled at his father's jest. He ran a hand through his tousled hair and sighed, "aye, perhaps I should clean up a bit."

"Ye ought to. T'day's the Lord's day, and we best not appear as rough as our conscience!" Patrick quipped. He resumed his grooming with steady hands, as he gazed with focus into the scratched and stained mirror.

"Right you are, Father," James conceded, allowing a natural grin on his face as he turned to leave the room.

Before leaving his parents to continue getting through their morning routines, James glanced around the small, hoary room that the two had made a storied bedroom. James always enjoyed taking in the many trinkets and mementos that adorned the room's shelves and walls. Patrick and Lilas' journey from the plantations in Ireland to the colony in Pennsylvania, and then down the Great Wagon Road to Mecklenburg County, was shared by many of the townsfolk and their elders. It was that pilgrimage, and its many trials and tribulations, that united their people as one.

Leaving his parents in the glow of their shared laughter, James turned and carried on down the hallway. As he neared the bedroom, wails filled the air—a chorus of discontent heralding his return. He found Margaret, her youthful presence and light smile an ever-present cure for the angst of their children, whose screams each fought for dominance in the morning air: Cynthia's cries for attention, and Patrick's cries for nothing in particular.

"Here, my love," James said tenderly, as he reached out to take their infant son Patrick from her. The boy's cries quickly softened to a whimper. Just as soon as baby Patrick had become easy with comfort and calmness, did a loud and sudden voice re-emerge from the hallway:

"Aye, that must be my namesake making all that racket! It seems he's inherited my talent for causing a ruckus."

With that, baby Patrick regained his wrath.

James turned to see his father, Patrick, leaning heavily on his cane but grinning broadly as he stood in the doorway. His eyes sparkled with mirth as he reached out to take up his infant grandson.

"Off you go, then," James said, as he gladly placed his infant son into the arms of the child's grandfather. With Cynthia now darting past the two Patricks to meet her grandmother at the end of the hallway, James turned toward the stairs leading up to the bedroom, where Margaret was already beginning to lay out their clothes for the church service.

Inside the bedroom, Margaret stood before their modest wardrobe, her slender fingers deftly sorting through the garments as she selected their most suitable attire. James looked on, his thoughts churning like storm-tossed seas as he contemplated the journey that lay ahead–and the secret he had not yet found the courage to share.

James nodded, swallowing hard against the lump in his throat, and readied himself for the day's worship. And though his heart was heavy with the knowledge of what was to come, he compartmentalized it all, one hour, one minute at a time.

In the sanctuary of their shared chamber, James and Margaret moved with practiced grace, as each spouse tended to the other's needs. A soothing smile graced her lips as she watched him shrug into his waistcoat, his lean fingers fumbling with the buttons in his haste.

"Here, let me help you," she offered, stepping forward and capturing his hands within her own. The warmth of her touch was a balm to his frayed nerves, and he felt a rush of gratitude for her steadfastness.

As they continued to dress, the first of their morning conversations began to flow.

"James, what happened last night? At the courthouse, with the militia?"

His hesitation was short-lived. James stood to meet his wife.

"Margaret," he said slowly, "the militia, everyone in the county, has resolved on independence. They won't officially announce it until tomorrow, but... that's their decision".

Her eyes widened at the enormity of his words, a mix of pride and worry flitting across her expressive features. She reached out, her fingers brushing against his cheek as if to anchor herself to him.

"I - I don't understand. Independence from Great Britain?" Margaret asked.

"Aye." James responded, unsure of how prepared he was to pair reason and logic to the passionate acts of the night before.

Margaret raised her eyebrows in perplexity. "How? How can one county declare independence from an empire?"

James glanced down at the floor beneath him, searching desperately for the right combination of words.

"We will not be alone," James said, his blue eyes now returning to meet Margaret's concerned glance. "This... declaration... it will go before the Congress in Philadelphia."

Margaret reached for James' hand and responded hesitantly.

"Then it will not be a county versus an empire. It will be a continent."

Without breaking eye contact with his wife, James placed his hands over Margaret's and answered,

"Better than a continent, my love... it will be a country."

For the first time in minutes, Margaret looked away from James. She walked a couple of steps towards the door leading into the hallway before looking back at James with a teary-eyed smile.

"I love you. And I know together we will be safe." She nodded before stepping out into the hallway.

"I love you too," James replied. Margaret was now gone, and for the first time all morning, James' heart began to physically gnaw in a way that nearly brought him into a sheer panic. The sting of all that had been left unsaid quickly brought warm tears racing down his face. James wept as quietly as he could, and with a buried silence, went to join his family.

Outside, the day was a picture of serenity, the sky a tapestry of soft clouds that shielded them from the sun's harsh gaze. A gentle breeze rustled the leaves of the trees that lined the dirt road, where a parade of townsfolk marched towards the nearby church house.

Having remade himself into the predictably calm man that his family knew, James closed the tavern door behind him and spoke to his wandering daughter.

"Come along now, Cynthia," James called to her gently.

As he swept his little girl up into his arms, James fixed his attention upon the small patch of dirt on her navy gown dress. James chuckled at his daughter's ability to dirty her dress in such a short time. With baby Patrick held firmly in the arms of Margaret, and his parents following just a few short steps behind him, James led his family toward that plain stone church that lay just down the road.

The walk took about twenty minutes. Despite walking alongside many other families, the dialogue spoken around him all felt indiscernible and alien. James could only pray that he did not appear outwardly as burdened as he felt within.

As they arrived at the open churchyard, his chambered trace became broken by the hallowed bells of the church. Their familiar melodies echoing distinctly across the rolling frontier. Here, at the forming of the congregation and the gathering of the clans, was James' refuge from pain.

James Jack stood among his family at the edge of the churchyard, his heart doing its best to find some degree of calm rhythm. He surveyed the sea of familiar faces, searching for those who had shared in the fateful meeting the night prior.

Just as James had steadied himself long enough to turn and speak something light-hearted to Margaret, a sudden and violent barking caused his clever joke to dissolve only syllables into its delivery.

"Argh!" James cried out as the fierce barking continued to erupt.

Margaret quickly turned to her husband, her eyes wide with concern at her husband's overreaction to the barking hound; moments before joining his startled state at the clashing of another sudden sound.

"Neigh!"

Now towering over the heads of the many men and women gathered in the church's courtyard, was the neck and head of a beautiful brown mare. Her brilliant colors a jarring juxtaposition to her hideous yelps and cries.

"Thud!" crashed her hooves, repeatedly, as she fought desperately to release herself from the rope which bound her to the post, and in proximity to the snapping hound.

James and his family looked on in a moment of hesitation as the horse's owner tried impotently to calm her.

"Pilgrim! Easy girl! You are okay!"

The dog barked relentlessly. Whatever had kept the creature on the farside of its fenced yard had become defective, and now the mutt was directly against the fence. Its mangy black fur and oversized teeth were now visible to Pilgrim, and it was enough to send her into hysteria.

With his children and wife behind him, James continued to watch as John Haigler—known in the county by the inoffensive but accurate descriptor, *"the cripple"*—attempted fruitlessly to contain his out-of-control horse.

When it became clear that the dog had no intentions of ceasing its torment of the mare, and that the horse risked breaking free of its binds and stampeding through the crowded churchyard, James stepped forward to meet the creature with whom he shared an internal distress.

James! Watch for her hooves!" warned his mother Lilas.

Unaware of what ingenious plan he had for calming the anxious beast, James approached. Unwaveringly, he stood before the raging steed.

"Easy now." James reached a hand for Pilgrim's snout, but she continued to rear aggressively on her hind legs. Her constant cries whisked with the endless barks of the black-furred hound, and the hollers of the congregation.

"Stand back you fool!" yelled John Haigler, as he lifted his cane, ready to strike Pilgrim, who was now mere seconds from shaking herself loose from her rope binds.

"No!" James turned to John and in a single motion, grabbed John's cane mid-swing, causing a momentary silence in the crowd. John stumbled backwards; his eyes avoiding contact with James'.

James looked back at Pilgrim, and putting all his focus beyond the barking of the hound, he whispered to the freighted mare.

"You and I..." James placed a hand along the horse's chestnut brown hair. "We are both creatures frightened... are we not?"

Pilgrim continued to snort and whine.

James calmly shushed the mare before continuing.

"The Lord is good to all..." James stopped to look gently into Pilgrim's brown eyes,

"... and his tender mercies are over all His creation."

James continued, and within a minute, Pilgrim had come to a calm. The hound found himself exhausted from barking, and the congregation regained its lively demeanor.

Finally breaking his trance with the chestnut brown mare, James looked back to John "the cripple" Haigler, and nodded his head humbly.

"I am much obliged, Mr. Jack," murmured John Haigler, his left hand gripping his curved walking stick tightly, and his right hand extended to shake James'.

"Glad I could be of help." James shook John's hand, before turning back to see his family, whose faces all shared smiles of relief and the remains of laughter, surely brought upon by some wisecrack from Patrick.

"By God, how did you calm it?" asked a smiling but curious Margaret.

James lifted Cynthia up into his arms and turned to his wife.

"I suppose I just said the same concord I use to settle that one!" James pointed to the giggling boy in Margaret's arms, and smiled as Cynthia pulled on the ends of his brown tricorn hat.

With the senior Patrick now in the lead, the family joined the procession of backcountry Presbyterians into the shelter of their modest "meeting house".

The faint scent of candle wax and timeworn wood filled James' nostrils as he stepped into the hallowed sanctuary. Motes of dust danced in the shafts of sunlight that pierced through the stained-glass windows, casting a kaleidoscope of colors upon the worn wooden pews. He followed his parents, Margaret, and the children to their usual spot, where they would soon join their fellow congregants in worship.

As James settled into his seat, and with the commotion in the courtyard behind him, he once again felt that gnawing pain from within his chest. To distract his thoughts he began rapidly searching the populating pews to see who all had come for today's service. He regretted his attempt at distraction when Thomas Polk's steely gray eyes met his, instantly returning James' thoughts to the county courthouse.

In horror, James watched as Thomas rose from his pew, intending to walk directly towards him and discuss further the events in the courthouse.

James let out a sigh of relief when Pastor Joseph Alexander spoke, sending all to take their seats in the pews.

"Good morning, brothers and sisters," the pastor began. His voice resonated throughout the chamber as he called the pews to order. "Let us begin our service with a moment of prayer."

James bowed his head, silently beseeching divine guidance and strength for the journey that lay ahead. As the pastor led the congregation in worship, James grappled with a tumultuous storm of emotions — fear, doubt, hope, and determination all vying for dominance within his soul. The pastor's words seemed to echo his inner turmoil: "Lord, guide us in times of darkness, and grant us courage in the face of adversity."

The service continued in the manner of a traditional 18th-century Presbyterian ceremony. Following a communal confession of sins, the congregation received an assurance of pardon. The pastor, who was among the few in the church's company fully literate, read aloud scripture from the King James version of the Bible.

As James listened to the pastor's impassioned words, he reflected upon the elder's particular use of the English language, and the strategy in which he led the congregation through the divine. With curiousity, James wondered whether someone had informed Pastor Joseph of the militia's grand conspiracy.

All the same, James' heart was heavy. Towards the end of the service, he reflected momentarily on how little he had broken his gaze from the pulpit.

It was then that Pastor Joseph's commanding voice spoke once more.

"As we face our daily trials and tribulations, let us reflect upon the words of the 10th Psalm, where David reminds us all of our Lord's sovereignty over all the Earth. Wherein David quoth the Lord in saying that 'He answers from on high and gives encouragement to them'".

James knew it was nearing time for Pastor Joseph to lead his flock in the singing of the Psalm, a tradition as ancient as the blood that flowed in each of their hearts.

Pastor Joseph looked upon his beloved bible, and after having read the scripture before all those present in the sacred hall, spoke and said:

"Let us now gather our voices to unite in praise and supplication..."

The Pastor paused, as if in deep reflection, before continuing. "As we seek the Lord's guidance in these trying times."

The first notes of the melody filled the air, pure and haunting, as the congregation sang.

"The Lord will ever reign as king

His throne will always stand

The heathen nations of the world

will perish from his land

Oh Lord the native ones desire

Your answer from on high

you give encouragement to them

and listen to their cries

For you defend the fatherless

and those who are oppressed

so that from fear of mortal man

the helpless may have rest."

James wept quietly.

"James," Margaret whispered, her hand finding his. James embraced his wife's hand, but once again, felt anxious at the thought of explaining his tears.

With a grace and tenderness that needed no conditional understanding, Margaret simply placed her hand upon his. James swallowed softly and, using his other hand, brushed away the tear that lingered on his cheek.

"It's just... the words of the psalm. They're a powerful reminder, don't you think?"

Margaret smiled softly and looked up at James. "Yes... yes they are."

As the congregation dispersed, James gathered himself cooly and prepared to lead his family back to their home in the tavern. Before he could get out of the sanctuary doors, Thomas Polk came to complete his aim from before the service.

"James," Thomas Polk called out, cutting through the gentle hum of conversation that surrounded them. "A moment, if you please."

James nodded to his wife and children, reassuring them with a tender smile as he stepped away to join Polk. He could see the seriousness etched in the lines of the older man's face, the fire of determination burning within his eyes.

"James," Polk said, his voice low and steady, "We have penned the Mecklenburg Resolves. These words shall guide our newly independent country on the path to righteousness and freedom."

"Indeed," James replied, his chest tightening at the thought of the crucial role he would play in delivering this message to the Continental Congress. "And what would you have me do, Mr. Polk?"

"Ride at first light tomorrow," Polk advised, his gaze unwavering. "I shall gather the townsfolk at the courthouse so they may hear the declaration read aloud before you depart on your journey."

James nodded, absorbing the gravity of his task, while his mind's conjured vivid images of the arduous road ahead. The fortitude in Thomas Polk's voice served as an anchor, steadying him amidst the storm of emotions that threatened to consume him.

Determination coursed through James' veins, as strong and unwavering as the roots of the ancient oak trees that adorned the landscape. The air was heavy with the scent of blooming wildflowers and the promise of a new beginning for his people.

"Very well, Mr. Polk," James answered. "I shall begin my journey at first light. May our words resonate within the hearts of those who hear them."

"Aye," Thomas replied, his eyes shining with conviction.

In a surprising display of emotion, Thomas embraced James in a hug and whispered into his ear. "We place our trust in you, as does the Lord. Ride with speed and safety, my friend."

With a nod of farewell, James turned to rejoin his family, feeling finally ready to share with them the burden of his duty.

As they walked along the dirt road, the sun dipped below the horizon, casting long shadows across the land. A soft breeze rustled the leaves overhead, as barred owls hoot in the distance.

As the door to the tavern swung open, the beacon of lit candles guided the family within. Cynthia and baby Patrick felt thoroughly fatigued and ready for sleep. James waited at the base of the steps, while Margaret laid the two children in their respective bed and cradle.

After the familiar silence of his two children falling asleep, his wife rejoined James, and together, they sat before the tavern fire.

"James, I know your heart is troubled. You mustn't worry about this declaration."

She paused, leaping from her seat and going to kneel beside James, who continued to look into the rapid motion of the flames.

"We will be safe here among the hills. Together."

James stood from the wooden bench and looked into the face of his beloved wife. Her honey-brown eyes were full of a faith that James so desperately sought not to break.

James lifted his brown tricorn hat from his head and placed it on the wooden bench, before taking both of his wife's hands into his.

"My dear and sweet Margaret. You will be safe. As will Cynthia and Patrick. My father will see to this."

James kept Margaret's hands interlocked with his.

"Why do you say these things in such a way?" Margaret asked anxiously.

"I am the courier of our people's declaration. I will ride to Philadelphia to deliver it to the Continental Congress."

The flames now danced wildly around the silhouette of the young couple.

Margaret stood silently, her eyes fixed on James', though warm tears filled them.

"You cannot do this. James, you will die." Margaret pleaded. "Why must it be you?"

"Because I volunteered."

"But why would you-"

"It is the right thing to do, my love. For our children, for our family, for our people."

Margaret steadied herself and studied her husband's face, searching for any hint of doubt or uncertainty. Finding none, she nodded solemnly.

"If you believe this to be your duty, then you have my trust."

With those words, she drew James into a deep, steadying embrace, her love wrapping around him like a shield.

After a long hug, Margaret ascended the stairs to their bedroom, and James began his journey towards his parent's chambers.

His heart buoyed by Margaret's unwavering faith, James sought out his elderly mother, Lilas. As James' entered into the hazy quarters, he found her sitting alone in bed, her hands busy with a needle and thread. As he approached, she looked up and chuckled.

"You surprised me today with that steed. What on earth possessed you to do such a thing?"

James approached his elderly mother and sat alongside her on the bed.

"Duty, I suppose."

"But it was not your horse."

"No, but I knew I could help. When you and Father sacrificed so much of your time and toil to help build Charlotte during her virgin winters, was that your cross to bear?"

Lilas grew more firm in her speech. "It was a sacred duty."

"Then you will understand why I have volunteered to be the one to deliver our people's cry for freedom, dear Mother."

Lilas' back became fully erect, and within the constraints of her feeble frame, did all she could to question James.

"Our cry for freedom?"

"Aye, Mother. The militia gathered under our previous moonlight and declared Mecklenburg County free from Great Britain.

James paused, reaching to hold his mother and her frail hands.

"To finish the worthy toil that you and Father began. To make full our deliverance into Eden."

Lilas took a moment to gather herself.

"And you shall be its deliverer?"

"Aye, Mother. It is my duty."

Lilas had no need for further discussion. She held her son close and began a brief prayer over him.

Once they reopened their eyes, they discovered Patrick Jack standing in the hallway—his expression making it clear he had been there for several minutes.

Patrick said nothing, but signaled James to come to him. Forgetting at once his age of nearly three decades, James gladly obliged his father's request. Once upon the tavern's back porch, Patrick took a seat in his favorite rocking chair, and clenched a pipe between his yellowed teeth and a contented smile. As the sun set rapidly over the horizon, James began to speak.

"Father,"

Patrick tore his eyes from the sunset, his wrinkled face deepening as he studied his son's solemn expression.

"Sit down, boy," Patrick motioned to the empty chair beside him, removing the pipe from his mouth. "You do not need to relay it once more."

James took a seat, feeling the familiar creak of the aged wood beneath him. He swallowed hard and let the silence of the moment attempt to soothe his soul.

Finally, Patrick spoke, his voice thick with pride. "My boy, out of all of my sons, I have always known you to be a man of courage."

James looked down at his brown boots, feeling guilty about his father's words; he felt as far away from courageous as one could be.

James resumed his silent stare into the setting sun. Patrick continued.

"All of us... we pay heavy tributes for building our world. None of us have long to stay, none of us get to. This is your due season."

"You have my blessing, and the Lord's as well."

Patrick coughed on a puff of his tobacco smoke before continuing.

"But remember," he added, a mischievous glint in his eye, "if you cross paths with any redcoats, be sure to give them my regards and let them know that this old Irishman has no love for their haughty king."

James laughed, the tension between them dissipating like the fading light. "I will, Father. I promise."

Chapter 4: Farewell, Christian Soldier

The dirt was soft yet sturdy, and the clearing was void of the tall grass that marked the countryside's rolling hills. A stone cross stood at the center of the opening. Approximately five feet tall, the cross displayed carvings that defined the traveling Scots-Irish who carried it. Triquetras and other homages to the trinity detailed the cross's arms and base, while the large circle at its core signified ancient roots. The cross stood enduring, while at its base, James Jack prayed.

"Father," James whispered meekly into his closed palms, "help me, please. Make sense of this journey and bring goodwill to Margaret, Patrick, and Cynthia." James took a deep breath in and steadied his lips, "to my mother and father, bring peace."

James continued.

"Abide with me through the day and into the night. Keep my pace steady and my course straight."

"Make use of my cause for Your will."

James wiped away a single warm tear that now appeared. James cleared his throat and opened his eyes, looking upward at the cross, whose head now felt towering.

"Father, help of the helpless... help me. Amen."

James rose from his knees, the fabric of his trousers now dusted with dirt.

He looked across the empty churchyard and proceeded towards the home of John Haigler.

As he approached John's home, the scent of wood-smoke wafted through the air, mingling with the earthy aroma of the surrounding countryside. The door creaked open, revealing John's crooked form leaning heavily on a gnarled walking stick.

"Ah, James!" John greeted him warmly, his voice carrying a slight tremor as he pushed open the door. "Come in friend."

"Thank you, John," James replied, stepping into the modest dwelling. As James entered the mostly one-room home, the comforting smell of a warm bowl of porridge greeted him, topped off with a thin layer of honey.

Upon closing the door, John turned to James and smiled before pointing to his bowl of unfinished breakfast, offering some to James. "Please help yourself if you'd like! I've got plenty to spare," James politely declined, and the two men stood amicably by the room's unlit wooden fireplace.

"I never got the chance to thank you properly for helping to calm my horse down yesterday." John said as he spoke between spoonfuls of his porridge. "She's a gentle creature, truly. The bark of that mutt was enough to shake poor Pilgrim deeply, make her forget her might."

James watched as John raised another spoonful of porridge to his mouth.

"How is she now?" James replied. "Is she settled?"

"Aye! She's calm as can be," John remarked.

"Good, I'm glad to hear," James replied. "Listen John, I must confide in you a great secret whose truth will be shared to all the townsfolk here soon."

John lowered his spoon and glanced at James, his eyes gleamed with quiet laughter.

"I know of the journey you are preparing to take, my friend. And I know why you are here today."

Surprise seized James, and he fiddled with his tricorn hat in an awkward silence.

"Why then, John, am I here today?"

John chuckled, and with as much strength as he could muster, lifted himself from his wooden chair with the help of his cane. John motioned James to follow with his hand.

"Come. She should have finished feeding by now."

James knew better than to ask how John Haigler knew of his journey, but imagined it's likely all curious minds of Mecklenburg had long since uncovered the whispers shared between the trees.

It did not take long for the two men to come to the end of John's small cottage and into the overgrown yard. There in the yard stood the chestnut brown mare that James met the evening prior.

Pilgrim. She looked far more relaxed in the comfort of her owner's lush lawn, safe from any black-furred hounds.

"How did you know of my intentions today?" James asked, while standing quietly, watching Pilgrim graze softly.

John's eyes softened with understanding, and he nodded slowly. "I know how critical this journey is, James. My horse, she has been my companion through many trials. Her gentle temper allowed even someone like me, with this wretched leg, to ride."

He motioned to his twisted limb, a reminder of the harsh realities that earned him his moniker.

"Her strength has been my solace through trials, great and small," John continued, turning to face James directly.

"There'd be no greater companion for your journey."

John's gift of intuition and the avoidance of his long prepared speech spared James, who simply extended his hand to John.

"Thank you, my dear friend," spoke James, his voice rich with gratitude.

"I promise to care for her as though she were my own and return her safely to you."

"Of that I am sure," John replied. With his quivering right hand still embraced by James, John lifted his cane with his opposite hand and pointed it towards the unbothered mare.

"Please, she is all yours."

James strode across the tall green grass and approached the gentle steed, praying that her embrace yesterday was not a fluke of nature.

"Pilgrim, is it? A very fine name."

James let out a light laugh as the creature seemed to nod her head in response to the question. James turned back towards John.

"There must be something I can do to return this favor?" James lowered his tricorn hat into his hands.

John dismissed the gesture with his good hand and shouted back.

"You can deliver our edict to those assemblymen in Philadelphia! And you can deliver this old man from the jaws of the bloodthirsty English!"

John nearly toppled over from his grandiose gestures, but caught himself and finished by saying,

"That, dear James, will be how you may repay me."

James bowed his head in humility and smiled.

"By God's grace, I just might."

James lept atop Pilgrim, waved goodbye to John Haigler, and began the short ride to the steps of the county courthouse, where all of Mecklenburg County had gone to gather.

As James neared the courthouse, he could hear the sounds of the crowd swelling like a tide; a sea of faces awash with hope, fear, and determination.

James' eyes darted anxiously, looking for his family whose company he had been in an hour earlier.

A large ring of townsfolk, who were frenzied and visibly full of intense dispositions, surrounded the county courthouse. James did his best to remain far enough back as to avoid detection. As James rode several yards behind the outer ring of the mass of Charlotteans, his family finally came into view.

They were busy: Margaret did her best to keep baby Patrick's mood upright, and Cynthia's physical frame upright—and out of the ever-tempting puddle beneath her. Meanwhile, Patrick and Lilas Jack focused on unpacking the supplies they had brought in on the family's donkey: a cloak for warmth, dried pork and hardtack for sustenance, a compass, and a small blade.

Quickly, James dismounted, and led Pilgrim towards his kin. Their arms opened wide to welcome him.

"Oh, James," called Margaret. "Look at this crowd who have come for you."

James turned and looked at the large rally of rebels before turning back to his wife.

"They've come to hear it for themselves, to see if the whispers are true."

James kissed Margaret, then turned his attention to Cynthia and Pat.

"Would you believe what I found in Mr. Haigler's yard this morning, love?" James pulled a Bluebell flower from his coat pocket, and placed it into the hands of his little girl. Dressed, of course, in her favorite blue dress.

Cynthia giggled and grinned, and James felt overcome with joy and sadness.

James watched as his elderly mother began transferring their supplies from the family donkey onto Pilgrim, focused on completing this last act of motherly love. While Patrick came and embraced James with a reassuring hand on his shoulder.

"There hasn't been a turnout like this for a Jack since Uncle Bill got put in the pillory for public drunkenness!"

James laughed and turned to help his mother load the last blanket roll onto Pilgrim. Then in union, the family waited together among the cluster at the courthouse.

After a short while of waiting, the courthouse doors swung open with a resounding creak, and the crowd fell silent as Thomas Polk emerged, clutching a document of singular importance.

James and his family watched on as Thomas stood at the top of the courthouse steps and spoke.

"Good people of Mecklenburg County and Charlotte town," Thomas Polk bellowed, his voice booming across the square. "I stand before you today to read aloud our Declaration of Independence!"

The crowd cheered with a bravado that rivaled the strongest summer thunderstorm. Margaret discretely grabbed hold of James' hand as Thomas began to read.

"Let it be known," Polk continued, raising the declaration high above his head, "that we the citizens of Mecklenburg county, do hereby dissolve the political bands which have connected us to the Mother Country, and hereby absolve ourselves from all allegiance to the British Crown."

The uproar from the crowd dwarfed even that of the night in the courthouse.

Thomas continued.

"Let every ear of the British legion know we do hereby declare ourselves a free and independent people, who are, and of right ought to be, a sovereign and self-governing Association, under the control of no power other than that of our God!"

Even after being present for its conception, Thomas' rendition of Abraham's words was enough to stir in James' heart the impossible courage he had spent his nights in prayer for.

"Liberty!" The cries echoed through the throng, men and women alike raising their fists in a show of solidarity.

"Let the world bear witness," Polk declared, his voice soaring above the clamor, "to the maintenance of which independence, we solemnly pledge to each other, our mutual cooperation, our lives, our fortunes, and our most sacred honor."

As Polk shouted the final words of the fiery Mecklenburg Declaration, James became realigned on the great journey ahead of him. James then watched as Thomas lowered the parchment paper and pointed directly towards him.

"Bold patriot, the courageous courier, indeed - Charlotte's greatest hero!" Thomas proclaimed. The people erupted in cheers and applause, their voices carrying on the warm breeze that rustled through the trees. James felt heat rise to his cheeks as he stood there, basking in the adulation of his peers.

Thomas descended the courthouse steps, his gait slow and determined, his eyes locked onto James'. As he approached, the crowd parted to create a path between them, their eyes following Thomas' every step.

"Here, my friend," Thomas said, extending a rolled parchment to James. "This is the Mecklenburg Declaration of Independence and Mecklenburg Resolves. Guard them well and deliver them swiftly."

"Thank you, Mr. Polk," James replied, shocked at the steadiness in his own voice. He took the precious documents, carefully stowing them away in his brown haversack bag.

As the parchment disappeared into the bag, James' thoughts raced, contemplating the long road ahead. How many miles lay between him and his destination in Philadelphia? What dangerous snares waited to cut short his endeavor? The faith of Charlotte's pride was now anchored upon James' resolve, and it compelled the tavern owner to valor.

The echoes of the crowd's cheers continued to fill the air, as Thomas leaned in closer to James, his voice a low yet urgent whisper.

"James, there is one more task before you set forth on your journey to Philadelphia."

James leaned in closely to Thomas', wishing desperately to not blunder any portion of his aim.

"What must I do, sir?"

"Ride first for Salisbury, our neighboring town," Thomas instructed, his gaze fixed intently on James. "There, you must have the declaration and resolves read into the record by the county magistrate. Only after the completion of this task shall your true journey north begin."

James nodded in understanding. A sense of momentary relief overcame him, as he could now see his journey broken down into executable stages.

"Godspeed, James," Thomas whispered, his eyes filled with the same fire that burned within James' heart. "May your journey be swift and your return triumphant."

"Thank you, Mr. Polk," James said, clutching his friend's hand. "I will deliver our discourse to the Congress, and they will join in our genesis."

With a last nod, James turned to face the cheering crowd once more, their voices now a clarion call, as he navigated once more to be in the company of his family.

With the haversack bag containing the declaration now placed securely over his shoulder, James approached to see Pilgrim fully packed with the supplies brought by his mother and father. Standing in front of Pilgrim, sorted in descending height and posed as if to form a blockade, were the members of his family.

The unruffled demeanor of a departing hero became susceptible from the sight, and James whispered.

"Father, mother, my love..." James sighed, his voice heavy with emotion. He drew his wife close first, her slender form trembling ever so slightly in his arms.

"I will return home within a month's time, and all shall be better for this sacrifice," he whispered into her ear, his breath warm against her inviting complexion.

"James," she responded, her voice barely audible as it quivered between sobs, "we will dream of you every night."

Releasing her gently, James then bent down to lift his infant son, Patrick, cradling the small bundle tenderly in his mighty arms. He pressed his lips to the child's soft forehead, feeling the fragile breaths that fluttered beneath his kiss.

Beside him, his young daughter Cynthia stood, her wide eyes brimming with curiosity as she clung to her mother's skirt. James knelt before her, cupping her cherubic face with his weathered hands, and gave upon her a gentle kiss as well.

As James stood, Cynthia pulled aggressively at Margaret's skirt and motioned erratically for her father's attention.

"What is it, Cynthia?" James calmly asked his young daughter.

Margaret let out a petite laugh and handed Cynthia something from her pocket.

"She spent hours making you this. She is very proud."

James could now see that in the palm of Cynthia's hands was a simple and unadorned cross necklace, made of some natural wood native to their lands. A piece of twig, masterfully shaped and kept circular with string, surmounted its cross section.

"I helped her just a little." Margaret chuckled as she wiped away a tear.

As James turned the homemade necklace onto its back, he noticed a small inscription carved into the foot of the vertical beam.

"J.J."

"She also wanted to make sure you didn't confuse it with anyone else's homemade necklace."

James wrapped his daughter in a warm and prolonged hug.

"My sweet blueberry. Thank you for your gift. I love you."

Knowing exactly how Cynthia would want to conclude the exchange, James lowered his head like a knight at his dubbing. Cynthia stood to her feet and placed the leather cord of the necklace around her father's neck.

James stood and turned to his parents.

Lilas embraced her son in a protective hold.

"Go with God, my son, and may He shield thee from perils."

"With love, Mother," James replied, his heart swelling with tender devotion. "I shall be home in short order."

As the winds of destiny stirred around him, James felt the weight of his father's large hand fall upon his shoulder.

"James, my boy," Patrick began, his voice rough with emotion yet steady with conviction, "there is naught for you to fear. You will reach Philadelphia without hindrance, and travel that road as effortlessly as you did when you were but a boy."

A wry smile touched the corners of James' mouth as he nodded, drawing upon his father's faith in him like a warrior donning armor. "Thank you, Father. I will make you proud."

"I have no doubt." Patrick clapped his son's shoulder firmly, imparting a silent promise. "I will hold down the fort here in your absence. Ride swift and true, son. We shall meet again soon."

James raised his hand, waving farewell to his family as he strode towards Pilgrim. The faithful steed heaved with anticipation, her dark eyes reflecting the fire that burned within both horse and rider.

"Come, Pilgrim," he whispered, his voice tinged with reverence. "We have a long road ahead."

Mounting his mare, James urged Pilgrim forward, her hooves thundering against the dirt road as they raced towards the horizon.

With Cynthia's cross beating softly against his chest, James increased his speed as he and Pilgrim began their departure from the steps of the courthouse.

As James and Pilgrim thundered down the dirt road towards Salisbury, a sea of townsfolk gathered on either side, their faces alight with fervor. Men, women, and children raised their hands to clap and cheer, forming a living corridor for the hero and his steed to pass through. The sun cast its golden beams upon them, illuminating the scene like a divine benediction.

"Go, James! Make us proud!" cried a young woman, her cheeks flushed with excitement.

"Godspeed, Jack!" shouted an elderly man, waving his cane in the air.

"James Jack!" Voices rose in unison, the chant carrying across the breeze like a battle hymn. "James Jack! James Jack!"

The chanting continued to swell, bolstering James's mettle as they raced into the summer day. He raised his hand in a last farewell; the wind whipping through his hair, tugging at his clothes as if urging him onward.

"James Jack! James Jack!" The voices echoed through the air, a chorus that reverberated throughout the essence of the adventurer.

James focused on the path ahead, his spirit filled with an unquenchable fire.

"James Jack! James Jack!" The chant faded into the distance as he and Pilgrim disappeared over the horizon, their purpose unwavering, their hearts steadfast, and their resolve unbreakable.

Chapter 5: An Unthinkable Proposal

For brief and passing moments along the trail, there were spells of cool wind. They came quickly and did not linger for long. After only five miles of riding from the steps of the Mecklenburg courthouse, a sleek towel of sweat had gathered between the collar of James' brown coat and the permanently sun-burnt skin upon his neck, which produced a bizarre blend of an unpleasant heat and an unseemly chill.

For Pilgrim, the day of non-stop riding from Charlotte had been far more accommodating. Aside from the periodic break to feed on grass along the road, or to drink from a level creek, Pilgrim had provided a pace upon which James placed great confidence that the journey to Philadelphia may in fact be a brisk and rather uneventful one.

As the two companions ventured forward on their way to Salisbury, the meek symphony of rustled leaves and crying hawks became overshadowed by the shifting stomps created beneath Pilgrim's hooves; from a path of dirt and clay to a road of cobblestone. Just ahead of James stood a small post sign and the distant sounds of civilization. The cool winds grew mightier and the thin strap of James' haversack bag bounced timidly upon his chest.

As James entered the boundaries of Salisbury, he glanced down at Pilgrim through the presence of her thick brown mane, and chuckled.

"Well Pilgrim, let's get this done in time for supper."

Upon entering the town, James observed it was slightly larger and more cultivated than what he had left behind in Charlotte. Along the cobblestone streets of Salisbury the buildings were more plentiful, and their constructions were sturdy frames of brick and lumber.

Placed upon a now strolling Pilgrim, James looked upward towards the tall and narrow windows teeming on either side of him. Using his tattered brown tricorn hat for shade from the sun, James glanced upwards upon young maids weaving threads through a loom large enough that it would have taken up half of his family's loft above the tavern.

In an open window on the opposite side of the road, James saw young boys playing with crafts of a simpler kind. The string that was tied to a small round ball, and the rudimentary wooden figurine of a man known by many names, who, with a bit of puppeteering, could be made to dance and jig. James knew them all. Similar to every other facet of backcountry life, the children who played with these toys were also the ones who constructed them.

As he proceeded further into the town, James spotted the courthouse, its noble facade standing out among its structural peers. For although everything material in James' world was younger than that of a single generation, the fine craftsmanship of the brickwork and the symmetrical design of the large courthouse kept it alone appearing mint.

In this place that felt so familiar and yet so distant to his own backcountry home, James mused intermediately while dismounting from Pilgrim, who appeared grateful to be finally at ease. James patted her crest affectionately before leading her towards the hitching post by the courthouse steps.

Less enthusiastic to quip a witty joke for his equestrian companion in the presence of passing pedestrians, James simply smiled an easy smirk at Pilgrim, and turned to face the steps leading up to the courthouse; the haversack bag secured firmly around his shoulders.

Steadying himself for the task ahead, James ascended the steps, his boots echoing against the firm stone. He placed his hand on the brass door handle and swung it open before him. Leading with his muddy leather boots, James stepped firmly into the courthouse's chambers.

With the massive oak door behind him, James surveyed the bustling courthouse entryway. Near the courthouse coordinator, a conversation was audible. As James walked nearer, it became clear it was a matter of law.

Inside a small room next to the main hallway sat an older gentleman with silver hair and a well-kept wool coat and matching cravat, and opposite this gentleman sat two figures who seemed physically diametric. The silver-haired gentleman spoke.

"Well now, gentlemen, what brings you before me today?"

The taller of the two inquiring men spoke first, his lanky figure extending into his gnarled fingers, now joined in a fist on the table.

"Ah, Justice Brown, it's a matter of utmost importance, a matter of land, as you may well imagine. My neighbor, Josiah Mott, has taken to claiming land that's mine, and I intend to see this injustice righted."

Before Justice Brown could respond to the concerned citizen, the friend of the concerned citizen spoke up.

"Well, I wouldn't say claiming... not exactly." The short and plump man paused with great clumsiness. "It's more like... it's more like... uh... *overlapping*, I reckon."

Intrigued but mildly amused, the town justice, Elijah Brown, turned back to the lanky gentleman who bore a striking resemblance to a scarecrow before continuing. "Overlapping, eh? Well, we'll need to hear more before I can make a judgment. Benjamin, it is? If you please—tell me what's happened."

All too happy to explain the situation, Benjamin Booth leaped from his chair and explained,

"You see, Justice, my land stretches far and wide, from the old oak tree by the creek, all the way to the stone wall by the pasture. It's been in my family for generations! But now, here comes Josiah Mott, claiming that his land extends—" Benjamin gave the justice a clear visual with his hands waving dramatically through the air - "far beyond where it ought to! Why, last week, I found him planting corn in my field!"

In concurrence with this explanation, his friend, John Dunn, turned to the exhausted justice with a rapid head nod of agreement.

"That's right! Corn, right in the middle of Benjamin's patch! I told Josiah, "You can't plant corn there! But he said, 'The ground's mine!' And, well... It looked like Josiah's corn. But I don't think it was."

Benjamin jolted his beady eyes down at John in frustration.

"It wasn't his corn, John! It was my corn, in my field, where it's always been!"

A vexing corn maze of his own making now completely engulfed John.

"I wasn't saying it *was* his corn, Benjamin. I was just sayin'. It looked like it. But you're right, it was your corn, just..." John stared at Benjamin. "not quite ready yet, if I'm being honest."

Benjamin now seemed completely oblivious of the town justice still sitting opposite him. "John, this is not about the corn, it's about the land!" Benjamin finally turned back to Justice Elijah Brown. "Josiah Mott! He's taken more than his share, and now he's using his corn as proof he owns my land! The man's got no respect for property!"

James watched on from the hallway in complete bewilderment.

After about half a minute, Justice Brown finally raised his head out from his clapped hands before speaking to the two men.

"Alright, alright, let's not get too tangled up in the corn, gentlemen. You're here because you claim Josiah Mott has crossed the line—literally, I presume. I shall issue a summon for Mr. Mott, and we can meditate on this issue on another day."

Justice Brown lifted a feather quill from his desk and dipped its end into a container of ink. While still looking down at a blank sheet of parchment, he asked the two men,

"The name is Benjamin, yes? And John? What are our surnames?"

"Booth" answered Benjamin. And here next to me is "John Dunn -"

"Esquire" interrupted John.

"Pardon?" asked a flustered Justice Brown, whose raised face told a tired tale of irritation.

"Just wanted to make sure you got the 'Esquire' part down for me," replied John, who wore a very sincere grin.

"That seems -" started Justice Brown.

"Me too!" interrupted Benjamin. "Just so you don't get us confused with any lesser men."

"Noted. Dismissed, gentleman." Justice Brown stood to show them out the door, where James Jack still stood, haversack bag in hand.

As the three men processed out, James stood patiently at the edge of the door. When the two "esquires" had turned the corner, the silver haired, and now notably exasperated, Justice Brown turned to James.

"My apologies for the wait." He reached out his right hand and extended his best foot forward.

"My name is Justice Elijah Brown. What can I do for you?"

James returned the gesture, and while shaking his hand, replied,

"Justice Brown, my name is James Jack. I carry with me a sensitive document that the town court must read and record."

Elijah's eyes appraised James for a moment before he replied, "Very well, young man. Follow me." He led James into his office; pulling the door near, but not to, a close.

After both men sat down, James continued.

"Justice Brown, in the afternoon hours of yesterday, I left from the town of Charlotte on a mission to deliver this document to the Continental Congress in Philadelphia."

James reached into the haversack bag, and for the first time since being handed it by Thomas Polk, unfurled it for the town justice to bear witness.

"It was the great battle in the north, sir. When the men of the Mecklenburg Militia learnt of the slaughter, they... no... *we* felt it was God's directive that we declare ourselves free of the king."

The Justice's eyes scanned the document without pause or reprieve.

"This..." the senior man interrupted himself. "Please, Mr. Jack... continue."

"Our meeting elders, upon completion, deemed it imperative to present our declaration to the North Carolina delegates' meeting in Philadelphia. The Congress' support and unification are the cause."

Justice Brown's eyes finally came to a rest as he finished reading through the final stanza of the declaration. As he lowered the incendiary document onto his desk, he looked up once more at James.

Justice Brown cleared his throat and whispered.

"And of Salisbury? Your purpose here today?"

James looked down at the unfurled document, and while reaching into his haversack bag to present the supplemental "Mecklenburg Resolves", said to Justice Brown.

"Mr. Thomas Polk, a man whose name I know you have acquaintance with, instructed me to make Salisbury my sole stop along the route. For we must have these declarations read into the court's records, and kept in perpetuity."

After a quiet moment of reflection, Justice Brown chuckled and breathed out a light sigh.

"Mr. Jack, here you are among friends."

Justice Brown pushed the two documents back towards James as he rose from his chair.

"Come, Colonel Kennon, our head of court, will be more than happy to hear you read the words of your kin."

James placed the haversack bag back over his shoulders, but kept the declaration and resolve grasped firmly in his hands. Exiting back out of Brown's chambers, James followed the town justice down into the central gallery.

The droning discourse of the assembly continued to ripple as James Jack and Justice Brown entered.

Seated around the assembly of Rowan County officials were approximately a dozen men, and at their head, sat elevated above the rest of the chamber, was Colonel Kennon.

Justice Brown turned to face the Colonel.

"Sir, I have with me Mr. James Jack, who brings forth a document of great importance." Justice Brown then turned to James, prompting him to speak.

"Sir," James starts, "I humbly request permission to read this vital message into record here in Salisbury, so that it can be preserved for posterity."

Colonel Kennon considered James' request and, after exchanging glances with Justice Brown, nodded solemnly. "You may proceed, Mr. Jack."

As James unfurled the documents, his hands trembled ever so slightly. He breathed deeply, drawing strength from the patriots who had entrusted him with this task.

As he read, the words flowed like a river, imbued with unyielding conviction and resonant with the spirit of rebellion. As James' voice filled the chamber, the Mecklenburg Declaration of Independence and Mecklenburg Resolves served as muses, tasked with rendering vivid images of liberty and defiance in the minds of all present.

"...and to the maintenance of which independence, we solemnly pledge to each other, our mutual cooperation, our lives, our fortunes, and our most sacred honor. "The finality of the declaration hung heavy in the air as James' lowered the parchment, his blue eyes swapping stunned surveys with those of the rapt assembly.

James locked eyes directly with Rowan County's highest legal official. The two men peered into one another's consciousness for a lingering moment, until Colonel Kennon stood from his seat, prompting all other members of the assembly to rise as well.

"Your people have chosen a path of significant resistance."

James cocked his head in suspense.

Colonel Kennon looked once more into the courier's ocean blue eyes.

"Godspeed, James Jack."

With a gracious bow of his head, and a great joy in his heart at the success of his primary trial, James turned to exit the courthouse chambers. As he made his way through the courthouse's grand entryway, the sun's rays streamed in, casting an ethereal glow on the burnished brick floor. James was now overcome with a sense of relief as he anxiously awaited his return to Pilgrim.

Despite a growing hunger at the base of his stomach, James looked forward to returning once more onto the quiet and wooded road. As James walked with a sense of confident urgency back towards Pilgrim, she began to rise from her relaxed position on the lush green grass.

Right as James was preparing to reach out to his companion, something interrupted their reunion.

"Mr. Jack," called out a cold, cutting voice from behind him. The lanky figure of Esquire Booth emerged from the shadows. His eyes narrowed with contempt. Beside him stood the portly Esquire Dunn, his jowls quivering with barely contained rage.

"You're off rather quickly, aren't ye?" pressed Esquire Dunn, his tone dripping with insinuation. "You have no wish to sojourn Salisbury for but a moment longer?"

James tensed at the sight of the two men, who he quickly recognized as the ones responsible for wearing Justice Brown's temper and mood prior to James' meeting. Yet while the scarecrow-esque Benjamin Booth and the cannon-ball built John Dunn remained an absurd presence, their tone had now grown severe.

James faced the two men, attempting to maintain a calm demeanor. "Gentlemen, what is it you wish to discuss?" Although his words were measured, apprehension raced through his mind.

"Your treasonous speech, Mr. Jack," sneered Esquire Booth, his face reddening. "You dare to stand before the court and spew such seditious filth?"

Taken aback by their offense, James chose his next words carefully.

"Gentlemen, may I remind you that the words I conveyed today belong to legions of aggrieved colonists," James' voice was firm, and for a moment he felt hesitant over the threatening tone of his speech. He continued with a softer tongue: "It is our right to seek freedom from tyranny."

"Freedom?" scoffed Esquire Dunn. The two men began to jolt and shift violently, rapidly closing the space between themselves and James. "What you speak of is rebellion and chaos, fool! You call that freedom?!"

The cries of the esquires now crescendoed into screams that would tower over even those of baby Patrick.

"Aye," replied an ever steady James, "Aye, I do indeed call it freedom!"

James turned his back on the two red-faced loyalists and reached for a clearly disturbed Pilgrim.

"Traitor!" bellowed Esquire Dunn, his portly form twitching with indignation. "This man is a traitor to our king!"

"Aye!" chimed in Esquire Booth, his lanky frame looming over James like an ill-tempered scarecrow. "A worthless Englishman, this blackguard is!"

Despite the gravity of their words, there was an inherent silliness about the two men.

"Your words hold no sway here," James countered, striving for calm de-escalation. "I have delivered my message, and it is not your place to judge its worth."

"Blasphemy!" Esquire Booth roared, his face reddening like a ripe tomato. "His Excellency Tryon should have hung all you bastards when had the chance!"

"Enough!" James exclaimed, his heart growing flustered as memories of the doomed "Regulator War" roused. "Perhaps his 'Excellency' will come to regret his clemency", James said sternly.

James was now fixated on the two men as they circled him, unaware of the crowd that had formed around them.

"Traitor!" Esquire Dunn snarled, his eyes ablaze with righteous fury.

"Peace, sirs," James implored, his hands raised in a gesture of surrender. "I mean no harm, only to complete my duty."

The two loyalists drowned out his pleas with their relentless verbal assaults. With each passing moment, the crowd surrounding them grew larger, drawn in by the unfolding spectacle.

To seize the declaration, Esquire Dunn lunged forward, his pudgy fingers clawing at James' precious haversack bag. With a surge of adrenaline, James unleashed a powerful blow, his knuckles striking Dunn's cheek with the force of a blacksmith's hammer. The corpulent loyalist crumpled to the dusty ground, his mouth agape in shock and pain.

"Enough!" cried James, his voice now full of anger at the predicament of the groping loyalist. "Calm yourself!"

Yet even as John Dunn lay vanquished, Esquire Booth, lanky and proud like a stork, reached into his coat, his intentions clear and sinister. But before Booth could reveal the weapon, a firm hand from the crowd intervened, seizing Booth's arm in an iron grip.

"Unhand me!" screeched Booth, his voice shrill with indignation. "I am an officer of the court!"

The man who had come to James' aid glanced down at the furious esquire with eyes ablaze with contempt.

"You are but a rabble-rouser, Booth."

Esquire Booth pulled himself free from the man's grasp. Stepping over Esquire Dunn, who still laid dazzled on the cobblestone, he turned to face the throng that had assembled to witness their confrontation, his gaze pleading for support.

"Do you not see the treachery this man carries with him? He self professes that he and his kin seek to sever our ties to the crown!"

Amidst the commotion, James could hear the meek whimpers of Pilgrim, whose companionship he now wished above all else to share alone, far away in some quiet frontier.

At first James said nothing, but readied himself like a firm anchor in troubled seas. At last, James turned his head in full acknowledgement of the dozens who now surrounded him and spoke.

"Judge for yourselves, citizens of Salisbury!" he urged the onlookers, his voice steady and strong. "I have come to share the words of my people - words of liberty, of unity, of hope."

"Words of treason!" snarled a rattled Benjamin Booth, his spindly frame trembling with rage.

A hush fell upon the crowd. Pilgrim's persistent whimpers and neighs were the only sounds for a several dawdling moments.

At last, men from the crowd step forward.

"Dunn and Booth," one large man's voice bellowed, "you are alone in this belief! None here wish to do anything but support our fellow Scot!" His voice thundered, rallying those around him to stand steadfast.

The gathered onlookers responded with a muttering of agreement, their expressions uncompromising.

"Traitors!" Esquire Booth spat, his words dripping with venomous disdain, his disgust at his neighbors now unable to hide the tremor of fear that coursed through him. He glanced toward Dunn, seeking solace in their shared cause, but found only a mirror of his own trepidation reflected in his ally's eyes.

As Esquire Dunn and Booth looked upon the faces of those they had sought to sway, they realized their efforts had been in vain.

As the fervor of the crowd swelled like a tempestuous sea, a burly man stepped forward, his muscles taut beneath his sweat-streaked shirt. "Let's tar and feather these tory rats!" he blared.

The crowd hollered in agreement, their collective fury igniting into a blaze of righteous indignation. Men surged forth, pinning Booth on the ground alongside Dunn with a grip that extended no reprieve. The two loyalists cried out in terror, their pleas for clemency drowned out by the rallying cries of the townspeople. Their eyes, once filled with arrogance, now shimmered with tears as they faced the wrath of Salisbury's patriots.

James watched in shock as the mob made quick work of tearing the mismatched articles of clothing from the shuddering bodies of the esquires. He searched desperately for the strength to scream above the chaotic clamor of the crowd.

"Enough!" James' voice cut like the steel of a sharpened cutlass.

"Leave em' be."

The blue eyes of James Jack beheld the frenzied scene, taking in the fear etched upon the faces of the fallen esquires and the zealous determination of the now-silenced mob.

"Show them mercy," James implored, his voice heavy with conviction. "Banish them from your town, but let them leave with their lives." James looked down at the men with a sense of pity.

Contemplating the orders of the courier, the men of the town eventually acquiesced, and released their hold on the trembling loyalist. They nodded in silent agreement, their faces full of disappointment at the suspended punishment. The two esquires scrambled to their feet, their humbled glance never once meeting the eyes of their erstwhile captors.

"Go," James commanded, his voice cold as ice. "You are strangers to this land and its country. Do not return."

Amidst the shine of orange skies, John Dunn and Benjamin Booth scrambled to their feet, with marks of intense desperation etched across their faces. The two men wasted no time in gathering themselves, acutely aware of the heavy gazes that followed their every move.

With his hands still secured around the declaration, and his back pressed up against Pilgrim, James watched the esquires make their escape. The men hastily mounted their steeds tethered at the courthouse steps.

The men dug their heels into the flanks of their mounts, urging them forward. A parade of uneasy hooves struck lines of gravel, and the fleeing shadows of the esquires were painted wide by the twilight vista of the sun.

The esquires were never to set foot in Salisbury again.

The silence of the crowd was broken abruptly by the swelling chants of the amused patriots.

"James! James Jack!" The jubilant shouts of the townspeople grew into a mightly crescando. An uncomfortable sensation of unearned accolade overtook James, similarly to how it had felt that fateful night in the courthouse. James watched as the assembly of smiling rebels swarmed around him. Suddently, he felt the warmth of their hands clasped onto his shoulders. He then heard their offering of heartfelt words of support.

"God be with you on your journey, James!" cried one man, his eyes shining with hope.

"Bring us freedom, brother," another implored, his grip firm and resolute.

As the well-wishes shrouded him, James took a moment to absorb the scene before him, freely inviting their passion to seep into his reluctant spirit.

"Thank you, my friends," James finally replied. "I will deliver the will of our people to the delegates meeting in Philadelphia. I will carry before them your courage."

The townspeople nodded in solemn agreement. The faith the men now placed in the manager of Pat Jack's tavern was unwavering, unconditional, and enduring.

As James' turned to leave, the crowd of patriots parted before him, forming an honor guard of sorts, their eyes never leaving his figure as he strode back to Pilgrim, who patiently awaited her master's return.

With the sun dipping low in the sky, casting the sprawling backcountry before him in an amber orb, James mounted Pilgrim once more, his heart racing with adrenaline.

"Come now, Pilgrim," he whispered to his mare, her flanks anxious with anticipation beneath him. "We must make haste towards Virginia."

And thus they set forth, their silhouettes mere shadows against the fading light as they traversed the rugged terrain that lay between them and their destination. The wind whispered through the trees, carrying with it the scent of pine and wildflowers, while the earth crunched beneath Pilgrim's crashing hooves.

"Are ye frightened, lass?" James asked his faithful steed, his voice barely audible above the steady rhythm of their journey. "I admit, I am shaken by our encounter with those loyalist dogs."

Pilgrim, in response, snorted softly and flicked her ears, as if to say she shared her master's trepidation, but would not be deterred. Emboldened by her steadfastness, James straightened in the saddle, his gaze fixed on the distant horizon where the promise of independence beckoned like a siren's call.

And as the last rays of sunlight dipped below the horizon, James and Pilgrim pressed onward, their spirits buoyed by the words penned in that unthinkable proposal.

Chapter 6: Eyes on the Inn

The dirt road upon which Pilgrim strode had become routine and with no unwanted excitement. James made frequent breaks to eat portions of the hardtack biscuits prepared for him by his mother and to drink from the water in his canteen. As the squall from the encounter with the esquires in Salisbury faded, it came to be replaced by the churning storm clouds of an impending thunderstorm.

"I don't believe you're due for a bath quiet yet, are you Pilgrim?" James joked.

James could feel the pressure in the air drop, and he knew the time drew near for Pilgrim and him to find shelter for the night. The sun continued to race below the horizon, painting a stretched shadow of the two companions as they galloped into the boundaries of the minor backcountry town of Bruce's Crossroad.

"Dice and cards," James said with a nostalgic smile. "This is the town where my father used to purchase them for the tavern."

James had become more than comfortable speaking to Pilgrim as though she could listen and respond. It was his primary defense against a debilitating sense of isolation.

Guided by the shadows cast by the setting sun, James arrived at a shabby inn that bore the same name as the village. Situated at the bottom of a hill, and animated only by the occasional gust, the inn appeared as though it had been forsaken years ago.

Though chipped and worn, the creaking wooden sign above the entrance still remained partially legible.

"BRUCS CRSSROAD,"

Cognizant of the need to find shelter as soon as possible, James dismounted from Pilgrim, and tied her loosely to a post in front of the rundown shanty.

"Stay here, Pilgrim," James whispered to his trusted companion, patting the horse's walnut mane. "We'll be warm and dry tonight."

James left all of his supplies resting on Pilgrim, taking only the ever-valuable haversack bag with him as he pulled open the door to the inn.

The grimy state of the inn and its neglected gallery immediately overpowered James as he entered the dwelling. As he walked, his boots stuck to the weathered floors, made syrupy from the uncleaned spills of ale and beer. Only tobacco smoke filled the air, and dust hazily covered the entire room. Faded, hole-ridden linens covered the tables where roughened men sat, speaking in hushed tones and casting suspicious glances around the room. In stark replacement to the sound of the fiddler at Pat Jack's Tavern, the only music at Bruce's Crossroad was the scratching of rats and the whistling of wind coming through loose shutters.

Knowing he would still be more comfortable within the decaying walls than in a vicious downpour, James approached the stout man behind the inn's counter.

"Good evenin', sir," greeted the innkeeper, the details of his face hardly discernible beneath his grizzled beard.

"Name's Luther Waldon, keeper of this humble abode. What can I do for ye?"

James stood at the counter, his hands resting on the leather haversack that hung at his side - its precious contents always weighing heavily on his mind.

"My name is James Jack. I need a room for the night, if you have one available. And a stable for my horse."

"Aye," Luther replied quickly, his voice gruff and rumbly. "Aye, we've got a room available. That'll be two shillings."

James reached into his pocket to produce the coins before realizing they were not in the left pocket of his trousers. James moved the haversack bag out of his way and placed it onto the counter so that he may retrieve the coins from his right pocket, only to realize the pouch was not there either.

James had left his pouch outside with Pilgrim.

After bumbling awkwardly for a moment, James rose his head to meet the eyeing innkeeper.

"My apologies sir, I seem to have left my coins with my steed." James now stood there, one hand in his pocket, and one hand still atop the haversack bag which sat before him on the counter.

Mid-sentence, the innkeeper cut James off.

"Right," stated Luther. "Your horse has some use for shillings?"

"No. I will walk back to her and retrieve your payment."

"So you forgot your coin purse, but not this?" Luther pointed at the haversack bag.

James' whole body froze, and Luther laughed.

James could hear the rain begin to pelt the wooden shingles on the roof.

"Son, it is starting to rain," Luther said menacingly. "You and your greedy horse are welcome to rest here, but I demand you share with me whatever you carry in that satchel," Luther said, lifting his bruised and burned hand to point at the haversack James clutched tightly.

James was deeply confused by the innkeeper's sudden interest in the haversack bag.

"Sir really I-"

"It's starting to rain pitchforks and hoe handles out there boy, now's not the time to be shaking like a leaf in the wind."

James began to haggle.

"It is not bread."

"No matter," replied Luther. "A cold serving of salted pork would do me well."

"It is not ale."

"No matter, water is better for my constitution anyhow."

"Sir, I insist that nothing on my person is of value to you other than the shillings I owe you, please-"

Luther laughed again as the rain cascaded into a torrential downpour.

James was becoming desperate. He could only imagine the restlessness Pilgrim felt in the hail of cool water, not to mention his mother's bundle of supplies. James' worried how long it would take before the downfall weakened Pilgrim's health. Reluctantly, James considered placating the inquisitive innkeeper.

At a crawl, James reached for the haversack bag.

Luther's focus was single-minded, and he resumed his list of predictions.

"I suppose you could fit a small jar of sugar in that bag of yours."

James lifted his head, temporarily perplexed by the strange comment. He resumed slowly reaching for the opening of the bag as Luther rambled on.

"Or maybe a flask of smuggled molasses or tea," Luther sighed. "It'd be a bit small to resell, but I could certainly make my own application of it."

Luther pointed to a stack of molasses on a shelf behind him. Proudly, he remarked,

"Aye, and Charlie told me the stamps on the bottles read of the highest purity this side of the Atlantic."

James paused, his eyes twinkling with strategy as a bolt of lightening temporarily illuminated the dank inn.

"Could you read me the brand on your smuggled tea? If it is 'Twinings', I might have a trade for you," James stated cooly.

Luther grew hushed.

"I can bring it here for you to read."

James now knew his way out of this quandary.

Confident that the illiterate Luther Waldon would be little more than disappointed at the "smuggled" good hidden away in the plain haversack bag, James prepares to pull the declaration from its resting place.

In that instance, the shouting of a man lounging in an unlit corner of the inn interrupted James.

"Waldon, did I hear you say you needed something read?"

"Aye, Charlie! Get up here!"

The color drained from James' face when his began to focus on the figure of Charlie, still masked by the dim lighting surrounding him.

A crimson red coat, and a cocked black military hat.

The British soldier remained lethargic in his chair, moving with no haste to meet Luther's summoning.

In a complete panic, James quickly pushed the declaration back into the haversack bag as he stumbled back from the counter.

"I must go-"

"Relax boy. Charlie gets his share."

Charlie had now risen from his table and was finishing some words with a fellow soldier before beginning his slow walk towards Luther and James.

"Really, it's no concern. I must be gone-"

"Mr. Jack," Luther's expressions were creeping from amused to irritated. "There is truly no need for a faint-heart. You will trade me your smuggled goods for this Twinner tea and a warm bed for you and your precious nag."

James' flusteration had reached a boiling point. Bright flashes of lightning and deafening claps of thunder raging outside the deteriorating walls as James desperately attempted to interject.

"It is not smuggled good-"

"Whatever lad! Whatever is so precious in that bag, you were prepared to trade!"

All eyes in the inn were now fixed on a shrinking James Jack, and as Charlie closed the space between himself and the crumbling exchange, James stepped back meekly.

"I am sorry."

James wasn't sure to whom the apology was truly addressed. The spitting and foaming smuggler, Luther Waldon, surely couldn't have been the intended recipient. James theorized that perhaps the real addressee of his apology was his family and friends back home, for the sin of having made their priceless parchment so vulnerable in the early hours of its maiden voyage. Or perhaps, more simply, James was apologizing to Pilgrim, who likely felt abandoned and frightened in the eye of the raging wind and rain.

"Come back here!" Luther barked and roared at the sight of his enigmatic trade retreating.

James refused to turn his eyes away from Luther and Charlie, and could only hope his feet delivered him to the door through which he entered.

In the dimly lit and cluttered design of the inn's gallery, James collided with barrels, patrons and tables, before finally placing too much faith in too large a step backwards.

"Crash!" The haversack bag swung in the air as James tumbled over a barrel seat and hit the sticky wooden planks on the floor of the inn. The music of the inn was now the symphony of laughter arising from the patrons at Bruce's Crossroad.

The crashing of the thunder mixed with the screams of Luther and the mocking of the patrons was a piercing clamor, but with the sight of Luther restraining an advancing Charlie, and the sight of the door now ahead, James proceeded out into the tempest, with the haversack covered in the interior of his coat.

The hurling of large raindrops made a raven-black night even harder to see through, and the sounds of the late-spring thunderstorm obscured all others.

"Pilgrim!" James yelled frantically.

His brown tricorn hat providing only the smallest respite from the rainfall. James searched wildly after realizing Pilgrim had broken loose of the binds that kept her at the post in front of the inn.

"Pilgrim, please!" James began to grow hopeless.

As the storm raged on, James' spirit lifted upon hearing Pilgrim's familiar neighs in the treeline. Taking great care to keep the haversack completely dry beneath his coat, James broke into a sprint toward the spot on the woods' edge where Pilgrim neighed and snorted.

"Pilgrim, hold on!" James cried out.

There beneath the widest oak tree she could find, Pilgrim had done her best to stay covered from the drenching.

"I guess you got your bath after all, girl."

Moving with a clear lack of dexterity, James quickly undid the buckles which kept the assortment of his parent's supplies fastened to Pilgrim's croup behind James' saddle. As James reached for the larger of two blankets that his mother had securely rolled, the various pots, sacks, and tins began to fall halfhazardly into the damp soil beneath him.

"Here, Pilgrim."

James took the partially dry blanket and tossed it across as much of Pilgrim's body as it would cover. Pilgrim let out a soft nicker in a pitch that almost resembled gratitude.

With the storm still raging onward, James took the second, smaller blanket, and began equipping the blanket as a Feileadh Mor, the traditional garb of his Scottish highland ancestors. The heavy folds draped around his body like a cloak, shielding him from the relentless rain. He then set about fashioning a rudimentary tent, using the sturdy limbs of the surrounding trees to support the makeshift structure.

With the haversack bag now secured under an additional layer of protection, James fixed his eyes forward, into the vast and black wilderness ahead.

James sank onto the damp ground beneath the tent, his mind awash with thoughts of home and all that he had left behind. His wife's gentle laughter, the warmth of their hearth, the camaraderie of his kin. James fought to place memories of warmer nights ahead of the terrible sounds of thunder, and the bright sparks of white lightning that soared down around him.

"God, thank you for your mercy," James whispered to himself. Removing his left hand from underneath the earth-green blanket, James lifted Cynthia's homemade cross up to his drenched lips, and kissed it.

The broken shutters of the inn swung violently in the gale. Mighty pine trees groaned under the force of the storm. As bright lightning and roaring thunder churned above him, James dreamt of home.

Chapter 7: Death is the Sentence

A bright sun now toiled to dry the dampened earth, replacing the luminous strikes of lightning that had labored all night to cleave the heavens. Booming claps of thunder were replaced with the familiar waking calls of mourning doves and northern cardinals.

James lifted his head from the dirt and instinctively reached to ensure that the haversack bag had remained dry under his threaded blanket. After confirming its steadfast survival, James then rose to his feet to examine the state of Pilgrim, who rested contently beneath the damp shade of a young longleaf pine tree. It was only after taking the time to study his companion that the overpowering musty smell of her wet coat and mane struck James.

"Jesus, Pilgrim", James chuckled to himself as he walked over and rustled her to wake.

"Come on friend," he said, patting the horse's neck affectionately. "We have much ground to cover."

Now atop Pilgrim, with all items packed and ready to restart their journey, the two made their way from the treeline back towards the main road north into Virginia.

As they approached the inn, James could not help but notice the number of patrons similarly mounted on their horses, preparing for the day's travel. A fleeting thought crossed James' mind, questioning the ultimate destination awaiting these strangers, but he eventually dismissed the thought.

"Let us make haste, Pilgrim," James urged, blue eyes focused on the horizon. "The Virginia border awaits."

Within the hour, many travelers sojourning north along the storied Great Wagon Road momentarily joined and then separated from James and Pilgrim. Keeping the haversack bag always close in his sight and often brought forward from his side so as to sit upon his lap, James felt confident while exchanging pleasant smiles and glances with numerous passersby along the route.

The entire reach of the road had been, from the time he left Charlotte, surrounded by an endless, and often indistinguishable forest cover. Yet something haunting had now befallen James, a persistent pull into something sinister and worse still, familiar.

Atop an eerily quiet Pilgrim and an even more silent wilderness, James felt tiny. He did his best to rationalize himself out of this feeling of dread, but he could not do it. James heard the sounds of a barred owl hooting ominously in the distance, and as James twisted his head across the now empty road to spot the creature, his tattered brown tricorn hat froze in a moment of sudden and nauseating familiarity.

There on the side of the muddy dirt road was a massive dead tree, buried partially in the suffocating soil beneath it. James halted Pilgrim for a moment as James heard the comforting whispers of his father and his mother. James thought about the warm tarp that had once covered him on this road, and of that gift of invincibility he felt so sure would last forever in the presence of his dear parents.

He thought about that frigid boy, scared and alone in the mouth of a consuming forest.

With Pilgrim now brought to a complete stop, James kept his head turned to his right. James glanced upon the details of the rotting timber, as its multitude of decay marks began to entrance him. Chief among these natural features was a colony of hardened fungi, each sprouting from the tree like cancerous lumps. James' dismounted from Pilgrim, and approached the piece of natural debris with the same caution and reverence one might use when nearing a tomb.

Like a young child awkwardly descending a small ditch, James worked his way down to meet the features of this carcass more intimately.

Once at the fallen tree's level, James lowered himself onto his right knee and placed his brown tricorn hat on his left leg. With a singular focus, James began to examine the seashell-looking-mushrooms protruding from the weakened wood.

"Muir... the seas," James whispered to himself. "I wish to see you with my own eyes one day."

Without warning, James' musings of a tranquil shoreline were harshly interrupted by the sound of Pilgrims' whimpers.

James turned from the tree and looked back towards Pilgrim, who stared intensely, meeting James' perplexity. James then turned his head to the left, slowly, as to delay the escalation of his sudden horror.

There on the road, staring back at James, were the soldiers from the inn.

Unlike the darkness which covered the finer details of the men the night before, James could now take full stock of the soldiers in their handsome red uniforms and statuesque appearance. Eclipsing all other physical features shared between the two men was a wide grin that stretched far beyond where it ought to have ceased, and piercing brown eyes which laced with venom the first words they spat upon James.

"Whatcha got in your pack, Jack?"

James froze in place as the two soldiers turned to one another and laughed.

The one soldier began slowly riding his steed forward, closing the yards between himself and a comatose Pilgrim.

"We weren't sure when you'd ever stop," quipped the advancing soldier. "We just figured eventually you'd stop to take a piss or something."

James' eyes darted in between the two soldiers and Pilgrim, who had refused to break her gaze with James.

The advancing soldier halted about seventy-five feet from James.

"Whatever you have in that damn pack of yours is worth something mighty, or else you'd have just sold it to Waldon back at the inn," shouted the soldier in the back, who now rode slowly to meet his stopped partner.

"Throw us the pack and you are free to go," promised the forward soldier. His intense and unnatural smile has not broken rank since James first noticed him.

James could hardly believe he had found himself in such an impossible bind. He was in no position to barter and knew defiance was likely a death sentence.

Yet with Pilgrim's gaze now apparently full of understanding, and her head bowed as if ready to sprint, James charged atop the road and lept for his ever-ready steed.

In one harsh and rapid motion, James threw his body upon Pilgrim, taking only the fraction of a second he needed to assure the haversack bag stayed joined to him throughout the rapid movement.

Pilgrim squealed like a swine for slaughter, and before James could register it, she had carried them both over a hundred feet of the speckled dirt road.

"Stop!"

The demands of the soldiers were barely audible over the stampeding sounds of their stallion's hooves impressing into the ground below.

James gripped Pilgrim's reins. Her swift pace jerked James unexpectedly, blurring the world around him into a green and brown blur. Leaves whipped against his face as tree branches reached to ensnare the desperate pair.

"Fly, Pilgrim, fly!" James implored, his voice rising above the thunder of hoofbeats.

The scent of damp earth and dew-laden foliage filled the air, mingling with the bitter tang of fear and sweat. James' breath came in ragged gasps, his heart pounding like a drum as the thunderous hooves of the soldier's steeds grew nearer.

Through the tangled veil of branches and leaves, James stole a glance behind him. The two soldiers were bearing down, their scarlet coats stark against the verdant landscape, swords glinting in the dappled sunlight. Their marionette grins refusing to fade. Every fiber of James' being screamed for relief, to give in to the relentless inevitability of capture.

Still, he kept on. With a surge of determination, James leaned low over Pilgrim's neck, urging her onward. The mare responded with a valiant burst of speed, her powerful limbs eating up the ground as she raced through the underbrush.

The thunderous hoofbeats of Pilgrim and her pursuers reverberated through the dense forest, a cacophony that echoed beyond the trees. Suddenly, the war drums fell silent.

"Crack!" The source of the sudden blast was made evident by its immediate successor, a whizzing whistle sent inches from the corners of James' tricorn hat.

"Fire again!" cried one soldier, his voice a snarl of authority and rage.

James turned in shock, only to behold that his grinning pursuers now wielded the gleaming barrels of two pistols leveled directly at him.

With a deft hand, James worked to steady the trembling Pilgrim. He could do little other than to keep her focused on the coarse sod before them.

Bullets rang out in intervals which grew alarmingly close by the minute. Finally, James did what he could to respond.

Steady to ensure one hand remained gripped on Pilgrim's reins, James reached into his coat and wrapped his fingers around the cold, reassuring weight of his pistol. Desperation lent him speed as he drew the weapon forth and geared it towards his pursuers.

"Crack!"

Though he could feel Pilgrim beginning to ride erratically, James kept his body turned just long enough to see that his bullet landed somewhere between the tree he woke up under that morning, and the stash of smuggled molasses at Bruce's Crossroad.

"Curse my aim!" James hollered at himself. Pilgrim snorted anxiously in between pounding waves of painful breaths, as the buckles holding his mother's supply of food, gear and other provisions gave way. James watched in horror as his only inventory of goods tumbled onto the trail behind him.

With his blood now hammering from within every inch of his body, James fumbled desperately with the powder and ball, struggling to reload his flintlock as Pilgrim's hooves rumbled beneath him. The wind whipped at his face, tearing at his clothes and stinging his eyes.

Removing his one hand from Pilgrim's reins, he whispered to her while balanced precariously as she raced across the unforgiving terrain.

"Steady girl."

With his pistol jammed, James heard one soldier approach so closely that the sound of his sword clashing against its mount could be heard above the thundering of hooves.

James summoned every ounce of focus he could muster, as he worked diligently to load his pistol. His heart pounded in his ears, drowning out the clamor of hoofbeats and the baying of the wind. At last, James released both hands from Pilgrim's reins, twisted his torso, and let out a wild scream as he pointed his dark brown flintlock square into the chest of his pursuer.

James pulled the trigger.

The pistol's report rang out like a clap of thunder, triumphant and terrible. The bullet found its mark, passing without pause through the crimson-stained coat of Cornelius Smith. A look of shock and disbelief crossed the soldier's face as he toppled from his horse, crashing down onto the hard ground with a sickening thud.

James turned forward, tears now swelling in his eyes. His body involuntarily hugged onto Pilgrim's mane, not daring to turn back again. All he could do is hold on tightly to the still racing Pilgrim, and dream vibrant scenes of the tavern fiddler, in a futile attempt to drown out the excruciating sound of Charles' cries for his fallen friend.

Charles Campbell, the remaining pursuer, brought his steed to a dramatic halt, his face chiseled with horror and disbelief. Perhaps out of some noble sense of obligation, James turned back and managed one last glance at his wake. Laid upon the dark and slick road, he saw that Cornelius' wicked smile had remained plastered upon his lifeless and contorted body; and that an expression of raw misery had now replaced Charles'.

As he watched Charles fall to his knees over the wretched body of his partner, James bowed his head as if to pray.

"Forgive me, my foe," James whispered, before urging Pilgrim onward, her hooves pounding out a requiem for the fallen as they leapt from the road and vanished deep into the Virginian wilderness.

Chapter 8: Welcome to New Bern

The greased axels of the wagon creaked and groaned as they journeyed across the wooden bridge, its thick beams darkened by years of rain and ceaseless waves. Brilliant rays of sunshine greeted the esquires as they crossed the Trent River's shimmering waters, replacing the rain from earlier in their journey. The unvaried melody produced by travel across a piedmont frontier yielded to something neither John Dunn nor Benjamin Booth had ever heard: a river's song. At the joining of the Neuse and Trent Rivers, the sounds of nature created a symphony wholly unique, one that heralded both men to their arrival in New Bern, the thriving capital of Colonial North Carolina.

"Behold, the bounty of civilization!" jested Benjamin, his voice lush with a degree of genuine sincerity. His ever-enthuastic friend John echoed his companion's sentiment. The streets of New Bern were rich and teeming with activity; well-dressed gentlemen engaged in animated discourse, while elegant ladies strolled along the cobblestone promenade, parasols twirling lightly in their hands.

"I've not seen these kinds of colors since before we left Bristol," remarked John. His gaze drifted from the covered wagon and over the peaks of the Swiss architecture that adorned the landscape. Buildings were painted in bright hues of red, blue, and emerald, and their peaked roofs reaching skyward, as if to grasp at Heaven itself.

With purposeful intent, the two esquires directed their wagon through the bustling thoroughfares, each of their beady eyes drawn to the grandeur of the vessels that floated along the river's surface. Amidst a dance of smaller craft gliding effortlessly through the waterways, tall ships, their sails unfurled like angel wings, lay at anchor.

The esquires both leaned out of their small conestoga wagon to get a better view of the ships anchored along the rich blue river. As their wagon turned the corner to become fully a part of the cobblestone street, the men turned to one another as Benjamin spoke.

"It's definitely not Salisbury."

As they ventured deeper into town and away from the sight of the seafaring behemoths, the men continued to be amazed by the liveliness of the colonial capital. As the men glanced upwards, the steeples of churches greeted them, standing starkly against a cloudless sky.

With John Dunn and Benjamin Booth under the reins, the wagon continued along the fanciful path of South Front street. The dry scent of the stones beneath their wagon's wheel were intermediately laced with the salt-infused wisps of the oceanic rivers.

As the men rounded the wagon over the last bend in their long journey, the resonance of something regimental grew unmistakable. Through the infrequent break in thick hedges, the two men could see shadows of crimson red. At one point, John Dunn, seated closest to this manicured barrier, looked upward and saw the Union Jack flying proudly in the river-breathed breeze.

Fixed atop the blue canvas of the fluttering flag was the diagonal white cross of Saint Andrew, rested just below the scarlet cross of Saint George, whose depiction together told of the union between the ancient kingdoms of England and Scotland.

The esquires had turned the last corner of their expansive journey and now glared upon their awaited destination: the governor's palace.

"By God."

Both men descended from their wagon; Benjamin falling to the ground under the unsteady support of gangly legs that had been bent too long.

As he rose to his feet, he joined John in a state of humbled awe as they watched the exhibition of the British empire displayed upon this small Carolina parcel. An eight foot tall wrought-iron fence adorned with gold accents lined the perimeter of the premise. A large stable housing the governor and his men's many steeds joined the massive brick dwelling on one side, a two-story kitchen extended the grand home on the other. The kitchen's primary working hands, the enslaved Africans forced to supply all manner of labor to the grand home, walked timidly before the palace's many patrolling soldiers.

From the tulips and pansies that bloomed in the palace's parterre garden, to the crows that sat atop the royal coat of arms mounted to the home's mighty front facade, every eye bore witness to the king's presence and might.

As John Dunn drew in a sharp breath through his oversized maw, his brown eyes widening as he took in the imposing facade, which towered before the lawn. "By the grace of God," he whispered, "I have never seen such a sight."

"Nor have I," confessed Benjamin, equally struck by the grandeur that lay before them.

After standing in awe for what probably appeared to the local population a rather unreasonable length of time, the two men awkwardly began approaching the tall black iron gates guarding the palace's main entrance.

As they reached the palace's gates, the legion of redcoats working diligently around the grounds quickly noticed their out-of-place appearance. After much waiting at the black gates by the two anxious esquires, two soldiers began marching towards the men.

The esquires glanced at one another, their eyes darting between themselves and the approaching soldiers. Just as soon as the two soldiers were within earshot, Benjamin Booth cleared his throat and raised his left hand dramatically into the air before beginning to shout: "We, the noble esquires and honorary baronets of this fair land, demand an audience with His Excellency, Gov-"

"Clang!" The sound of the senior soldier striking his sword against the wrought-iron fence caused both esquires to fall back in fear.

"Remove yourself from these grounds at once!" commanded the stern and fearful guard.

"Sir, we have -" pleaded John.

"Vanquish yourselves from our sight this instant!" Ordered the second soldier, who had now fixed his bayonet-led rifle upon the two anomalous visitors.

With both sets of arms raised in a display of non-combativeness, and in a manner completely out-of-style with how they had envisioned it the last several days on the road, the esquires sheepishly and with quaking voices finally revealed their cause for visiting the home of the royal governor:

"We bring news of a rebellion in the backcountry!"

The one soldier kept his rifle set directly upon the two cowering men, while the other stood in a moment of contemplative silence.

"Indeed!" interjected John Dunn, stepping closer to the gate and lowering his voice conspiratorially. "We bring news of a great rebellion threatening to inflame not only this colony but the entire continent!"

The senior soldier lowered his rifle slowly, revealing a face stained with concern and doubt.

"News of a rebellion, you say?" the guardsman's voice boomed.

"Aye," replied the esquires with a newfound confidence.

The two soldiers turned and looked at each other in a solemn exchange of worried glances.

"Lieutenant Jones, bring me Morrison."

The younger of the two men turned to his superior and nodded dutifully.

"Yes sir, Captain Walker."

With this brief but telling exchange, Lieutenant Jones quickly walked away from the two curious esquires, and down the cobblestone road toward an unknown destination. Once he was out of sight, Captain Walker turned back towards the two esquires and ordered,

"Follow me."

The esquires watched as Captain Walker pulled open the gold-tipped iron gate. Once Captain Walker opened the path, the esquires silently fell into formation and followed the decorated British soldier onto the formal lawn of the governor's palace.

The smells of sea salt and turpentine from the docks gave way to the aroma of cooked mutton and freshly baked bread from the kitchen. The enslaved who worked both in visible range and out of visible range mostly ignored the out-of-place backcountry loyalists, as did the rows of British soldiers who cleaned their rifles and made use of their time on every corner of the guarded palace lawn. As the esquires approached the steps to the door of the palace, their minds raced. With as much subtlety as the ungraceful Benjamin Booth could muster, he turned to his peer and whispered,

"Is it 'your excellency' or is it 'your grace'?"

John Dunn shrugged his shoulders haplessly and responded,

"Don't know. Just remember to bow your head."

As Captain Walker pulled open the cream door to the palace, John turned back towards Benjamin in a motion so uncoordinated he nearly fell down the steps he'd just ascended.

"Your hat! Don't forget to remove it."

The men removed their tricorn hats, revealing knots of unwashed hair on Booth, and a marked bald spot on Dunn. With a nod of gratitude to Captain Walker, they entered the refined realm of the governor's mansion, which was known across the colony by a different name: Tryon Palace.

The esquire's eyes drank freely from the opulence that now surrounded them. Gilded moldings adorned the marble white walls, whose height reached far beyond the men's reach. Fine tapestries woven with threads of gold and silver depicted scenes of great battles and triumphant victories. At the instruction of Captain Walker, the two men sat nervously upon fine furnishing which, like much of the material composing the palace's interior, must have had its origins outside the confines of the colony.

As the men sat anxiously awaiting their meeting with the royal governor, they noticed the piercing stare of marble busts, whose formless eyes from identities unknown, brought upon the esquires a feeling of nearly unbearable consequence.

Lieutenant Jones walked with a focused purpose beneath the shade of magnolia and dogwood trees which had been planted along the side of the cobblestone streets. With the palace now out of his view, Jones turned down a less crowded street and towards his much less elegant stop: the county jail.

Jones mused about how an uninspired architect had built the small white building with as little imagination as possible: completely square and with one black door and two barred windows on either side. The only unique feature of the unassuming white cube that was the county jail, was the part completely unseeable from the road; the hidden staircase, and the underground dungeon within. After pausing beneath a particurally shady magnolia to catch his breath from the hurried pace, Jones wiped a line of sweat from beneath his cocked black hat and hesitantly placed his bronze key into the door of the county jail and opened it, unearthing a suffocating darkness.

As Jones walked into the nearly pitch-black room, his lack of sight narrowed all of his senses upon the wretched smells of misery and waste. The assaulting presence of rancid meat, damp stones mixed with ammonia and mildew, and what felt like the stale breath of some unfathomable beast, shaped the room.

Upon retrieving the lantern attached to the wall beside the door, Jones cautiously waded through the uninviting space, his military boots periodically overtaken by the scurrying of prison mice.

"Officer Morrison! This is Lieutenant Jones. Where are you?"

As Lieutenant Jones listened intently for some clue as to if Morrison was even in this misleadingly sized prison, he heard a response come from within the unknowable abyss surrounding him.

It wasn't words that answered Jones' calls, it was screams. Screams of methodical torture and hopeless wailing. Cries for unanswered mercy and unfulfilled moments of physical reprieve.

A symphony of suffering that stood to make the stewards of Hell jealous.

With this, Jones knew where to find Edward Morrison. He lifted the newly found trap door and began his descent down the accursed stairs.

The inexhaustible screams of pain did not end until Jones was over halfway down the stairs, and as he crept over the last step, Jones turned to see a much larger room than upstairs.

Unlike upstairs, there was a light in the underground dungeon. A series of candles hung from the unpainted brick walls, and beneath their flickering illumination was a scene that caused Lieutenant Jones to feel as a stranger might feel if he was dropped into the center of another man's home: alone, unwelcomed, and paralyzed with fear at the thought of attracting the notice of the large man whose back he now faced.

Before Jones could speak, a shivering man stood up from the crude table where Edward had presumably tied him moments before. His partial clothing could not hide his spiritual nakedness. He stumbled and tripped back into his cellar, of which there were approximately six on either side of the damp room.

"Officer Morrison?" inquired the shaky Lieutenant Jones.

The man said nothing, and continued to handle some blade, his back remaining turned on the Lieutenant.

Jones grew angry and spoke once more.

"Officer Morrison! This is Lieutenant Jones and I am ordering you to turn and face me!"

After waiting a couple of seconds, the man responded coldly,

"Have the foxgloves begun to blossom?"

Aware of the pressing schedule he was under to gather Morrison for their meeting with the royal governor, Jones approached the shadowed man, shouting as he went.

"Edward Morrison! I am commanding you -"

At last, the large man turned and faced Lieutenant Jones, towering over him as he calmly asked once more,

"Have the foxgloves begun to blossom, Lieutenant?"

Edward, whose shoulder length black mane and icy green eyes looked down at a still defiant Jones, continued,

"And the Lilacs, Jones. What about them? As you watch over the subjects of Martin's gardens, you should know enough to tell me."

Jones took a small step back, but kept his eyes locked with Morrison's.

"Quit your bitterness and come with me."

Edward laughed. His explosive burst of noise startled the cautious lieutenant.

"I have more to guard in my kingdom than Rose Bushes and garden hares," snickered Edward.

He lifted his blood-stained dagger and aimed it at the dozen prisoners still cowering in their wet cells.

"My day's duties have just begun."

Edward turned from Jones and began walking towards the first cell on his left. The emboldened orders of Lieutenant Jones interrupted the sound of a prisoner whimpering.

"It is His Excellency who demands your presence!"

Edward abruptly halted his walk and whispered coldly.

"I was not aware the governor could stand the presence of a low-born."

Jones replied aggressively, "you will not refuse the governor's command!"

Edward punched his bloodied dagger into the bars of the prison cell before turning and barreling towards the cornered lieutenant.

"If the royal governor wishes to see me, he may do so himself. I will be damned to heed the barking orders of some novice high-born prance!"

Despite being outsized by nearly half a foot and out-aged by nearly a dozen years, Lieutenant Jones held his ground and responded calmly.

"We have guests from the backcountry. They speak of a rebellion and wish to share this news with His Excellency. You must help secure these men... if their intentions are false or prove threatening to our governor."

Edward took a step back, finally breaking his gaze with Maddox Jones. Edward glanced down, his heart in conflict over rather to issue a jeer about being the royal governor's selected bodyguard, or to embrace the bubbling curiosity now within him. Reluctantly, the stubborn soldier chose the latter.

"The prisoners can wait. Take me to these backcountry tories."

With the lantern in Jones' right hand, and the bloody dagger still in Edward's left, the two men ascended the dungeon stairs and began the journey back to the governor's mansion.

The esquires had remained patiently seated upon the velvet bench under the watchful glare of the marble busts opposite the grand parlor.

While the men anxiously fiddling with the buttons on their jackets and loose threads on their trousers, a sudden noise arose as the esquires watched the heavy oak doors of the waiting room swing open, revealing a dour-faced servant.

"His Excellency will see you now," he intoned solemnly, gesturing for the esquires to follow him.

The two men rose from their seats and once again followed the lead of men far more assured within the walls of the governor's elegant home.

The esquires entered through the oak doors and found themselves in a chamber that left the men speechless.

The two men felt utterly humbled by the scale of every feature in the expansive room. Massive portraits of King George III and his wife, Queen Charlotte, hung on one side of the accented walls. Portraits of aristocrats the esquires could not hope to name hung adoringly along the remaining portions of the walls. Gold accented furniture gleamed and glowed, standing in stark contrast to the dark wood paneling that lined the lengths of the mighty room. And there, at the end of the long and singular panels of oak wood on the floor, sat an opulent desk, and at its helm stood a man adorned with privilege, yet haggard with burden: the Royal Governor of North Carolina, Josiah Martin.

The esquires performed a head bow so extended and unnatural it almost appeared they hurt themselves.

Governor Martin wore a gentle smile, and walked around the side of his large oak desk, keeping one hand gliding along the surface as he went. Once he reached the front of the desk, his silk blue coat, laced with gold adorning and black trousers, came into full view under the sunlight from the large glass windows surrounding the men.

His white wig was placed upon his head with precision, and his blue eyes seemed to tell of a man whose soul had aged faster than his flesh. He placed his best foot forward and spoke to the esquires.

"Welcome to New Bern. I have been told you traveled the road all the way from Salisbury. Please tell, what impelled you to travel this distance?"

John Dunn turned to his friend Benjamin Booth before speaking, his words stammering at the start.

"Your Excellency... I... we... have traveled from our homes to tell you of a great rebellion forming in the hills of the backcountry."

Already knowing the contents of this first statement, but nothing beyond this, the Governor Martin listened intently.

"Please, continue."

John Dunn continued.

"Your Excellency, it is Charlotte, and the people of Mecklenburg County. There, the men of town have written and fixed their names upon a parchment, declaring themselves free of yours, and His Majesty the King's rule." John paused, and Benjamin Booth finished his thoughts.

"There is a rogue. A scoundrel by the name of James Jack, who is racing to bring this parchment... this treason of his kin, to the Continental Congress in Philadelphia."

Governor Josiah Martin stood in silence for what felt like an endless occassion, before slowly turning from the esquires and walking uniformly back behind his large oak desk.

The room was now filled with the presence of the esquires, Captain Walker, Junior Lieutenant Jones, Officer Edward Morrison, and their superior,

Lieutenant Roger Smalls—all waiting anxiously to hear Governor Martin's response.

At long last, the words spilled from his lips, the passion behind them subtly betraying the man's stoic appearence. Governor Martin's pleasant face had now contorted into an unmasked snarl.

"By God," swore Governor Martin, his words dripping with bile, "these traitors shall fail in their seditious schemes."

With a sudden and unexpected swing of his fist, Josiah Martin turned back the men present in the stately room. The veins on Josiah Martin's forehead bulged like the roots of towering oaks as his clenched fist slammed down upon the polished mahogany desk. The impact sent a tremor through the lavish chamber, momentarily shocking its witnesses into complete silence.

"I will not be undone by some backcountry Carolinian rogues!" The Royal Governor roared out in fury, his voice booming like thunder over the rolling seas.

The wrath of Governor Martin was contagious, and it spread quickly through the hearts of the men in the halls of Tryon Palace.

"Your Excellency," interjected Roger Smalls, the governor's trusted lieutenant and head of his forces, "we must act swiftly to quell this rebellion before it spreads any further." Lieutenant Smalls voice was firm, yet tinged with an undercurrent of urgency.

"Indeed," agreed Governor Martin. His blue eyes had cooled to a unruffled demeanor, but his movement persisted with intensity. Aflame with an intense hatred for the news now laid upon him, Governor Martin removed himself from behind his desk and returned to stand in the center of the half-circle of witnesses.

The esquires stood timidly, as Governor Josiah Martin turned to face his lieutenant directly.

Lieutenant Roger Smalls, a devoted and professional servant of the crown, stood ready to receive his commands.

"First, Lieutenant Smalls, I charge you with organizing a unit to march on Charlotte," Josiah lifted his finger and pointed aggressively.

"Root out these traitorous scoundrels and let them feel the severe consequence of their rebellion!"

Lieutenant Smalls, feeling no less hatred than his superior for the Mecklenburg rogues, answered calmly and with a steadiness in his voice.

"We shall carry out your orders with swift and unyielding precision, Your Excellency."

As Roger prepared to depart from the grand room and begin organizing his mission, the esquires shifted uncomfortably where they stood, their thoughts ringing like a blacksmith's hammer. *What hell had they just brought down upon their backcountry neighbors?*

"Second," Josiah declared, his voice echoing out like a trumpet's blast among the opulent splendor of his office, "I shall pen my frustration and beseech our most gracious Majesty the King for support in this dire matter." He strode purposefully to the grand mahogany desk, which dominated one end of the room.

Seating himself with impressive ceremony, he dipped the quill into the inkwell; the blackness staining its tip as he prepared to lay bare his soul upon the parchment. "His Majesty must realize the perilous situation we face. These treacherous rogues threaten the very foundations of his realm, and we must spare no effort in quelling this rebellion."

As he wrote, the words flowed from his hand like the coursing waters of the Trent River, their power and eloquence matched only by the depth of Martin's despair.

The royal governor labored before the parchment for several minutes, the gnawing doubt of the letter's value in the present war festered within him, like a persistent worm burrowing through his mind. *What if his efforts were not enough? What if in the three months it would take for reinforcements to arrive from London, this fire of insurrection spread too far, too fast?*

"Who," Martin muttered, an edge of despair sharpening his tone as he rose from his chair and paced the length of the extravagant chamber, "could hunt down this rogue headed to Philadelphia, and bring him to heed?"

Amid Governor Martin's lament, a shadow detached itself from the ornate walls of the chamber, taking form as it stepped forward. Edward Morrison, his countenance cast in ironclad resolve, stepped into the light that danced upon the room's gilded surfaces. His green eyes, cut like that of a dragon, quickly met with those of the harried governor.

"Your Excellency," Edward uttered, his voice a low and steady hum, "I stand before you, prepared to undertake this mission. Let me be the instrument of your will, the hand that plucks this traitorous serpent from your garden."

The room fell silent, all eyes now fixed on the towering frame of the dutiful soldier. The esquires, who only moments before had been embroiled in their own heated conversation, now watched with rapt attention.

Josiah studied the man before him, noticing the tight clinch of his jaw and the raging inferno behind his emerald eyes. "And what makes you believe, Officer Morrison, that you are the one to bring this rogue to heel?"

Edward's lips curved into a dry smile. "I have tracked fugitives through the wilds of this untamed land, stalking them like beasts through the densest forests and darkest nights. I have fought at your side and bled the veins of your adversaries in your name, Your Excellency. My loyalty is unyielding, and my purpose unwavering. This 'James Jack' shall never deliver his seditious message if I am granted leave to hunt him down."

A flicker of hope sparked within Josiah's chest, and the downtrodden governor lifted his chest and held Edward's gaze, seeking any sign of doubt or hesitation, but finding none.

"Very well," the governor declared, his voice resonating with newfound determination. "Edward Morrison, I charge you with intercepting James Jack and seizing the declaration he carries. You shall return both to this palace so that justice may be served."

"By my honor and my life, Your Excellency," Edward vowed, dropping to one knee and bowing his head in a show of fealty, "I will pursue my quarry relentlessly until I deliver it to you, dead or alive."

"Rise, Edward," Josiah commanded. "Your valor and initiative are commendable. Return to your young family and prepare yourself for the journey ahead."

"Thank you, Your Excellency," Edward replied, standing tall, his eyes gleaming with fierce determination. "I shall make haste and not disappoint you, nor our king."

"Go forth, then," Josiah affirmed, watching as Edward bowed once more before striding from the grand east wing, every step echoing his unwavering fixation.

As the door closed behind Edward, Josiah turned his gaze upon the esquires, who had remained silent witnesses to the unfolding events.

"Gentleman," he began, his tone softer yet still commanding, "you have done your King and country a great service. As a token of my gratitude, you shall have a shelter in the palace for as long as you would like."

"Your Excellency is most kind," Benjamin Booth responded, his eyes wide with surprise and appreciation. "Your generosity honors us."

"Indeed," John Dunn chimed in, equally awed. With a breathless sigh between beaming lips, he exclaimed, "we shall forever be in your debt."

"Think nothing of it," Josiah dismissed, a flicker of a smile playing on his lips. "The crown must reward loyalty."

With a flourish of his hand, Josiah bid the esquires farewell as a palace butler escorted them away. Their footsteps echoed through the grand halls, leaving Governor Martin in a sudden stillness, interrupted only by the rustle of parchment on his desk.

Turning slowly, Josiah strode across the lavish chamber, each step punctuated by the rhythmic tapping of his boots against the polished floors. He halted before the towering window that overlooked the front lawn of Tryon Palace, his eyes surveying the verdant expanse with a mixture of pride and dread. Under the shine of an early-summer sun, the illuminated and immaculate grounds of the palace became hustling as the legion of soldiers became aware of the happenings in the colony's backcountry.

"O mighty land, how shall I ensure thy protection?" Governor Martin murmured, his voice laden with a resentful burden. The son of a Caribbean planter, and the heir to an established lineage of British authorities, the dutiful administrator was determined to not let his, the ninth tenure of royal governorship over North Carolina, be the last. As the threads of his kingdom became frayed by the insidious whispers of rebellion, Royal Governor Josiah Martin became irate.

Spurred by an anxious jolt, Josiah walked to the opposite end of the room, and glanced out over the rippling waves of the Trent River.

"By the grace of God and King, I shall prevail," he vowed, his voice resolute with conviction. "Carolina will not fall."

Chapter 9: An Instrument of Justice

A single church bell tolled as the morning fog lifted over the restful streets of New Bern, and the earliest rays of the sun settled upon an already risen Edward.

While the aroma of fresh cornbread waifed from his kitchen, Edward sat atop a tree stump in his lawn, looking out contemplatively over the still waters of the Neuse River.

"Edward! Come inside," Sarah, Edward's wife, called for him from inside their small home. Edward lowered the sword which he had been sharpening since before the sun had began its long ascent over the vastness of the Pamlico sound, and he turned to join the company of his beloved.

"Fresh cornbread this morning," said Sarah. Edward, a man of towering stature and fierce demeanor, stood before the hearth as flames danced in his frosty green eyes. The brass buttons on his blood-red uniform gleamed like miniature suns. His hands, calloused from years of wielding sword and musket, lovingly caressed the hilt of his saber - an extension of himself, the instrument of justice that had served him well.

"Sarah," he said, his voice a deep rumble resonating throughout the modest cottage, "I promise you, my dear, this shall be a swift endeavor."

Her short red hair curled at the base of her petite shoulders, and her sulking blue eyes gazed downward as she wringed her hands anxiously.

"Edward, I understand not why you wish to do this," she whispered, her voice wavering. "You can still tell his Excellency that you have decided against it."

"I cannot."

"But it is not your obligation!" pleaded Sarah.

"It is all my obligation."

Edward turned from the morning fire, walking over to face his trembling wife directly.

"This is an opportunity, Sarah. The governor told me himself."

"How can you be sure that he speaks the truth this time? How can you know?"

"Should I bring this bastard to him, dead or alive, then he shall have no choice." Edward reached for Sarah's hands. "Should I do this, the governor has promised me a lieutenant's commission."

Sarah jumped to her feet and paced.

"But Edward -"

"My love, this is nothing more than a jaunt in the brush, a 'morning's pursuit'." Edward searched desperately for the words that would placate his wife's worries.

"It is a simple matter. I will hunt and bring to justice this frontier filth, just as I did during Governor Tryon's 'War of Regulation.'"

Sarah looked back anxiously.

"You remember, don't you love? Lieutenant Smalls and I, we trapped those fools like vermin."

Sarah smiled lightly.

"Aye, I remember."

"This is no different. A quick foray into the forest, and when I return, we shall have all that we've ever wanted."

"All we've ever deserved," corrected Sarah.

"Be well, my love." Edward kissed Sarah goodbye as he set off through the front door of the cottage, ready to mount his stallion, Eclipse.

"Trust in me, Sarah," called Edward as he walked towards his jet-black steed. "I shall return victorious, and when I do, our family shall finally know good fortunes."

"Where are you riding?" Sarah called.

"West," Edward stated plainly. "From there, I will reach into the minds of my companions in the piedmont."

"Edward," Sarah ran to him, now sitting atop Eclipse, "I love you."

Edward looked down through Sarah's copper-red hair and said with great affection,

"I love you too."

The dawn was setting, and the winds blew west. Edward Morrison was on the hunt.

Urging Eclipse forward, Edward set off on his journey west, charting his course. By the strategy of all frontier adventurers, Edward knew to travel upstream along the banks of the Neuse River, following its southern branches at every split, until eventually arriving in the rural county of Wake. There, at its seat, Bloomsbury, would be where the king's men found refuge among the hills.

With a relentless hatred for the rogues in rebellion, and a thirst for tribute from his governor, Edward raced Eclipse along the riverbanks towards a frontier that would be frightened to see his wrath return.

Three Nights Later

On a tall and sturdy tree branch sat a red-tailed hawk, his yellow eyes following a white-footed mouse, as it nervously crossing an open part of the dirt trail that ran along the Neuse River, now little more than a large creek.

In the ears of the white-footed mouse, the sounds of the Neuse's waters overpowered his world, colliding and rushing over smooth stones in its path. In the eyes of the white-footed mouse, the blades of grass were towering, and the open dirt road was as vast and unforgiving as an ocean.

The white-footed mouse had one aim: survive. Scurry across that patch of earth without notice, and he may live. Yet if seen, some primal nightmare predator would surely consume him.

When the earth shook, the white-footed mouse scurried in terror.

The red-tailed hawk watched, confused at first, when the white mouse he stalked quickly scurried off the road and into the tall grass along the banks. Instantly, the hawk noticed the powerful black stallion that raced towards him.

The hawk lept from the tree branch and surveyed from above.

In his red crimson coat and his black tricorn hat, Edward Morrison raced along Eclipse in a position that suggested they had not rested but for brief breaks for three straight days.

With sweat dripping from his forehead, and his shoulder length hair greased from the physical toil of a three-day ride, Edward was in no desire to halt now. He knew his destination was close. As the river grew narrower and narrower, and the plains turned to rolling hills, Edward knew that the British outpost of Bloomsbury was near.

The sun dipped below the horizon, casting a crimson hue over the land as Edward and Eclipse traversed the winding path toward Bloomsbury. The scent of blooming wildflowers filled Edward's nostrils as he filled the forest with the rhythmic thud of his steed's hooves.

Instead of a proper town fit with homes or shops, Bloomsbury was recognizable first by the large clearing in the woods, left unfinished in parts by a sea of tree stumps, and second, by a primitive frontier fort: its perimeter, an area no larger than the yards around Pat Jack's tavern, were protected by wooden palisade walls, and a single wooden gate.

Plain and simple wooden barracks filled its interior. Stationed in the outpost's single watchtower, a dutiful soldier of the empire, watched as the midnight black Eclipse galloped towards its gate.

"State your name, soldier!" the watchman called down to Edward.

"I am Edward."

The watchman was on the verge of chuckling at the stranger's omission of his surname, but the Edward's glare was potent and overflowing with poisonous hate. The soldier thought better than to laugh.

"I need your full name, soldier."

"Open the gate and I will give it to you."

Reasoning that it was not worth elevating Edward's frustration, the soldier motioned for his men to open the wooden gate.

"Let him in!"

Edward raced Eclipse into the outpost. He dismounted with practiced ease and tethered the horse to a nearby post before striding toward the door, his thoughts focused on determining the quickest path to intercept the rogue named James Jack.

"What can I do for you?"

Edward left the soldier with no response, and instead marched past him, and directly towards the center barrack of the outpost.

"Sir!" called the guard, running after Edward.

As Edward pushed open the door to the center barrack, the creaking hinges of the imperfectly cut door signaled his arrival.

Edward fully expected to be greeted by the boisterous laughter and camaraderie of his fellow soldiers. Instead, a hushed silence filled the room, punctuated only by the pitiful whimpers of a broken man.

As Edward approached the circle of soldiers that surrounded the mourning man, who was knelt down in the circle's center, Edward noticed each of their faces were somber and weary, as if bearing the weight of a thousand sorrows.

"What happened here?" inquired Edward.

"Alas," the soldier sighed, "tragedy has struck our ranks. Our brother-in-arms, Cornelius, has fallen in pursuit of a vile miscreant."

"Who shot him?" asked Edward, plainly.

The soldier, who was kneeling over the corpse of his comrade, slowly turned to face Edward. His eyes told of a man who had gone days without sleep as he spoke.

"Verily, this rogue refused our command to reveal the contents of his haversack bag, and so we gave chase," Charles continued, his voice cracking under the weight of his grief. "But alas, our pursuit ended in tragedy, for my dear friend lies dead, felled by the hand of this vile criminal."

"We were gaining on him," Charles continued, his voice gaining momentum as the events replayed in his mind. "We closed in, surrounding him in a clearing bathed in the dying light of day. It was then that he turned to face us, an air of defiance in his stance, his eyes wild yet calculating. Before we could react, he drew a pistol from his belt and fired."

Without allowing even a moment to process Charles' account, Edward coldly replied,

"Why did you want his bag?"

"We suspected him of carrying smuggled goods."

Growing increasingly curious about Charles' encounter, Edward rapidly approached him and the stiff cadaver of Cornelius, armed with several eager questions.

"Tell me again, what set your eyes upon this man? Did you retrieve his name? What was his appearance? Where did you last encounter him?"

Shaken by Edward's lack of restraint in the face of a fallen soldier, Charles gave a slight grimace and a shallow swallow before answering.

"Cornelius and I were manning our stations at Bruce's Crossroad in the county of Guilford. This was when we first encountered the rogue." Charles' eyes were fixed on the sunken cavities of his comrade.

"The name was Jack. He rode upon a brown mare, and his attire was that of a frontier clodhopper. This is all I can recall."

Edward could not believe his good fortune. Eager to uncover the answer to his last question, he did his best to be considerate of the still-grieving Charles. Awkwardly, Edward placed his hand on Charles' shoulder.

"Charles, I am ever sorry for your loss. If you help bring me to the last sight of this 'Jack', I will kill him in memory of Cornelius."

All the heads in the circle of British soldiers turned and looked at Edward, most wearing perplexities. Edward restarted.

"I will bring him the King's justice, in honor of our fallen brother."

To this, Charles at last rose to his feet. He turned and faced Edward, before letting out a sigh and saying,

"It is no short ride back to Guilford County. If we leave now, we may arrive before nightfall."

"Bring me to that place of villainy, and I will see this rogue in chains," assured Edward.

Together, the two men walked away from the outpost. As Edward gave one last glance to the darkened blot that speared the chest of Cornelius Smith, his heart became poised on bringing this rebellious reaper to justice.

"I shall follow you along the path," Edward shouted to Charles. Edward lept atop Eclipse and began the trek to the place where James Jack made his stand.

The hills grew steeper while the soil's top layer remained a red clay. Sparse bursts of light filtered through the dense canopy of the trees above, casting dappled patterns on the forest floor. As Edward and Charles approached a small clearing in the road, they observed the signs of a recent tumult lay scattered like fallen leaves.

The earth bore the marks of scuffle, hoofprints, and bloodstains. Scattered across the road were the many supplies James had brought from Charlotte: his compass and most of his dried provisions, all now devoid of worth.

"Here we are," Charles choked out, his voice heavy with grief as he gestured to the scene before them.

Edward's eyes took in every detail, the fierce determination within him growing stronger. He dismounted Eclipse and stepped closer, examining the ground with precision. Edward lifted one of the opened pouches off the road and held it close.

"He dropped all of his provisions," he said while laughing. "I'm surprised flying biscuits did not slay you."

Charles took no pleasure in the jest and spoke solemnly while pointing towards the treeline ahead of him.

"There, where the bushes are crushed and flattened, is where he fled."

Edward quickly sprung to his feet, the curls of his black hair falling beneath the cover of his tricorn hat, as he strode over to examine more closely the parting in the foliage.

"He just rode into the tanglewoods?"

"Aye, like a fleeting wraith."

Edward took a deep breath and, while closing his eyes, tried to imagine the condition of the man who now navigated through the constraints of the trapping underbrush; the man who killed the soldier on the road, the man who brought the royal governor to fury, and the man who brought Edward to his supreme task.

"Mr. Jack." Edward let out a nefarious laugh.

"Mr. Campbell," Edward turned to face Charles' one last time, "rest easy knowing that your friend shall have vengeance."

"God willing," Charles answered meekly.

As Charles watched Edward begin his slow descent into the consuming wilderness, a red-tailed hawk cried from atop a lofty tree, performing a lone departure hymn.

Eclipse's raven black hide and Edward's crimson red coat grew fainter and fainter in the veil of the woods, until the cry of the red-tailed hawk ceased, and all sight of the soldier halted.

In the endless chaos of a new world wilderness, Edward Morrison was on the chase.

Chapter 10: A Remote Wilderness

Pilgrim's nostrils flared as she explored the roots of a large American Sycamore tree. Bowing her head, she gently walked over the cool soil, finding the softest damp grass to graze upon.

Pilgrim enjoyed her meal without concern or pause and was only for a moment interrupted by the sensation of a small tree branch falling onto her back.

She jumped. Frustrated by the break in her feast of rich forest turf, Pilgrim strutted a couple of steps away from the base of the towering sycamore, and looked upward.

Her eyes searched over the sturdy branches and green ocean of blooming leaves to find two brown leather boots, perched precariously atop the second highest tree limb.

Her eyes continued upwards as she saw that the brown leather boots belonging to the dangerously unstable legs of her guardian, whose arms rested on the highest branch, and his blue eyes surveying beyond the peaks of the forest canopy.

"This wa-", James stopped himself mid-sentence after discovering how unwise it was to free a hand to point at this height. James steadied himself.

"This way ahead, Pilgrim. I believe we are indeed headed north."

Pilgrim continued to enjoy her meal, as James did his best to not plummet from the Sycamore's peaks.

After finally rejoining his brown boots to the solid earth below, James gathered Pilgrim and continued on their journey. Her place of feasting left yet another trace that the two voyagers had been through this stretch of backcountry frontier.

The setting sun showed James he was heading due north, but beyond that, he was lost. The violence at Bruce's Crossroad had kept James and Pilgrim racing for several hours, and once they had decided that it was safe to rest, their place in the vast wilderness was unbeknownst to them both. With fewer provisions and more challenges than he had foreseen, panic came for the humble tavern owner.

Yet for all the afflictions he had endured when faced with his fellow man, the isolation of the Virginian wilderness was a surprisingly welcomed alternative.

As long as he could keep himself and Pilgrim free of further hardship while in these woods, James felt confident his path would still lead them to his destination in Philadelphia.

James gripped the haversack bag, its strap laid permanently across his torso.

As the afternoon turned to evening, cool winds teased James' skin; and as the thought of another lonely night crossed his heart, doubt crept into James' mind like a serpent slithering through the underbrush.

Reasoning that this indistinct patch of wilderness was as sufficient as any other, James dismounted Pilgrim and took a seat upon a fallen tree.

Anxious at the act of opening his only remaining pouch of hardtack biscuits, James reached in and felt a conflicting sense of gratitude and despair: gratitude that God had allotted him even the slightest aid in the form food along his journey, and despair that the biscuit in his hand was the last in the bag.

In the stillness of his unraveling exodus, James stood from the dead tree and fell to his knees.

He removed his tattered tricorn hat and placed it on the lifeless, toppled timber. James lifted the leather cord of Cynthia's necklace from his neck for the first time in the weeks since he departed Charlotte, caused a light pang as he pulled it from his skin.

James placed the celtic cross necklace next to his hat. James then placed the single hardtack biscuit before the cross in an act with a ritualistic, almost sanctified reverence.

With the cool wind at his back, James pushed the grubby knots of his dirty blonde hair aside before bowing his head and clasping his hands in prayer.

"O Father, almighty and everlasting God, in your infinite mercy, take pity on your wayward son. Set in my heart the course out of these devilish forests, and give me the valor to see your will done. Amen."

James remained knelt in silence for several minutes. The blackness of his closed eyes a canvas for imagining the warmth of his wife, and the embrace of home.

James retook his seat atop the rotten tree and ate the last morsels of his bread with deliberation.

Pilgrim watched on, the whites of her eyes now blanked by massive brown pupils.

Pilgrim whimpered softly.

Over the last few days that James had spent wandering through the forest, he had become accustomed, and even numb, to the many familiar noises of the wilderness. The drumming of little woodpeckers and chattering of squirrels were as commonplace as the sound of laughter was in the late-hours at the tavern. The distant screams of a bobcat or the periodic howls of coyotes were naught for raising concerns. Even the sounds of Pilgrim's whimpers were not unfounded, and could usually be sourced to the ending of a tasty sup.

What was unfounded, and what caused every hair on James' back to spike with terror, was the pounding thuds of another horse's hooves.

In a state of disbelief, James launched himself from his seat and darted his eyes towards the direction of the galloping steed, unable to see anything beyond the rows of trees. Pilgrim's whimpers continued to grow. In a moment of pure desperation, James picked a path inverse of the one he had been blazing, and in an act that cringed him to partake, he struck Pilgrim and instructed her with a hushed whisper to run from him.

"Go Pilgrim! Into the forest! Run!"

Pilgrim hesitated for a moment. The deafening gallops of the stranger grew nearer and nearer.

"Pilgrim please!" James struck her hide once against, and this time, she bolted west into the foothills of Shenandoah.

With Pilgrim now charging out of sight, James lept behind the rotten tree and down into a ditch. Hastily, James buried himself in leaves, twigs, and dirt. Unsatisfied with his disguise, but without the time necessary to alter even one detail of his position, James laid motionless in the ditch, while plump beetles began to march across his face.

James laid paralyzed in the ditch, and he focused his senses beyond the aching of his bladder, to hone his ears on the thundering of horse's hooves. After weeks alongside Pilgrim, James had become convinced he could recognize the clapping of her hooves along cobblestone, dirt and mud. The pounding of hooves that James now listened too was not the steady rhythm of Pilgrim's gallop, this was the unholy tapping of a thousand fingers upon a helpless earth.

The charging of the hooves gave way to a lumbering pace, before eventually coming to a stop. As James did his best to discern what was transpiring on the opposite side of the rotten tree, his entire body seized with fear when he remembered what he had left atop the fallen tree: his tricorn hat and Cynthia's cross.

A gray wolf spider crawled curiously up James' hand, who wouldn't dare move it for fear of causing noise. James listened on for the tortuous revelation of who this man was that now joined him in the frontier's desolation.

Gripping the haversack bag as if he were his newborn son, James listened as a terrible sound probed through both his ears.

"Thud!"

The stranger had dismounted his horse. The sound of soft and untraceable footsteps followed.

James prayed internally. Praying this stranger be perhaps a friend. Praying most of all that he leaves without incident. As James contemplated what on earth may be his recourse should the traveler look to where James lay half-hidden, his ears listened to another set of harrowing noises. A wicked laugh accompanied the words, sounding as if Satan himself had spoken them.

"Are you lost, Mr. Jack?"

The malefactor stalked the site where James sat comfortably just minutes prior. As James listened to the sounds of leaves rustling and twigs snap, all he could do was hope that Pilgrim had covered enough ground that she was no longer in sight of the inquiring wraith.

Then the monster spoke again.

"J.J."

He chuckled.

James watched helplessly as he caught sight of the man's enormous arms lift above his head, as he placed his daughter's necklace around his neck.

"A wonderful gift for the governor."

Rage boiled within James, but as he reached for the blade that he knew would not prove fatal, and remembered that his pistol was almost certainly not loaded, all he could do was catch glimpses into the nightmare unfolding behind the horizontal tree.

The pursuer was massive. His crimson red uniform appeared more like a massive quilt upon his frame, whereas it had appeared a small throw on the soldiers at the inn. Two flintlock pistols, a saber sword, and a lethal dagger were on his belt.

James observed as the man squatted closer to the ground and studied the marks left by the fleeing Pilgrim.

In horror, James watched as the large man exploded with speed as he leapt atop his sable mare, positioning her to take off on the trail left by Pilgrim.

"No," James whispered weakly.

With the man's back turned, James reached for a nearby stone and threw in into the shrubbery several yards north.

The quick plunk of the stone falling through the shrubs, followed by the swish of leaves and soft shifting of twigs, pulled the purser's eyes away from Pilgrim's tracks.

The man walked his horse the short distance towards the thick assortment of bushes and forest debris. While preoccupied, James scurried from his position, and sprinted from his position in the ditch into another hideaway—this time standing behind a large oak tree.

From the barrier of the large oak tree, James watched restlessly as the man dismounted his steed and began searching through the assortment of trees and bushes.

With Pilgrim now vanished to the wind, and the path to locate her open, James contemplated his escape.

Just as James went to take his first step out from behind the tree, he heard a sudden noise coming from the massive figure, which had now resumed standing.

Although his back remained toward James, the mysterious man now held James' brown tricorn hat in his hands. The curly black hair of the fearsome stranger flowed down the back of his head, and James listened closely as the mysterious man began, not to speak, but to sing.

It started off so quietly that James could not discern the song's words, but eventually they grew louder.

And louder.

In a cold and flat tone, the mysterious man hummed and sang an ancient song from the isle of Great Britain – *The Three Ravens*.

He hummed its word with a deadly tone.

"As I was walking all alone, I heard two ravens softly groan. One said to the other near, "Where shall we feast, my dear?"

"Down in that hollow, dark and deep, a fallen knight lies fast asleep. No soul knows he met his fate, but hound, and hawk, and fickle mate."

"His hound is off to chase the hare, his hawk soars high in open air, his lady's found a new embrace, So we may feast without a trace."

"You'll perch upon his shattered crest, and I'll pluck eyes from above his breast. With golden hair, we'll weave our bed, And rest our young upon his head."

"Many a man so proud and bright, lies lost in shadow, far from sight. None shall know his name once told, but the crows who feast upon his soul."

As the massive stranger continued to sing, James sprinted into the punishing wilderness.

The stranger's song continued in repetition.

As Edward's lullaby reverberated across his mind, James tripped and fell over fallen limbs and tree roots. With the setting sun fading beneath the horizon and the forest becoming cloaked in midnight black, James desperately searched for Pilgrim, as the stranger continued singing his sinister ballad into the damning doom of the dusk.

"Down in that hollow, dark and deep, a fallen knight lies fast asleep."

Chapter 11: Shadows Over Shenandoah

J ames crept through the dark. His breath was shallow, and his heart hammered so violently he feared it might betray him. He measured each step forward, the damp leaves beneath his boots muffling his passage. The trees loomed around him, their gnarled limbs reaching skyward like the twisted fingers of the damned.

The woods were suffocatingly silent.

Too silent.

Not a single cricket chirped, nor did the distant cry of an owl break the stillness. It was a silence so complete it gnawed at his senses. James swallowed hard, tasting the damp chill in the air. He tightened his grip on the strap of his haversack, forcing himself to move, though his body screamed for stillness.

The crisp winds that glided over the immortal peaks of Shenandoah stalled just long enough for James to hear an all-too familiar sound.

"Snap!"

James stopped cold.

Somewhere behind him, a twig had broken beneath the weight of something deliberate.

Not a deer. Not a fox.

Something that moved with patience.

He turned his head ever so slightly, peering through the dense blackness. The trees sat in a tangled mess of shadow and moonlight, their twisted forms shifting in the faint breeze.

"Father… Christ, please," James pleaded underneath his muted whisper. His trembling hand drifted to the knife at his belt, fingers tightening around the worn handle.

James wet his lips and whispered into the dark, knowing in his heart the futility of his attempt.

"Pilgrim."

The forest spoke nothing.

His stomach twisted. James' itched to call out again, but he dared not. He strained his ears, hoping desperately for the familiar shuffle of hooves against the forest floor.

Once again, the black forest offered nothing in return. Nothing but an oppressive sensation that beyond the towering trees and under the watchful presence of the moon, another soul trampled through these woods.

The dread had now clung to him like damp wool, pressing against his skin, seeping into his lungs. A deep, uneasy feeling curled in his gut, something beyond fear, beyond instinct.

James knew he was being watched.

James exhaled slowly, forcing himself to move. He had to find Pilgrim. He had to keep going. Before it was too late.

"Thump!"

James barely registered the moment his body hit the earth. His limbs had moved before thought, as impulse sent him hurling into the brambles of a low bush, its wiry branches clawing at his arms and the leather of the haversack bag. He sank into the dirt, pressing himself flat, willing the shadows to take him. A sharp thorn dragged across his cheek, but he did not move. He did not breathe.

Through the tangled brush, James saw it.

A glint of steel.

Faint, fleeting—but unmistakable. The blade caught a sliver of moonlight, the polished edge gleaming as it swayed like the welcome sign at his father's tavern.

James felt the earth beneath him, cold and damp, swallowing his fading warmth. Every muscle in James' body screamed for movement, for escape, but he did not yield. He willed himself into the earth, into the silence, forcing his chest to rise and fall in shallow, measured breaths.

Then—nothing.

The glint from the hunter's steel had vanished.

The woods held their breath; the world shrinking into that single, terrible pause. James felt his heartbeat slamming against the ground; he felt it in his throat, and behind his eyes. The stillness pressed down on him, suffocating, stretching time into something unnatural.

Then over the setting and distant fog - a chuckle.

Low. Amused.

"I know you're near, Jack."

The words did not rise like a question. They did not demand an answer.

They simply were.

James clenched his jaw, his teeth grinding as he fought back the primal urge to flee. His fingers curled into the dirt, feeling the dampness seep beneath his nails.

Then came the sound of movement. Slow. Unhurried. A predator in no rush to catch its prey.

Leaves rustled, twigs snapped—Edward was moving again. Not away, not toward, but just enough to remind James that he was still there.

Still watching.

Still waiting.

Once the torture was finished, James continued aimlessly into the unforgiving frontier.

James stumbled through the blackened forest for what felt like hours, though time had become an illusory thing, a phantom that faded with each step he took. The night had grown deeper, suffocating, and the trees—taller, darker—seemed to press in from all sides.

The path had long disappeared beneath a thick blanket of fallen leaves and tangled roots, leaving him no sense of direction, no comfort in the faint moonlight that filtered through the canopy above.

Each step carried James' further into the unknown, yet every direction felt the same, a twisted mirror of the one before.

James paused, wiping his brow with a sleeve, feeling the damp sweat cling to his skin. He tried to focus, tried to push aside the relentless panic clawing at his chest, but something was wrong. Something was—wrong.

The air shifted, just slightly. Turning his head with caution, James glimpsed a fallen tree; its massive trunk blackened, charred as if burned by some unnatural fire. Its contorted branches twisted upward like the skeletal remains of a creature long-dead. The hollow at its center beckoned him, a dark opening, yawning wide like the mouth of a terrestrial leviathan.

James, despite the chill creeping through him, felt an inexplicable pull toward it; like being on the handling end of a rope guiding a powerful field ox. Without understanding his own movements, James walked briskly towards the timbered carcass. James could not tell why. He could not think.

He crawled into the hollow, his body moving almost involuntarily. His hands scraped against the rough bark, his nails catching on the jagged edges. His breath came faster, and he peered inside.

The hollow of the fallen tree was dark—impossibly dark. A void that seemed to suck in the surrounding light, but then—movement. A faint, shifting form.

James blinked.

He leaned closer, twisting his body to fit fully into the darkness. His breath caught in his throat as James saw it; upon a moss-covered stone, there was a reflection.

Instinctively, James pulled away. Troubled by the sight of his own disturbed and lathered appearance. The road from Charlotte has become so broken and twisted. How alone he felt in concord with the damned.

Yet the rare opportunity to study his grimaced appearance drew James back into the blackened hallow.

With his body now completely interred in the woodland coffin, James gingerly lifted the moss-covered stone and examined the features of his emptied face.

His skin stretched taut over his hollowed cheeks. His hair appears thin and of dimmer color than when he set off. In his ocean-blue eyes, James saw some glimpse of that pleasant home that greeted Henry Miller all those weeks ago.

Yet as James took solace in staring into his father's eyes, a terrible sight pulled him away as his reflection—no, it wasn't just a reflection—smiled.

A slow, deliberate grin curled up the edges of the face in the hollow. It was twisted and jagged. The teeth, yellowed and sharp, were snarled as the ends of its grin reached unnatural lengths.

"No."

James stumbled back in horror, his flailing arms a useless instrument for breaking him from the claustrophobic vault. He backed up helplessly as the haversack bag was pushed over his back and fell in front of his eyes.

James crumbled from the mouth of the hollow, his body recoiled as terror surged through him like a breaking wave. His hand shot to his mouth, trying to stifle the scream rising in his throat. James scrambled to find his footing, desperate to get away from the nightmare that was the blackened and cursed hollow, but as he did—

"Crack!"

A sharp rifle report shattered the silent air, deafeningly loud. The bark of the collapsed tree beside him exploded, splintering into pieces. The force of the bullet missed him by inches, and James could feel the sting of the air in the wake of its passage, the wind from the bullet's flight grazing his cheek.

His heart pounded in his chest as his legs now shook like a wet sack of flour beneath him. His head shook desperately as he contemplated returning into the infernal passage beside him, or simply sprinting into the darkness, praying he would not be running directly into the massive arms of his pursuer.

As the guttural, mocking laugh of Edward Morrison echoed through the trees, James charged further into the forest. The sound of hooves, steady and thunderous, now grew louder, closer.

Edward was coming.

Adrenaline surged through his veins, and without a moment's pause, James dove into a thick underbrush off a large slope. James buried himself in the thick undergrowth, his body half-hidden among the thick, damp ferns and tangled roots. He squeezed his eyes shut, holding his breath, wishing frantically that Cynthia's cross was there to hold him.

The galloping grew louder, echoing through the woods like a storm. James could hear Morrison's horse getting nearer, the sound of hooves pounding against the earth, a steady, relentless beat. The laughter still echoed through the trees, carried on the wind.

Edward was close.

James stifled a gasp as the sound of hooves thudded in his ears. He didn't risk movement. He remained silent, not daring to make a sound. His hands and knees sank into the damp, spongy earth, as he crawled slowly and deliberately across the forest floor, thick with rot and decay. He dragged himself down the uneven terrain, breathing raggedly and shallowly, each exhale colder than the last. The ground sloped downward, and with one silent inch at a time, he wormed himself and the haversack bag down the descent.

To James' relief, the thundering of Eclipse's hooves seemed to have raced by his hide along the embankment. James sighed with equal parts relief and frustration as he reached a cluster of thick, gnarled tree roots that twisted into the earth like the bloated veins of some primordial behemoth. James continued to crawl and drag himself through the dense knot of roots, praying they would conceal him from Edward's prying eyes.

It wasn't long before James realized something else was wrong. His boots, brown and weathered from weeks of troubled wayfaring, had become ensnared in the dense tangle of roots.

The rough fibers clung to his feet, pulling tighter with each shift of his weight. James tried to pull free, but they were stuck, the toes of his boots caught in the deep crevices between the thick roots.

His pulse quickened, and his heart pounded. Panic rose within him, gnawing at his resolve. He pulled harder, his fingers scraping against the rough earth, but the roots held fast, not letting go.

"No, no, no—God, please," James begged meekly. Sweat broke out across his brow, joining the warm tears that stung in his eyes.

The panic was unbearable. He tugged harder, wrenching his legs this way and that, but the roots only seemed to tighten their grip. Like the clasp of a blacksmith's tongs, the earth held James captive. The smell of earth and decay flooded his senses as he kicked violently, like a trapped hare.

And then—he heard it. A soft, distant sound that made every hair on his neck stand on end.

A song.

The wind lifted and carried Edward' s voice, low and haunting,. The melody was slow and aching. Every word spilling with malice. The notes curled around the woods like a fog, and James wrestled helplessly with his earthen captor.

> "As I was walking all alone,
>
> I heard two ravens softly groan.
>
> One said to the other near,
>
> "Where shall we feast, my dear?"

Its creeping crescendo made the tormenting lullaby worse.

"No, no," James whispered, clenching his teeth, "not now. Please."

James pulled viciously at his boots, but they wouldn't budge. The roots were like iron, unyielding and merciless. His hands slipped against the slick surface of the bark as his desperation rose higher, the suffocating silence growing deeper with each passing moment. The lullaby continued, its eerie, melodic voice crawling through his veins, each word turning his stomach.

"Down in that hollow, dark and deep,

A fallen knight lies fast asleep.

No soul knows he met his fate,

But hound, and hawk, and ficklemate."

James kicked harder, and when he decided silence would no longer be an aide in his struggle, he screamed.

He screamed and flailed as he put all of his might into wrenching his boot from out of the tree's grasp.

"Thwack."

James' foot launched out of the maze of tendrils with a sickening rip of leather, breaking a surface root.

"Christ!" James exclaimed, falling onto his back, his head now throbbing with a fusion of material and immaterial misery.

As he looked up into the midnight sky, he saw a cauldron of bats glide into the starry sky. James' temporary trance was broken by the forming liquid at the base of his now freed feet.

He recoiled, gasping, his mind struggling to understand what he had just felt.

It was not rain. It was not sap.

It was blood - or at least it had all the qualities.

A thick, dark substance oozed from the fresh wound of the broken tree root. It soaked into the earth, staining the ground beneath him with its unnatural tint.

James looked down in horror, his pulse racing as he saw the roots un-dulating, shifting, moving like a snake he'd seen stalking the chicken coop back at home. The unfamiliar blood was now flowing, seeping from the deep crevices and through the veins of the roots. The entire mass seemed to pulsate like a human heart.

His breath hitched as James realized that in his passing lapse in focus, his boot had become ensnared once more in the spider's web of crossing tree roots. His sense of hopelessness grew even stronger when he realized it was not one, but two feet that were now hostage to the devilish snare.

As he listened to the squelching of the pulsating veins on the ashen-gray roots, James' reaching for the dull knife still on his belt when the sickening realization hit him all at once: The roots weren't just alive—they were feed-ing. On something. On him.

Panic surged. His mind raced as Edward's twisted melody came drifting in the breeze.

> "His hound is off to chase the hare,
>
> His hawk soars high in open air,
>
> His lady's found a new embrace,
>
> So we may feast without a trace."

James hacked wildly at the roots with the dull knife, his strokes desperate and sloppy. His hands were slick with sweat, the knife slipping from his grip with each strike. Louder than the singing or anything else, his heart pounded in his chest. His nightmare was relentless.

With one final, frantic swing, the knife bit into the roots with an effective cleave. He felt the roots give way, just slightly. Another swing—closer. One more—closer. His boots pulled free with a reverberating pop, and James gave into fright as he shoved himself forward, feverishly wringing to take control of his limbs.

James scrambled toward the safety of a nearby thorn bush, his breath ragged and sharp as he dove headfirst into its brambles, the thorns biting into his skin. In his heightened state of self-preservation, he hardly noticed the peels of skin he lost from the plunge.

James's heart thudded in his chest as he crawled into the dense thicket of thorns; the sharp, unforgiving branches biting into his skin with every twist and turn. His breath came in ragged gasps, barely contained.

Each movement was an agonizing struggle against the gnashing teeth of the forest. His brown coat and white linen shirt tore with each jagged edge. Nevertheless, he waded through the woodland's jaw.

As James' persisted through the thornbush, he could hear that Edward's footsteps were near. The slow, deliberate crunch of boots on dry leaves echoed through the thicket.

He could hear it now, that haunting lullaby, drifting through the trees like the reaper's refrain.

"As I was walking all alone,

I heard two ravens softly groan..."

The sound of Edward's voice seemed to remain in the air, the words crawling like centipedes into James's ears.

Shadows flickered under the setting moonlight, as James watched anxiously for any sign of his harrier.

James twisted his neck to look again, but there was nothing—nothing but the tangled mess of branches and shadows, the remnants of the thicket. He held his breath, trying to focus, trying to calm the panic rising in his throat. But then, just as quickly as it had come, the movement vanished.

And then—*hot breath*.

A rush of warm air against his neck.

It was so close, so terrifyingly close, that James could feel it against his skin, and could almost hear its rhythmic rise and fall. He froze, his blood turning cold in his veins.

He turned his head slowly, instinctively, his body frozen in place as the sharp thorns dug into him like a thousand pricking needles.

There—there it was again. The breath—familiar.

It was Pilgrim's.

A cold knot twisted in James's stomach as he blinked into the darkness. The form of Pilgrim was buried somewhere in the thorns. James had long lost his faith in his perceptions; the forest and Edward's cruelty had paralyzed them.

With enormous caution and hesitation, James began plodding through the thorn bush towards the hot-breath of the creature.

After reaching a small opening, James found himself looking eye to eye with his companion. The cruel spines of the thorn bush wedged her unnaturally in its heart, twisting and tangling her body. Her browncoat was now stained with a thin film of red. Terror beset her eyes.

"Oh Pilgrim," James uttered painfully. "Why have you come here?"

The horse produced no response, but her brown eyes gleamed in a show of relief at her steward's arrival.

James continued to shuffle through the piercing thorns, grabbing a hold of Pilgrim's reins and guiding her from the entrapment as well. Eventually, the two were reunited; bloodied, exhausted, and on the verge of collapse, but united.

The hours carried on and the long night drew nearer to a close. In the temporary absence of Edward's taunts and chants, James led Pilgrim on a path intended to obscure the predator's hunt.

James led Pilgrim through the creeks and swamps, encouraging her to wade through the cold, muddy waters. He had her circle back over the ground they had just crossed, muddying any tracks they might have left.

The struggle to keep Pilgrim quiet, however, was growing more difficult with each passing minute. Her hooves, once steady and confident, were now labored, dragging through the underbrush. The thorns, the jagged edges of roots, the painful gashes on her body—each wound caused her to wince in pain, her breath shallow and uneven. James could feel her trembling beneath him, could see the fear in her wide, brown eyes, mirroring his own.

"Shhh, Pilgrim," he whispered, his voice tight with desperation. "Quiet now, girl, we can't make a sound."

His pleas fell on deaf ears. The pain was too much for Pilgrim to endure, and her soft whimpers grew louder with each step. The bleeding gashes on her flanks painted the ground beneath her in streaks of red. James had no choice but to press on, encouraging her with quiet words and the occasional pat on her neck.

Dawn was approaching. James led Pilgrim across a rocky outcrop, the uneven terrain forcing her to slow her pace. Every step was a calculated move, a deliberate attempt to wipe away the path they had taken.

They did not stop until they reached a clearing; the sun rising behind them, casting its first light over the mountain ridge. James dismounted from Pilgrim, and in the same act, collapsed to the ground before placing himself upon his knees, his hands shaking violently as he gazed out over the valley.

Blood dripped from their wounds—his and Pilgrim's—and they were both exhausted, trembling from the wicked shadows over Shenandoah.

But for the moment, they were safe.

James bowed his head, and the words of a psalm he had learned as a child rose from his bosom and up through his bloodied lips. His voice was quiet and reverent, as he sang the words that he had felt as a boy were too mournful to be adjoining to the Lord.

A bloodied Pilgrim and vast mountain range were his audience.

His voice, which he had heard so little of the last several hours, croaked as he began the first verse.

"How long will you forget me, Lord?

Will you forget always?

How long, Lord, will you hide your face,

and turn from me your gaze?

How long must I be sad each day,

in deep perplexity?

How long will my opponent stand in triumph over me?

O Lord my God, consider me,

and give me your reply.

Light up my eyes, or I will sleep,

the sleep of those who die.

Then would my enemy declare,

'At last I've laid him low!'

And so my foes would sing for joy,

to see my overthrow.

But still I trust your constant love;

You save and set me free.

With joy I will extol the Lord,

Who has been good to me."

James did not weep, but remained on his knees as he surveyed the peaks of the Virginian frontier.

Blood and sweat dried in unison as the sun rose higher into the heavens. The warmth of its light touched his face, and for a moment, James allowed himself to believe that maybe, by the grace of the Father, he had a chance.

Chapter 12: Help of the Helpless

The water barely stirred as Pilgrim waded through the shallow creek, her hooves slipping against the moss-slick stones beneath. James sat slumped in the saddle, his bloodied body swaying with each step, his limbs sluggish from exhaustion. The creek ran silver under the cloudy sky, a sliver of quiet in a conniving wilderness. The air was cool, but sweat clung to the back of his neck, his feverish mind stirring with the ghosts of the past.

For three nights, they had kept northeast, chasing the constellations like they were lanterns guiding him home. Pennsylvania lay somewhere beyond the horizon.

Hunger had consumed James. Nights earlier, he had used up all his hardtack biscuits and jerky, and he now had to find sustenance from whatever the earth provided.

From atop Pilgrim, James saw that his steed was weakened in body and spirit. He thought of his promise to John Haigler that he would return her without harm.

James thought about all the promises he had once made in the comfort of his home.

James ran a hand down Pilgrim's neck, feeling the ridges of old scars, the fresh scratches from the thornbush still raw against her hide. The brambles had left their mark on both of them, etching their suffering into flesh. Under the gray clouds overhead, the gashes along her flanks looked like winding rivers of black, glistening where the water touched them.

As Pilgrim lumbered through the shallow creek, James' constant swaying abruptly ended when Pilgrim's steps grew slower and slower.

Pilgrim let out a sharp snort, her ears flicking toward something in the trees. James mustered his strength and lifted his head, listening for the ever-recognizable sounds of his adversary. Behind his red-rimmed eyes, James' mind was overflowing with a thrashing paranoia and dread. James let out a light and dry chuckle when he remembered his repulsion as a boy when Patrick would order him to scrap candle wax from the table or some other similarly dull task.

What James would not give for such mental mundanity.

Every snapped twig, every rustling branch, every distant whisper of wind against the leaves—Edward had made a phantom of the whole damned wilderness.

Another step. Another. And then Pilgrim stopped.

James straightened, blinking himself back to the present.

Pilgrim's breath came fast, her body rigid beneath him. Her ears pinned, her muscles tensed. She saw something.

"What?" James whispered, his voice throat dry and hoarse.

Nothing.

The woods sat still.

Then Pilgrim shuddered, backing a step. James cursed, gripping the reins.

"Pilgrim," he growled. "He is not upon us. We would know." James spoke with an unconvincing certainty meant more for his own fleeting assurance than that of his mare.

Pilgrim was now backing up slowly.

"Pilgrim, stop!"

She reared, the whites of her eyes flashed with intensity.

James barely had time to brace before she twisted, hooves flailing. The world lurched, and then, he was falling.

He hit the creek hard, the cold water closing over him like a cloak. His head cracked against a submerged rock, sending a splinter of lightning through his skull. The impact knocked the air from his lungs, his body momentarily paralyzed as the current slithered around him.

Then—a horror struck him more resounding than the pain.

The haversack bag.

James shot up, gasping, frantically pulling the soaked bag from the water. Its weight was wrong—it was too heavy.

"No, no, no—"

He ripped it open. The parchment stuck together; the ink beginning to blur. Those words—the words—

He staggered onto the bank, shaking hands, peeling the declaration apart. Black letters bled upon the edges, curling like the frayed ribbons on Margaret's bonnets. James gasped for breath.

"...the authority of the King and Parliament are hereby dissolved..."

The words of his kin were still well-defined on the parchment, but James feared for how long.

He needed to dry the bag. He needed to warm it.

James clenched his jaws and looked up at Pilgrim through his strains of hair as slick as tallow.

"Damn you, Pilgrim," James muttered.

Pilgrim looked at the man before her. James was kneeling on the banks of the trickling creek. His brown trousers were stiff from the long journey, and torn slightly at the knees. Scratches and patches marred his boots. Pilgrim watched as he removed the stained and weathered brown coat, leaving only a partially torn white linen shirt to cover his torso.

The tricorn hat had been lost deep in the wilderness. Another prize for his pursuer.

James appeared ragged. He smelt foul. He gritted his teeth and let out another yell.

"Damn you, damn you, damn you, Pilgrim!"

James smashed his fists down into the creek and looked up at his comrade. She remained standing in the creek, now unbothered by her frightful vision just moments earlier.

James shared a portion of his anger at Pilgrim, but saved most of it for himself. He looked down into the mud with hurt and whispered softly.

"Father, help of the helpless... help me."

His mind raced. He needed that fire. He needed the heat.

James threw himself up and down the creek's banks. He pulled smooth stones from their clay beds. With trembling fingers, he stacked them all into a pathetic attempt at a fire ring. He dug for kindling, fingers numbing in the damp soil.

He had found a few good stones, dry enough to strike. Another. Another. And then—

A fist-sized rock, blackened with age. Smooth. Unassuming.

He did not hesitate.

He tossed it into the pile.

Next, James took a dry piece of bark and sharpened it into a round stick, approximately eighteen inches long. The soaked ends of his white linen shirt sank as he reached out for another piece of timber debris—this one to be used as a board for the end of the stick to fit into. James collected his kindling and placed it in the small hole he had formed on the board.

Pulling a piece of twine from the hole in his trousers, James fastened it around the end of the stick and inserted it into the hole in the board. He then spun the stick.

At first, there was nothing but the maddening belief that this effort was for naught. All James could hear was the creek running, and all he could feel was the growing ache in his back and shoulder.

He spun and spun before a spark eventually began forming in the dry kindling below it.

James let out a smile and a sigh of relief. Still knelt over the fledgling fire, he turned to gather the stones from their pile. He could see that Pilgrim stood dutifully in the creek, guarding against shadows in the wind.

James placed the stones into the fire, careful not to extinguish the flames. After several minutes, the surface of the stones heated to a warm temperature, and James lifted his blistered hands, now heated by the temperate rocks. The touch was pleasant and calming. For a moment, James was in his bed above the tavern again; the smell of warm bread and pot pies wafted from the kitchen below. Together, this merry clan was preparing to praise their Creator and celebrate together their freedom from the crown.

James did not want to open his eyes when he heard the rocks begin to hiss.

James barely had time to flinch before the explosion began.

Shards of molten stone ripped through the sky, a burst of light and heat and violence. The searing white light swallowed James's vision, and the force threw him backward. A wave of burning pain erupted across his face and arms, his ears ringing so loud he could not think.

He gasped, clawing at the dirt, but the world tilted beneath him. Sparks rained down like falling stars. The fire had leaped from its pit, hungry fingers stretching outward, now catching onto dry leaves.

James squeezed his eyes shut, but the light burned through. His skin sizzled. His head pounded. The world reeled.

Pilgrim neighed and stamped her hooves against the creek-bed. As James laid out on the dirt, trying desperately to gather himself, he thought that his martyred mare may finally flee and abandon her foolish keeper.

But she approached him and lowered her head to meet his battered frame. Pilgrim nuzzled the length of his torn and pierced body as if to say to James he must rise to his feet.

Still looking into the cloudy skies, James laid motionless on the dirt. A simple cry broke from his cracked lips.

"I am sorry."

As James' eyes became tranced on the figures of the enormous clouds above, they became intermediately distracted by the dancing of a different haze; it captured his focus at the same moment that his nose noticed it.

Smoke. It was billowing into the sky.

James shot up from his horizontal position, tearing his sensitive back. His eyes darted around him as he realized that the fire caused by the explosion had spread like an ink stain on parchment, darkening the earth and crawling over the leaves and pine needles with lightning speed.

Frantically, James reached for his brown coat, still heavy with the water from the creek, and began swinging it at the trees, bushes and grass, now ablaze with a relentless inferno.

"Watch out!" James shouted to Pilgrim as her hooves pranced anxiously around the rising pyre.

The heat was so intense that it brought out the most severe pain for the many layers of wounds that adorned both James and Pilgrim.

As James realized that the fire was beyond mortal intervention, another realization struck him.

He had moved like a ghost for three nights, drifting silently and without a trace. Yet now, in the middle of the Virginian wilderness, he had created a mighty beacon for all to see.

"Pilgrim, be ready!" James shouted as he hurried along the creek bank, grabbing the haversack bag around his shoulder.

He dropped his water-logged coat upon the dirt, and when the force of the linens wrapped in the brown fabrics of his coat drummed against the dirt, that of another collision joined their sound: thundering hooves and pounded earth.

Now standing on his feet, one arm over the back of Pilgrim, James turned behind him in horror.

Through the inferno's blistering mouth, Edward Morrison emerged—his black horse, Eclipse, leaping through the yellow and orange flames with a hellish invincibility. His red uniform, a scarlet tongue, licked the fire's edges, and his hair—black as sin—cascaded like a dark veil over a severe and grim face. He leapt through the wall of flame with focused ease, and when the hooves of his of stallion crushed the ground below him, James could witness his purser's face fully. Beneath his steely green eyes, no song or laughter passed through his lips: only the cold, condemning silence of a man consumed by hate, a wolf closing in on its prey, relentless and inevitable.

As the scalding flames wailed around him, James threw his body atop Pilgrim and charged away from the devil.

Chapter 13: Black Bear

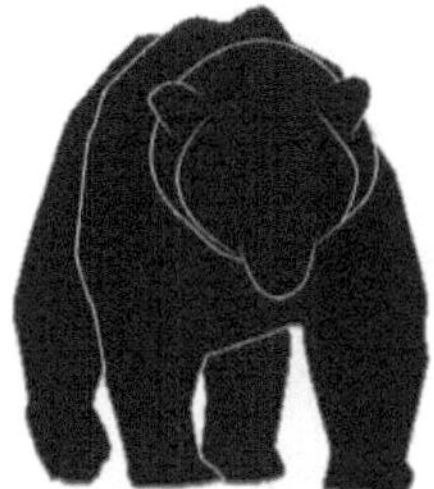

The growling of the fire was a low, thrumming hum in James Jack's ears, delivered on the wings of a blazing gust. Pilgrim's hooves pounded the earth, her breath was empty and choked by the smoke. The smoke had thickened into a suffocating haze that curled around them. The sickly orange light painted the world, and the shadows of trees and rocks loomed like ancient abominations. Pilgrim pushed forward, the fiery hell behind her growing larger with each passing moment.

The sound of hooves grew louder. Edward Morrison pursued like a relentless beast in its hunt. His horse, Eclipse, was faster—always faster—and the sound of their hooves was a dreadful beat layered over the forest's melody of death.

"Thud-thud-thud," the exchange of slamming hooves between Pilgrim and Eclipse was piercing.

James didn't look back, but he could feel Edward's searing gaze upon his back, white-hot like the flames that chased them. James gripped Pilgrim's mane, laced with blood and sweat, and urged her forward with a wordless plea.

Never more than several yards apart, James remained held in terror in anticipation of Edward's next move.

"Whoosh!"

A bullet whizzed past, far too close. Pilgrim's ears pinned back in alarm. Her pace faltered, but James wrenched her back on course. All James could do was harness the energy that chase-induced adrenaline had given him. All he could pray to do was keep Pilgrim steady and on her feet.

"Easy, girl!" James spoke into Pilgrim's pinned ears.

James could hear the clicking of pistols as Edward prepared for his next volley of bullets. Full of doubt that it would meet its target, James reached into his belt and retrieved his pistol. James quietly thanked himself from yesterday, for the single-shot pistol had stayed loaded. The constant threat of a stalking Edward was a solid case for keeping the flintlock ready for action. Lifting his bruised hands up from Pilgrim's reins, James turned his torso backwards, putting the sight of the burning bushes and inflamed trees in a blur.

His eyes sharpened from the blur right as the wicked face of Edward came into focus: his curly black hair, dragon-born green eyes, and massive figure jolted atop the galloping stallion. James aimed his pistol at the bared teeth of his opponent, but right before he pulled the trigger, he became distracted by the presence of something so entirely misplaced upon the breast of his crimson red coat.

A cross - made of twigs and made "celtic" by its imposition over a simple circle. It was Cynthia's. The one that was stolen by Edward on the first night of their encounter.

The sight of his daughter's craft launched James out of focus and sent his bullet flying far beyond the gaining presence of Edward Morrison.

Before James could turn away, he watched Edward's lip curl into a cruel smile. Edward drew his second pistol and fired.

The second bullet flew past them, but this time it was too close. Pilgrim shied violently, her hooves slipping on the wet earth. She bucked hard, throwing James forward, off balance. He held onto her mane, but the force of the motion sent him sprawling across her neck, and sent his pistol flying from his hand. For a moment, he was weightless, suspended in terror, before his limbs tangled around the closest refuge in a frantic, instinctive knot of survival. James had positioned himself too far forward on Pilgrim's neck. The mare whined in pain, and James shifted awkwardly to return to his saddle. The dodging of Edward's gunfire and the stumbling of Pilgrim over fallen trees, burning leaves, and hidden cavities in the dirt left James' frail body appearing as a tall ship might in a rocking storm; James' blood-stained and white-linen shirt billowing like the sails which carried his parents across the Atlantic years before.

He and his pursuer climbed the ascending landscape; the endless burning forest offered only one direction, as his tireless mare was sent upward. The oppressive denseness of the forest was such that James could not have known when they crossed over from forest to foothills to mountain.

It was clear to James now that he fought his enemy not upon the hills of Virginia, but the peaks of his own Mount Sinai.

Determination raged through James' raised veins, and he lowered himself onto Pilgrim's mane as Edward's bullets interchanged with the thundering of hooves.

Behind them, Eclipse pushed harder, a dark blur in the haze of smoke.

Pilgrim's hooves slipped again. The ground beneath them was slick with mud, and the scent of burning earth and wood filled James's nostrils. The fire was growing hotter, closer. He could feel it in his skin, the heat wrapping around him like a tightening coil. The furnaces of hell waited to devour a fallen rider.

Then, suddenly, Pilgrim tripped. Her legs buckled beneath her, sending them both tumbling toward the ground. James's breath caught in his throat as his heart skipped a beat. He braced himself, arms outstretched, but Pilgrim's instinct kicked in. She twisted, righting herself, and with a great heave, she pushed forward again, narrowly avoiding a catastrophic fall. James clung to her, heart racing in his chest as the fire raged on around them.

He could hear Edward's voice, cruel and mocking, close behind. James could feel the burn of the hunter's gaze even without looking back. There was no escape unless Pilgrim could carry him farther than she ever had before, and the weathered creature was losing momentum.

And then, as though the heavens themselves had intervened, disaster struck Edward.

Eclipse slipped into the mud, and the air suddenly filled with the harsh sound of hooves setting in unnatural ways. Eclipse's legs went out from under her, and she collapsed, the ground swallowing her in an instant. The beast let out a sharp cry as she twisted violently, her ankles breaking with a sickening snap.

Edward let out a desperate, angry scream as he was thrown forward, losing his iron grip on Eclipse's reins. The sound of his colossal form slamming into the ground registered in James' memory like the sound of a collapsing house. Even thrown from horse, James' mind conjuring images of the lethal soldier simply continuing the chase on foot.

With a quick glimpse behind his back, James knew he could disregard that threat. Edward was motionless on the forest ground, flames bolstering around him as they feasted on the corpse of Eclipse.

The two men were now separated by a gulf of mud and fire, and James had momentarily found a brief reprieve. But ahead, another turn loomed—a twist in the trail that promised danger anew.

As Pilgrim rounded the bend, the forest seemed to warp before James's eyes. The smoke, thick and swirling, blotted out the sky, casting the trees into shadows that danced like twisted specters. His heart was blasting in his chest, not from the exertion, but from the mounting terror. The heat of the fire crept closer, its presence an aching weight at the back of his mind, but it was not the fire that stopped his breath. It was what stood on all fours at the turn of the corner.

Through the smoke and the heat, the silhouette of the creature appeared.

A hulking shape, massive in its size and ferocious in its stance.

A black bear.

It stood in their path, its large body framed against the distant flames, its eyes gleaming like dark glass. Its teeth were bared, and it roared—a low, rumbling growl that quickly escalated into a sharp, guttural bellow—drowning out the shrieks of terror from Pilgrim's convulsing flesh; who was now face to face with the creature that had spooked her hours before. In the dark and frightened eyes of Pilgrim, the matted beast before her was simply the newest variation of the black hound who first haunted her in the churchyard back home.

The bear raised onto its hind legs, and Pilgrim reared in response, her hooves striking the fire-kissed air as it leveled with the beast's claws.

"Pilgrim, hold on!"

James reached for his dagger. The threaded ends of the short dagger waving furiously in the wind as the haversack bag jumped upon James' body.

The black bear towered several feet over Pilgrim, and the whiff of the creature's breath was rancid with decaying plants and rotten meat. As the bear let out another horrifying roar—this time almost resembling a guttural laugh—James returned with a scream of defiance.

A scream so harsh he tasted blood.

A scream so proud it steadied Pilgrim.

A scream so brave that the burning leaves shared whispers of it.

James Jack lifted his dagger and watched as the bear reared its enormous paws.

Pilgrim dodged the strike, and James gripped Pilgrim's reins tighter, the fingers of his left hand were slick with sweat. The fingers of his right hand continued to grip the dagger knife.

The bear's growl rumbled through the ground beneath them, a low, menacing vibration; the air thickened with the stench of fur and sweat, the beast's breath was hot and foul against the wind.

Still reared upon her hind legs, Pilgrim slowly walked back in terror. She whinnied in fear, kicking her hooves wildly, and her footing slipped on the uneven ground. Her body lurched as she twisted to avoid the bear's next strike, but she bucked in that moment of panic.

James could no longer hold on. He whispered a prayer for Pilgrim's safe return home, released his left hand from the rein, dropped the dagger from his right, and secured both hands on the haversack bag as he began his fall.

His body flailed through the air like a rag doll. He slammed into the earth, and his body tumbled down the hillside. A blur of pain and heat overtook him as the world spun wildly around him. His stomach lurched, and his head collided with the ground with a sickening thud.

He felt the sharp jolt of impact spear through his skull, and then, in an instance, the world folded in on itself. Everything turned to black.

Through the haze of his consciousness, James' could still hear the roar of the bear, and the distant clopping of Pilgrim's hooves.

Through the crackling of the fire, James could feel that the brooding, and heavy gray clouds had finally given way.

Rain pattered upon the dirt.

With the last ounce of his strength, James offered his broken flesh as cover for the haversack bag as he pulled it underneath himself.

As the icy rain fell, James could only focus on the pounding of his pulse in his ears, the searing pain in his skull, and then—

Darkness.

Chapter 14: The Queen Bleeds

Lieutenant Roger Smalls sat atop his stallion, staring out at the sleeping town of Charlotte. The night air was thick, heavy with the scent of damp earth and distant smoke. It was under a cloudless sky that the towering trees of Mecklenburg held their breath, and watched onward anxiously.

Behind Lieutenant Smalls, a dozen calverman flanked him. Their horses shifted restlessly beneath them. Beyond them, stretched along the narrow dirt road, stood two hundred and fifty regulars, their red coats catching the orange glow of the torches that burned in steady fists above their heads.

"They know we're here, don't they, sir?" came the quiet voice of Private Acker. The young soldier sat stiffly on his mount, his knuckles tight around the reins.

Smalls exhaled through his nose, a breath that curled in the torchlight like the smoke of a musket just fired. "Of course they do," he muttered. "A place like this—isolated, defiant, rotten with rebels—they can smell the king's justice before it arrives."

Acker shifted uncomfortably atop his steed. "So... we attack at first light?"

Smalls turned his head slightly, his lips pulling into something just shy of a smile. "First light?" he repeated, as if amused by the thought. "No, Private. We attack now." He raised his torch higher, letting its glow cast shadows over his scarred face. "The flames we set tonight will give us all the light we need."

Acker swallowed hard, his Adam's apple bobbing in his throat. Behind them, the regulars stood at attention, waiting for the word. The moonlight cast long shadows over the rows of uniform men.

The moment stretched, harsh and expectant, before Smalls finally broke it.

"The queen bleeds before the sun rises."

Then, with a sharp tug of his reins, he turned his stallion toward the town, and the line of redcoats followed, their torches lifting like the heralds of hell.

Lieutenant Smalls raised his right hand.

"Forward."

The army pressed on, hooves clattering over packed dirt, boots crunching against the dry underbrush. The road they traveled was nothing more than a crude, winding path through the Carolina backwoods, but the wagon ruts ahead gave them confidence that they were on the right course. Acker, still uneasy, looked over his shoulder.

"Odd, sir. Always thought the road into Charlotte was wider."

Smalls barely paid him any mind. His eyes were fixed on the parts illuminated on the narrowing path.

"These roads are barely roads at all, boy. Now keep moving."

The march continued, slow and steady, the flickering torches carving out a thin corridor of light between the darkened trees. After several minutes of marching and riding, the soldiers under Lieutenant Smalls began to become doubtful.

The path had narrowed to a near impasse; the underbrush thickening at the edges, closing in as if the forest itself now conspired to swallow them whole. The ground grew uneven, and the king's horses were now forced to step cautiously over concealed roots and loose stones.

"Sir, I believe we are lost," Acker said with a quaking voice. The novice soldier glanced nervously to his left and right, and saw that massive hills, dotted with hickory trees and blanketed under a midnight sky, encircled him.

Lieutenant Smalls ignored the cries of his inferior, and kept his eyes studied on the ruts left behind by Charlotte's traveling wagons.

"Snick!" Smalls boots hit the dirt with force as he dismounted from his horse. With the orange glow of his torch as his only aid, the veteran lieutenant buried his doubts and focused his attention on the winding ruts ahead.

Traveling several yards ahead of his men, the lieutenant curiously followed the marks of the wagons deeper and deeper into the narrowing crescent between the hills.

"What in God's name..."

The swift motion caused by the turning of the lieutenant's head caused the tips of the torch's flames to dance, his tricorn hat swinging through its flame. Realizing that the facial expressions of his men were as dumbstruck as the one surely painted upon his own face, he looked back to the source of his perplexity.

Unsure if he was looking at the origin or destination of the rut tracks, but knowing all too well that wagons do not begin or end in a ditch beside the trail, Lieutenant Smalls knew he had been fooled.

He lifted himself from his knees and his senses now focused on the distant, rumbling sounds coming from either side of the great hills that surrounded him.

A rustling. A shifting in the earth.

The soldiers near the front slowed, the men stiffening, hands tightening around their muskets. It was subtle at first—the low murmur of movement in the brush, the creak of wooden planks shifting in the night.

Then, from the darkness, they came. Rushing down the hills dodging trees and shrubbery alike.

A wave of small, wild-eyed goats.

They surged onto the path, bleating and leaping over the uneven ground. The animals scattered among the troops, slipping between the legs of the horses, startling them into nervous sidesteps, and causing their whines to fill the forest air. A redcoat cursed as one goat butted against his shin, nearly knocking him off balance. Another one of the goat's leaped wildly onto the back of a supply cart, its blacks hooves clattering against the wood before it tumbled down into the brush.

Private Acker barely held in a laugh. "What in God's—"

"Hold your fire!" Smalls barked as a few startled men raised their muskets. "They're just damned goats!"

The soldiers swatted at the animals with their musket stocks, trying to push them away. The bleating had become so great, that they could hardly hear anything beside it. In the chaotic storm of dashing goats, whimpering and shuffling horses, and a chorus of laughter and curses from the soldiers, another presence slowly began to dominate. Under the whisking light of their torches, the men could see the loose dirt, kicked up by the platoon of goats, had begun to shake and rattle. Then, finally, they heard it. Pounding hooves hurling down the hillsides.

Reinforcements had arrived.

A surge of cattle—large, hulking shapes with glinting horns—erupted from the darkness, their eyes wide and rolling, their nostrils flaring with panic. Reddish-brown bulls and cows alike barreled down the hills, flattening every blade of grass in their path.

Speechless at the sight, and still preoccupied with the butting of two dozen goats, Lieutenant Smalls and his men brought their torches to the hillside opposite of the descending herd of cattle.

They smelt them before they heard them, and they heard them before they saw them.

Hogs. Dozens of them.

They stampeded down the opposing hill, their sharp and curved tusks leading the charge. The squealing of the swinish brigade was deafening.

All Lieutenant Smalls could do was inhale deeply the barn-stained breeze of Charlotte, and holler to his men,

"Brace yourselves!"

Smalls began his sprint back to the reins of his stallion, hoping to at least be atop his steed when the stampede arrived; the soldiering goats, however, equipped with great skills of interfering, kept the lieutenant tripping and falling through the panicked mass of men.

From his vantage point on the ground, Smalls watched half a dozen cattle smash into a row of soldiers: one was sent soaring, before crashing only feet from where he laid. Another received a bull's horn through the torso, causing him to drop his torch, before crumbling to the ground beside it. Yet another reddish cow slammed into a supply wagon, causing it, along with the mare and her rider, to tip with ease.

Smalls could not muster the will to turn his head, and put a picture to the harrowing cries of the hogs behind him; but between the shouting of men, the blasts of fired pistols, and the bellowing of rageful pigs, the picture was as detailed as the finest portrait in the halls of the governor's palace.

Chaos had erupted.

The infantry broke ranks, scrambling to retreat out of the pit and back down the road. Muskets and pistols were fired, flashes of light illuminating the swirling dust and panicked faces. The crack of gunfire only worsened the frenzy, sending the cattle into even wilder confusion. Men dove aside, bodies colliding, orders drowned beneath the cacophony of hooves, screams, and snapping branches.

Smalls' stallion reared, and prepared to bolt into the night. Now back to his feet, the bewildered lieutenant yanked the reins of his horse.

With a furious gaze sweeping the madness, Lieutenant Smalls called out, "Hold the line, damn you!"

But there was no line to hold.

Lieutenant Smalls leapt back atop his horse, and from this view he could now see the crude fences placed along the hill's peaks, the ones that the rebel patriots had used to guide the animal's charge.

Having been made a victim of the rogue's trappings so early on in his night of conquest brought the lieutenant to a place of overwhelming hatred and rage.

He watched as the livestock, now tired from the frenzy, began to dissipate into the night. It had ended as quickly as it had begun. The trail was littered with scattered weapons and men left groaning in pain: some clutched their legs where the hardy skulls of goats had rammed, and the vicious tusks of hogs had burrowed. Others cocked their heads in a slow-motion daze, as they desperately pulled themselves from where they'd been thrown to the ground. Private Acker remained motionless entirely.

Smalls released a sorrowful sigh in the face of the chaotic carnage. Still he turned his stallion sharply, and rallied to his able-bodied men.

"Back to the main road," he ordered with the pointing of his left hand. "We ride for Charlotte. Now."

Bruised and humiliated by the trap, Smalls' formidable force gathered their wounded and their scattered weapons. The march resumed, slower than before, but no less determined.

The torchlight flickered as they pressed forward, their path now clear. The Queen City awaited.

The British soldiers, having regrouped after the chaos of the stampede, marched into Charlotte under the cold command of Lieutenant Smalls. The flickering torchlight cast jagged shadows over the small town, illuminating the crude wooden barrier erected at the main road's entrance. It was no grand fortress—just a hastily constructed wall of wooden beams and overturned carts and wagons.

Smalls reined in his stallion and lifted a hand, signaling the column to halt. Silence pressed down on them, broken only by the occasional snort of a restless horse or the distant creak of wooden buildings settling in the night. He lifted his chin and called out.

"People of Charlotte! You will surrender at once! Any who defy the king's justice shall suffer for their insolence. Step forward, and give us the traitor, James Jack!"

Smalls' voice echoed, swallowed quickly by the night. The town remained eerily still. No flicker of movement, no cry of surrender.

Then, from behind the barrier, a voice rang out—dry, edged with humor, and unmistakably unimpressed.

"Well now, if it's help getting through you need, why don't you go lasso one of them bulls we sent you?"

A chuckle rippled through the unseen defenders. Smalls' nostrils flared.

"We'll not waste our time on games," he sneered. "If you don't open the gate, we'll burn it down."

Without another word, the torches were flung forward. Fire licked hungrily at the wooden beams, hissing as it consumed the dry planks. The flames spread rapidly, curling themselves around the barrier's supports. Within moments, the structure groaned and splintered, collapsing in on itself in a cascade of sparks.

"Advance!" Smalls barked.

The redcoats surged forward.

The black gaiters at the feet of the British legion stepped through the singeing rubble, while the hooves of the officer's horses stepped over the browning rubble.

At the moment their boots hit the otherside of Charlotte's dirt-laid Trade Street, the gunfire began. From the rooftops, from the few second-story windows, from the alleyways—sharp cracks shattered the night sky. The redcoats reeled as musket balls tore through their ranks, men dropping to the dirt with strangled cries. Blood sprayed across dirt and stone, and the winding torches casted long streaks of crimson on the ground.

Smalls ducked low, yanking his stallion's reins to the side as a shot whizzed past his head. He snarled, "Return fire! Bring those bastards to the ground!"

The redcoats scattered, lifting their muskets skyward, firing blindly at the rooftops. Lead balls ripped through shingles, shattering windows and sending wooden splinters raining down. A patriot tumbled from a rooftop with a meaty smack, his musket clattering beside him. The order from their commanding officer was clear: engage, destroy, and dishearten the will of the rebellious traitors. With a force of Charlotteans rushing to meet the redcoats in the street, the fighting quickly devolved into a backcountry brawl.

Fast and chaotic were the qualities of every detail in every duel in the Queen City—shadows lept without pattern, gunpowder obscured the light from the moon, and men and women both screamed as steel clashed in alleyways.

After several minutes of practicing his saber on the backs of fleeing townsfolk, Lieutenant Smalls summoned a small band of his infantry towards him. He asked above the sounds of battle,

"Where is Pat Jack's Tavern?"

The band of soldiers pointed northward.

"Follow me," Smalls growled. While his army continued to grapple with the rugged resolve and resourcefulness of the people of Mecklenburg, Smalls peeled away with a handful of redcoats. They ducked through the fray, sidestepping the fallen as they made for their true target.

The lair of the legendary traitor, the den of their devilry: Pat Jack's Tavern.

It only took a few brief moments to arrive at the same yellow-painted sign that had welcomed Henry Miller several weeks prior. The glows of the soldier's torches mixed with the stark moonlight and blaze of the army's meddling, accompanied by the sound of shattered windows, gunfire, and women crying, made the non-lit essence of the tavern appear as if it had been placed in a feverish nightmare.

With the tavern standing dark and seemingly abandoned, Lieutenant Smalls dismounted his steed, and nodded to the soldiers flanking him. Under the swaying welcoming sign above them, the men drew their sidearms and began ascending the steps to the tavern.

One soldier stepped forward and swung open the door.

Inside, the large gallery was masked in darkness. The only light being the glow of the moon through the numerous windows lining the walls. What light there was in the empty tavern, showed it was spotless.

The soldiers began their advance, the torches illuminating over round wooden tables and barrel seats.

As the men reached towards the back of the tavern, they noticed a figure forming in the distance.

Sitting quietly in a rocking chair by the cold and unlit hearth, was Patrick Jack.

He was calm. Unshaken. The firelight outside cast deep shadows over his lined face, but his hands were steady as they rested on the worn stock of his Brown Bess rifle.

Smalls smirked at the sight of the elderly man.

"Come now, old man. You have the wisdom to surrender peaceably, don't you?"

Patrick Jack exhaled slowly. Then, in one swift motion, he lifted the rifle and fired.

The lead ball blasted from the end of his gun. It struck one of the soldiers square in the chest, sending him stumbling backward with a gurgled cry. His rifle fell to the ground with a thud, as gray smoke seeping from the muzzle of Patrick's musket.

The remaining redcoats roared in fury, rushing forward, seizing the old man by the shoulders.

They lifted him from his chair and began to carry him, the stubborn man dragging his feet as they went across the length of the tavern floor.

Across where the fiddler had played, and the men had played cards.

Across where the women had laughed, and the children had drawn art.

Across where James grew from a boy into a man, and where he first saw the honey-brown eyes of his bride.

Stepping ahead of the soldiers that restrained the elder Jack, Lieutenant Smalls peered out the open door, making sure Patrick could see well the devastation of Charlotte.

Then, from atop the highest step to Pat Jack's Tavern, they threw him with ruthless ease.

The frail and elderly frame of Patrick's body shattered as he tumbled down, his head striking the dirt with a nauseating crack. He did not cry out. The only sound was the rustle of his body settling at the bottom of the steps, breath shuddering in his chest.

Without sparing the pitiful man so much as a glance, Smalls tossed his torch within the open door of the tavern. He turned to his men,

"Burn it."

Torches sailed through the open door and windows, their flames exploding against the wooden walls. The redcoats walked the perimeter of the tavern, dragging their torches along the foundation. Smoke coiled up in thick, black tendrils, the heat curling the tavern's sign until the letters twisted and warped.

Patrick Jack lay motionless, his breath began to grow shallow.

Smalls knelt beside him, gripping his chin. In the fading gray eyes of his captive, Smalls could now see he was looking into the namesake of the tavern. He gripped the ears and hair of the dying rebel.

"Where is your son?"

Patrick's eyes, once sharp, now flickered with something distant, something unraveling.

Frustrated with the lack of answers coming from his white-haired prisoner, Smalls raised the buttstock of his rifle, ready to further split the crack in Patrick's skull.

As he prepared to descend his weapon, a war cry bellowed from behind him.

A detachment of Charlotte patriots pounced upon the redcoats, men and women alike, their weapons gleaming in the inferno's glow. Pitchforks thrusted forward, while muskets cracked in rapid succession and homemade clubs struck the jaws and faces of the men in red.

When pitchforks pierced the flesh of the lieutenant's horse, Smalls looked down at the bloodied ruins of Patrick Jack, brightened only by the glow of orange flames engulfing his shop and home. At this sight, Smalls reeled back, a smirk twisting his face. "Fall back! I have listened to the queen's death rattle."

In the sight of Patrick Jack's decline, the patriots continued to melee with intense rage. One soldier howled as a musket stock crushed his jaw, and another, with a knife buried in his thigh, staggered backwards and away from the fearless expressions drawn upon the faces of Margaret and Lilas Jack.

The redcoats turned and fled, chased by the rebels' fire and rage.

As the British retreated into the night, Margaret Jack and Lilas Jack fell to Patrick's side. Their attempts to offer even a single moment of comfort to the dying warrior was denied by the cruel journey he was now upon.

The flames of the burning tavern spat burning debris out onto the yard, and with the help of their fellow patriots, Lilas and Margaret lifted and moved Patrick several yards back from the closest source of warmth any of them had on that cool and windy night.

Finally, they knelt beside Patrick, their hands trembling as they touched his face, and ran their hands through his white beard. They whispered his name, and pleaded for him to hold on.

My lionheart, my love, please." Lilas collapsed upon her beloved.

Through the tears that swelled in her honey brown eyes, Margaret searched desperately across the eyes and lips of her once lively father-in-law, never knowing his to be without a clever remark, or a humorous observation, a word of kindness, or simply a silent presence meant to wrap his company in a calm safety.

This silence was malignant and without mercy.

Under a cloudless sky, the shield that had guarded the frigid boy on the road, and the steady pillar that the people of Charlotte had come to rely upon, passed in a manner that was antagonistic to his mortal ways.

Indignant and indifferent. Patrick suffered a death that was relentless.

The fire behind them consumed the tavern, and the black smoke carried James' home into the highest of the heavens.

Chapter 15: His Loyal Thieves

The rain had not been kind. The constant stream of water upon James' battered body had kept his skin fragile, and disrupted the healing of the unknowable number of scratches, cuts, and burns along his body.

The fires that had raged throughout the night were smothered, and now, as the morning sun filtered through the trees, a soggy and damp calm had taken hold of the forest. As the smoke began to clear, the scent of charred leaves and wet earth still clung to the air.

James Jack appeared as a forgotten corpse upon a distant battlefield. His white linen shirt was torn, and the presence of bright red blood had turned his brown trousers into a rusty shade.

James was alive, but his mind was suspended in a state of sleep that was crossed between pleasant dreams and inhuman illusions. The veins in his head pulsated with aching pain, as he laid motionless upon his earthen bed.

His thoughts were untraceable. The pain and toil of moving any part of his body kept him still; and the mental fatigue and stress placed James' in a state of dissociation that the strongest of the tavern's ale could not hope to achieve.

As James floated in between flashes from his childhood, to the birth of his daughter, to the long party had in the tavern after his wedding with Margaret, James could hear the rustling of shrubbery in the distance.

Coming in and out of focus, James was unable to muster any concern for the growing rumblings in the dirt. The sounds of boots crashing into the earth blended in effortlessly with the vivid dreams he wandered through.

Suddenly, James felt a kick. The toe of the boot struck James' weakened rib cage, and upon impact, it jolted him to reality.

The world spun, and he sucked in a sharp breath, his heart racing. He instinctively trying to move, but only managed a light shudder. With his nose caked in the dirt, he listened closely.

The shifting of the dirt gave way to voices—a low, murmuring conversation held just above him. Two men, their tone as callous as the hardhearted.

"Looks like he's still breathing," one of them muttered.

James' eyes snapped open. The men loomed over him, their figures blurry at first, and he thought for a fleeting moment that it was Edward Morrison's towering silhouette. But then the fog lifted, revealing two strangers.

"You're too late," the second man said with a laugh. "He's dead, Kit. Just like his horse."

James blinked away the dizziness, trying hard to persevere through a raging migraine. The men's voices faded in and out.

Paralyzed by his pain, but now cognizant that the two men were standing over him, James prayed that they would leave this enigmatic carcass to rest in the wilderness. James could feel the man place his foot upon his bruised side.

"Don't matter," said the first man. "We loot him, take the other horse, and be gone before sundown."

The two thieves rolled James' over with a crude yank, revealing the dry haversack bag that had been guarded from the storm by his body.

The movement caused James' vision to spin again. He groaned, his body screaming in protest, but his mind pushed through, a spark of clarity igniting.

James took in the scene—their mismatched clothes, their faces rough and covered with spotty black beards, and the large knives at the men's respective waist. These were highway thieves, opportunistic vultures.

The thieves stiffened. "Look at this one," Cyrus muttered. "Couldn't even tell if he was alive or dead." He spat on the ground beside James.

The second man, Kit, walked over to inspect James' haversack, which for the first time since the chase with Edward, now sat just inches out of James' reach. Kit squatted, and focused his eyes down to the bag.

"See this?" Kit grinned. "Ain't no way a dead man's carrying something like this."

The first thief, Cyrus, reached for the bag. The sight of Cyrus reaching for the haversack bag resurrected James to life. Without allowing any consideration for his immense frailty and pain, James jerked his body to the side, his arms shaking with the effort.

The thieves jumped back, their eyes widened with surprise. From their view, a dead man had been just been revived with the breath of life.

"Still got some fight in him, eh?" Cyrus said, his grin sharp and dangerous. "Would've thought you'd be long gone by now."

James didn't respond. His body was stiff, but he fought to stay conscious, to keep his wits about him. He kept his grip fastened on the straps of the haversack bag, and he craned his neck to look forward, past the ends of his bloodied boots. What he saw caused the muscles centered around his heart to ache with hurt.

Tethered to a nearby tree with coarse rope, Pilgrim dipped her chin in sadness. Her dirty brown mane fell over her eyes, as if she intended to hide her shame for becoming the thieve's captive.

James let out a soft cry to see his companion so close, yet so impossibly far from reach.

"Don't bother about your mare." Cyrus grinned and pointed to the left of James. "Least this one's still upright."

Laying twisted on the ground was the remains of Edward's horse, Eclipse.

Cyrus laughed, and Kit reached once more for the haversack bag. James wrestled against his pain and shouted hoarsely.

"You cannot!"

Once again, the two thieves were taken aback.

"I am more than certain of the fact that we indeed, can do whatever we please."

The two men both removed their large daggers from their belts, and pointed them directly into the sunken face of James Jack.

"Is this a mercy kill then, lad? You protest our robbery, and we end your suffering here in these woods?" Cyrus placed his dagger only inches from the surface of James' cornea.

James twitched his eyes to look past the blade and the thieves grinning visages. His eyes temporarily locked with that of Pilgrim's.

James then refocused his eyes on the thieves.

"You will not capture this." James broke his gaze with the thieves, to look upward into the cloudy sky above.

The Esquires faced twisted curiously, and both thieves looked around at the smoky forest around them; the twisted carcass of Eclipse, the deep gashes in Pilgrim, and the physical devastation that marked every inch of the man in front of them.

Cyrus scratched his scraggly goatee and set his dark brown eyes against James. He laughed, and refocused his rusty blade: pointing it first towards James, and secondly, at the haversack bag by his side. Cyrus remarked,

"What treasures you must carry."

James looked through Cyrus and chuckled internally at his own thoughts, "if only they knew".

As James gritted his teeth, he could see Cyrus turning to invite Kit over to him. James knew the men intended to rob him of his last possession, his most prized purpose. James knew he must not only preserve his ownership of the haversack, and the Mecklenburg Declaration within, but that he must somehow retrieve Pilgrim from the men. James could hardly move, his body still ached and gnawed from his escape from Edward. All James could do now was think and pray for the wisdom to unbind himself from his impossible lot.

With nothing but his steady courage and faith, James sat up straight, readying himself as the men came to seize his unknown treasure.

Cyrus and Kit reached past James, but he interrupted them.

"You think it is a treasure?" James rasped, his throat dry. His voice was hoarse from days of barely speaking, but it came out sharp enough to grab their attention. He wasn't sure what he was going to say, but the words spilled out anyway, desperation driving him. "That bag... it is not treasure. It is cursed."

The thieves exchanged skeptical glances.

"Cursed?" Kit snorted in laughter. "You expect us to believe that?"

James' grip on the haversack bag remained like that of a vice.

James nodded, more to convince himself than them.

"Aye. Cursed. By an Indian tribe far south of these mountains."

Cyrus and Kit turned to one another and shared an expression of genuine befuddlement. In unison, the men broke out into laughter.

"Is that right? Well in my pocket I've got myself a horse's feather and a hen's tooth!"

The unending stream of the men's cackling was distressing for James, as he desperately searched for the next thread in his deception.

"It is true, by God I swear it is."

"What tribe has placed a curse on your satchel?"

"The Cherokee of the Carolina mountains." James swallowed deeply, as he further committed himself to the tale.

"It is not the bag that is cursed. It is the token inside that haunts me."

It had been weeks since the marauding thieves had been in the company of civilization, and even longer since they had been the beneficiaries of proper entertainment.

In the isolation of the Virginian forest, the two thieves decided to, guardedly, listen on.

"So some tomahawk wielding redmen decided to curse you. What is it that's even in the damn bag?"

The beating of James' heart sped as he watched Cyrus and Kit refocus their attention on the haversack bag.

"It is an ancient object within the bag, it was cursed by the Cherokees priestly class. The long-dead, Ani-Kutani."

James did not have the clarity of mind necessary to tell if the tears forming in his eyes were a consequence of his devotion to the fable, or the bubbling of his unconquerable exhaustion. Nevertheless, he persisted.

"I stole it from a man. The curse is now mine to bear."

James wept gently. The thieves spent several minutes examining the innumerable injuries marking the oddity before them. They surveyed his visible hysteria. They concluded that by accounts, the battered fool certainly appeared cursed.

Still, neither man was fully convinced.

"And how'd a fool like you steal something of this value?" The thieves were now wondering if the stranger had an expertise to share with them.

"They gave it to me, handed it to me many moons ago, with the order to bury it."

"Bury it where?"

"At the site of their enemy's homeland."

"Well those directions sound rather indistinct. Who among this land isn't enemies with the Indians?"

"Their people warred for centuries with the Shawnee tribe; it is somewhere in these hills that I am meant to inter this wretched mark."

James could now see that the thieves were completely consumed by the tale.

"But fate evades me as to the exact parcel of dirt for which the vessel is to be entombed."

"And so I wander this land. Till this quest is completed, the curse will linger on me as the token's courier."

"I will die in this forest, by the hands of the curse; either nature-" James paused to look directly into the intensely focused eyes of the thieves, "-or man, shall end my suffering."

The thieves sat in silence for nearly a full minute. Finally, Cyrus spoke.

"Then perhaps we ought to just leave a blade in your belly, and put you out of your misery."

His offer seemed laced with at least an ounce of sincerity.

"It cannot be done."

"No, I am positive we could kill you," Kit chimed in.

"No. If you kill me, you will take on this curse yourself. It will follow you until you are laying alone in the dirt of the forest; chased by phantoms, your body burnt and bruised; your only companion, the rotten carcass of your steed."

Kit and Cyrus hesitated, their hands still hovering over the haversack, and their eyes darting in between bemusement and horror. Finally, they both straightened, and slowly withdrew their hands.

"Ghosts," Cyrus muttered, his voice tight with unease. "...fire, and I'd have to die alone in the woods?" He looked over at Kit.

"Bloody hell, Kit, I'd rather just take the horse and live to tell this tale in Winchester."

The two men looked back at Pilgrim.

"I think I'll name her 'Manitou', that way we never forget her savage roots."

Now completely disinterested in the contents of the haversack bag, the two thieves stood to their feet and began walking towards Pilgrim.

The panic in James reset as he rushed to his feet. Emboldened by his successful deception over the two men, he hurried after the men as quickly as his eroded strength would allow.

"Wait, you cannot take her!"

"For the last time fool, I am positive that we could."

"No, please," James began to plead. He knew he had to choose his next words very carefully. So far, the thieves had believed in the Indian fable, but James knew that if he overtaxed the tale, he risked straining it to a breaking point.

Pilgrim had to be rescued, a path would have to be found.

James put himself between the thieves and his horse, and permitted the madness of the moment to manifest in his intense blue eyes.

"If you steal my steed, the curse of the Ani-Kutani will spread to you both."

The two men sighed as they began formulating their responses.

"New rule, eh?" jeered Kit.

"No truly I tell you. Whatever man who steals from the accursed, will have the curse spread onto them."

"Care to offer a shred of evidence, you smooth-tongued rogue!"

James contemplated his response, his peripheral vision captured by the frozen remains of Eclipse.

"There."

James pointed at Eclipse's corpse, and the eyes of the thieves followed.

"That horse did not belong to me, but to a pursuer who had chased me from the Wagon Road in North Carolina."

"What happened to him?"

"His final fate is unknown to me, but I know he suffered greatly. His only steed lay dead upon the earth, and he is alone in this wilderness, now haunted by the same devilry that plagues me."

"Well what did he steal from you?"

James' mind thought of his daughter's celtic cross hanging from Edward's neck. James gritted his teeth and simply said,

"Something precious."

Kit and Cyrus exchanged a glance, the uncertainty on their faces deepening. James could see it in their eyes—the greed still lingered, but an opposing force had been awoken too. When they surveyed the unreasonable devastation around them, the words of the strange vagabond began to make sense.

Finally, Cyrus spoke, his voice lower than before. "So, this cursed thing," he muttered, "we just act as if we never crossed your path, and the devilry stays with you?"

"Until it kills me, aye."

Cyrus considered this for a moment, glancing at Kit, who seemed more skeptical but was no longer as eager to push forward. "If we give you back ''Manitou', what's stopping you from coming after us once you get your strength back?"

James' eyes darted to Pilgrim, who stood nervously at the edge of the clearing, the rope still tethered around her neck. His heart pounded as he realized that the fate of his only remaining companion rested on the next few words.

"For the short time that I have left, I have only one focus, finding the patch of soil I need to bury this accursed token." James spoke, keeping his voice even.

There was a long silence, the only sound was the soft rustling of the trees around them. James held his breath, watching as the thieves weighed their options. Finally, Cyrus sighed, rubbing his chin. "I don't know. It feels like a fool's gamble, either way. But a limped horse is nothing compared to this mess you're talking about."

Kit huffed, clearly disappointed, but his eyes darted nervously back to the bag. "Fine," he grumbled. "We leave the damned horse."

Cyrus looked at him one last time, and then back at James. "Well, lady luck's blessings, stranger. Thank you for the grand tale."

Cyrus and Kit wandered off down the beaten path they had arrived from, until eventually fading out of sight. Though they took every effort to appear unmoved, James could tell their fear of the Indians had been used effectively against them.

James slumped his back against a tree, and rejoiced that he remained in possession of his two greatest treasures on the road: the haversack bag, and his dear companion, Pilgrim. Pilgrim let out a soft cry as she galloped over, her brown coat still beautiful despite the marks and bruises.

James embraced her muzzle in a tight hug, and held her in silence for several minutes. Finally, he whispered into her arched ears,

"Almost there now, Pilgrim... just a little further."

Chapter 16: Blood in the River

For seven days and seven nights, James Jack and Pilgrim persisted through the woodlands and accompanying mountain ranges. Every night, James would pull his tattered body up the sides of the tallest - and as he discovered the importance of on his third night - the sturdiest tree in his vicinity. Once James had secured his position atop the highest tree branch, he would look up into the vast and humbling cosmos.

Some nights the sky was overcast with a tapestry of countless clouds. Other nights, the sky was radiant with thousands of astral gems; the candles of Heaven all shining in luminous accord. Each of the seven nights, James was generally able to spot two major celestial bodies. First, was the North Star. James could remember as a boy, when his mother would lead him out to an open space on a hill in Mecklenburg.

As James journeyed along with Pilgrim, he fought to remember the location's name.

"Stack-town?"

James shook his head.

"Stung-town?"

No, that definitely did not sound correct.

"Stumptown. That was what we called it, Pilgrim."

James chuckled as he remembered sitting upon a tree stump, as his mother explained that the same North Star that led the three wise men, was the one that watched over them every night.

The North Star continued to watch over him, and every night when the skies were clear, James would share a glance black. The permeance of the glowing orb kept him and Pilgrim headed towards their destination in Philadelphia.

From his birdlike perspective atop the highest branches in the forest, James would also examine closely the three bright stars that make up Orion's Belt. While watching the three stellar points rise in the east and set in the west, James was able to not only hone his directions out of the wilderness, but also find comfort in the memory of his truest guide.

His father.

"Remember, James," Patrick would say, "three stars for the three parts of our God: the Father"—he'd point to himself—"the Son"—he'd turn and point to James—"and the Holy Ghost"—where he'd always shout "boo!" or something similar.

James also remembered something else his father used to say about Orion's belt.

"It's not just God up there who watches over you, you know that right? My own mother and father, who left this earth long before you'd remember them—they offer their watchful eyes as well. All the named and unnamed Jacks that have come before you, they'll watch you too."

James chuckled when remembering how unintentionally threatening his father could make that last line of dialogue.

But like usual, his father was right. James climbed up the trees and spoke with his departed kin, the named and unnamed every night, and before he knew it, he and Pilgrim were resting in gentle meadows.

On the eighth morning since surviving the standoff with the thieves, Pilgrim delivered James to a meadow rolling with a variety of rich flora. Among the newly discovered vegetation was the plant yarrow. After crushing the plant with his hands into a soft ball of mass, he applied the remedy all over Pilgrim and himself. By reason of the fact neither him nor his companion died from the multiple infections that sought to ravage their vulnerable vessels, James considered the yarrow's effect a great success.

After two days traveling through the meadows with Pilgrim, James approached another series of woodlands, although these were a notably different manner of forest.

Unlike the diabolically scarce wildlife in the wilderness ruled over by Edward Morrison, this stretch of forest was teeming with life—particularly, in the trees.

James learned quickly the reverence one must be prepared to give to a nesting bald eagle, of which there were many upon the highest and sturdiest branches in the new grove.

Eventually, James' numerous close calls with the nesting bald eagles made him aware of what the mother eagle was bringing home for her chicks to sup on.

Fresh fish.

James knew that the Susquehanna River, his final physical barrier before arriving into eastern Pennsylvania, was near.

With a belly full of freshly picked berries, nuts and roots, and a back that was remedied well by the effect of the yarrow and other healing flora, James ushered Pilgrim onwards towards the sounds of the formidable river.

Before long, the two were standing at the outer boundary of the woodland grove. The Susquehanna river was massive, and unlike anything James had ever seen. James knew that from his current position, it was far too wide and treacherous to cross. For the remainder of the day, James listened to the cries of eagles as he journeyed further up the river's banks, hoping to eventually find a suitable passage for crossing.

Right before nightfall, James came across a neck in the river: a narrow bend that featured two natural islands in the river's center. James estimated that from his position on the bank to the first island, it may be about two hundred feet. From the first island to the second, it may be an additional two hundred feet, and from there, approximately one hundred and fifty feet to the opposing bank.

Knowing that this crossing could be burdensome on Pilgrim, James decided that choosing a crossing that could offer sources of rest would be vital.

James fashioned a rudimentary bed out of leaves and pine needles, and prepared himself for the night ahead.

As Pilgrim curled herself into a comfortable position beside James, they both listened to the constant cries of the bald eagles above.

If James was none the wiser, he might've thought that the flock of eagles had joined rank with the stars in the sky as the river's watchmen; their piercing yellow eyes in constant surveillance.

James could feel the morning sun warm his body, and turn the makeshift bed of pines and leaves up to an uncomfortable heat. James was relieved that it was not the sounds of the rivers that awoke him, for he had prayed that the rushing cascades would subside, and make the crossing less treacherous for Pilgrim. In lieu of torrent rapids, James looked upon a river that was far gentler.

After enjoying a small breakfast of berries and mushrooms, James leapt atop Pilgrim, and secured the haversack bag in its usual position upon his side.

"Well Pilgrim, do you feel ready?"

James watched as the mare appeared to snort in understanding.

With the sun now fully risen, and the promise of finally reaching their destination so near within sight, James ushered Pilgrim to take her first steps in the Susquehanna river.

Her hooves were placed firmly and without hesitation. James fixed their focus on the first of the two natural islands, their safe shores two hundred feet away. James could not see what the bottom of the river was composed of, but the sounds created by Pilgrim's hooves impressed upon James that it was neither dirt nor sand, primarily, but was something hard and solid.

Rocks.

James waded Pilgrim cautiously, as he feared every step she took might unknowingly lead them both into waters far too deep or violent. Fortunately, the water levels never rose above the tops of Pilgrim's legs, and its currents were never more than a mild tug on the adventuring galloper.

As they grew closer to the first point of land, James became entranced by the sight of bald eagles soaring through the air. As Pilgrim stepped out of the water and onto the sturdy terrain, James watched three different bald eagles dive down towards the river's surface; all three seizing smallmouth bass in the process.

As Pilgrim and James rested for several minutes on the island, the eagles continued to soar, glide, and hunt. Occasionally, they would perch upon one of the dozen or so trees that were rooted on the small islet. As James led Pilgrim to the bank, and set her sights on the next island approximately two hundred more feet away, he could feel his companion begin to tense up and neigh.

"Pilgrim, is it the river?" The mare seemed bothered by another presence.

"The eagles?" James inquired gently.

As the birds of prey continued to circle in activity above the two wayfarers, James was sure this was the source of Pilgrim's bother.

"Worry not, friend. They'd be foolish to mistake you for a trout." With a pat on her mane to reassure her, James steered Pilgrim back into the river.

Much like the voyage to the first island, the trip to the second river island was fairly unremarkable. The anxiety of unintentionally guided Pilgrim into a deep hole or other hazard was still present in James' heart and mind. However, all worry rescinded like the wind-draw waves on the shore, when Pilgrim once again walked herself and James upon the solid earth of the second island.

Sensing the growing mental and physical fatigue of his mare, James granted him and Pilgrim nearly an hour to rest under the shade of the island's cottonwood trees.

As the heat from the sun reflected off the river, it warmed and agitated the harsh blister that had formed along James' waist. Climbing atop Pilgrim to use her height as leverage, James pulled several handfuls of cotton from the branches of the shading trees. James fastened the loose cotton against his vengeful blister, hoping to keep it dry and covered from both the sun and the river.

To the sounds of crying eagles, a rippling river, and a slightly guarded Pilgrim, James ushered her back into the river to complete the final stretch of their crossing. One hundred and fifty feet of river stood between them and the long-awaited soil of eastern Pennsylvania.

As James rode upon the slowly moving back of Pilgrim, he could see that her brown tail was being pulled by a slightly stronger current then earlier in the crossing. James stroked Pilgrim's mane, and did his best to encourage her.

"John Haigler really wasn't lying was he? I couldn't have asked for a better companion for my journey."

James looked ahead, feelings of gratitude swimming through him to see the trees on the awaited bank grow larger and larger as they inched forward through the waves.

"Already halfway through, Pilgrim."

Suddenly, James began to feel Pilgrim's hooves shift atop the rough rocks beneath her.

"Steady girl, it is alright!" James rushed to reassure her.

Pilgrim began to panic and fret in a manner James had not seen for over a week of traveling. James convinced himself it must have been something in the river, perhaps a snake or some other foul creature.

The current's force seemed to be accelerating in concord with Pilgrim's frenzy. James knew it was better to allow Pilgrim the time to return to equanimity, rather than forcing her on under distress. The last outcome James could bear would be to be dropped into the river's embrace.

So James waited, assuming that Pilgrim would eventually muster onward by her own will.

Pilgrim was comatose.

Only seventy feet away from salvation, James watched enviously as a herd of white-tailed deer treaded effortlessly along the river's banks.

Suddenly, James heard a noise so sickeningly familiar, that it brought back all the terror from the Shenandoah valley in an instance.

Over the sound of eagles crying and the water cascading, James heard a voice emerge from the river island behind him.

""You've been a clever rabbit, Jack, but I'm a patient hound."

Standing on the shore of the river island was the enormous stature of Edward Morrison.

Before James had the time to charge Pilgrim out of the river and onto the safety of land, Edward steadied the silver flintlock in his hand, and fired.

The last thing James felt before being swallowed by the river, was the grazing of the bullet on his right shoulder.

The force of the river was unyielding. James had no idea if the depths of the water was too much for him to stand, his unsteady feet combined with the slick stones along the river bottom made it impossible for him to find out. His whole body was soaked in the water's vicious caress, and every hurt upon his flesh was now intensified tenfold. The blood from his most recent wound swirled in the river's wake, as James could only give earnest thanks that the bullet was far too north to offer any fatal injury.

The only part of his body that was not drenched in the icy river stream, was his one limb that acted completely on instinct as the rest of his body fell beneath the river's surface. With the precious haversack bag clutched in his right hand as tightly as a vine is to a tree, James kept his right arm raised directly vertical over the river's skin. Appearing to the eagles above as though the Lady of the Lake herself had replaced the blade of Excalibur with the worn leather of the haversack bag, James struggled beneath a suffocating river to keep his treasure safe.

James lifted his head from the river, and though his dirty blonde hair veiled most of his vision, his ears could hear a sound rise above that of the river.

"Crack!"

Edward's barrage of gunfire was unceasing, and James shuffled haplessly to avoid the bullets, save the Mecklenburg Declaration from destruction, and maintain his place amongst the living.

Unexpectedly, James began to hear Pilgrim stamping on the shores of the river's banks. After using his one free hand to brush aside his wet strains of hair, James could see Pilgrim rearing up on her hindlegs, and stomping in a display of distress at her master's peril.

James turned back to see Edward tossing his flintlock, now presumably out of bullets. James watched in horror as the phantom who had hunted, tormented, and punished him over the last three weeks unsheathed from his belt a large and meanincing cutlass sword. With an impossibly large step, the black-maned warrior stepped from the island and into the river's embrace.

James' psyche was a hailstorm of half-formed solutions, all interrupting one another at the rapid-realization they were utter fantasy: he could not wade out of this river any faster than Edward could close the distance, besides, unless he could calm Pilgrim to the point of allowing him to remount her, his odds against a saber-wielding Edward seemed even more grim if upon solid ground. What of the haversack bag? Even if James managed to throw himself between the reach of Edward's sword and the strap of the bag, it was almost a given certainty that the Mecklenburg Declaration would be lost and destroyed in the currents of the river.

From his helpless position twenty five yards from shore, James reached an inconceivable verdict: the bag would have to be thrown to the safety of the banks.

His right arm was already fatigued, nearly numb from its unnaturally maintained pose, as well as the bleeding wound from the grazed bullet in his shoulder.

James could see Pilgrim ahead of him, and could hear Edward rapidly closing the distance behind him. James prayed through the cascading currents.

"God, my Father almighty, please, please deliver me your mercy."

"Help me."

James focused all of his energy on his single task. The fury, the rage, the passion, the unsullied love of home and the will to serve for its liberation coursed in every ounce of the patriot's blood flow. Upon jagged and uneven rocks, the tavern owner steadied his weathered brown boots, and like the climax dance of an Irish reel, he placed his right foot forward, turned his body, and launched the haversack bag, sending it soaring above the river's grasp.

In the company of bald eagles the haversack flew. The force of the throw caused James to tumble back under the chilly water. As quickly as he fell, James pulled himself back above the surface to search desperately for sight of the bag. When at first he could not locate where it had landed, a sense of crushing doom washed over him.

"No, Christ please, no."

His dread was lifted, but shortly thereafter settled back upon him, when he finally saw the strap of the haversack bag hanging precariously off of a log two yards from the sanctuary of the shore.

James' watched as the haversack bag, and the precious document there-in, idled just inches away from the squeeze of the Susquehanna river. The terrifying presence of Edward Morrison was drawing unbearably close, and James had to prepare himself for whatever cruel fate awaited him.

All of a sudden, James' eyes were drawn back to the banks and the log just off shore.

Despite an onslaught of whimpers and shy hesitations, Pilgrim placed her hooves back into the river's rushing currents. She waded for less than a minute, and then, in a scene that would follow James the rest of his life, his beloved companion secured the strap of the haversack bag in her teeth, and carried it onto the safety of the dry shores.

Pilgrim had found her courage, and saved the declaration from destruc-tion.

"My dearest friend," James closed his eyes and whispered to himself.

Inspired by his mare's incredible courage, and determined to slay the dragon of his ceaseless disturbance, James lowered a hand into the river's bed, and secured his fingers around a wieldable sharp rock. Now face-to-face with the green eyed behemoth, James entered into the duel of his life.

Edward's sword swung in a wide arc, but James ducked low, narrowly avoiding the deadly blade. The water swirled around them, distorting both of their movements. The river's current seemed to grow stronger, as if plotting to place both men squarely within the other's reach.

With a roar, Edward advanced again, swinging the sword with brutal intent. But James was faster, moving with the flow of the river, ducking and weaving under the attack.

To James' dismay, the soldier suddenly shot out his free hand, and stran-gled the width of James' neck, pinning him underneath the water's surface.

James choked and screamed for air. The haunting image of Edward's green eyes, wild sable hair, and predator ivories distorted by the water's surface, was an appropriately demonic visual to go along with the sensation of being choked beneath the river.

After what felt like an eternity, James finally managed to kick Edward hard enough in the legs, so that the massive man lost his footing. With both men now horizontal in the rapids, it was a race to regain an upright position.

James managed to beat him to his feet.

Driven by a desire to see his enemy vanquished, James wrapped his hands around Edward's neck, and similarly attempted to make him the river's next victim.

Edward was simply too strong.

He hurled James off of him, and he was sent stumbling backwards in a large splash.

Looking to build off of his momentum, Edward charged James with his sword, and swung it at his heart.

Unbeknownst to Edward, James was still armed with his rock beneath the water's surface.

Within a second of Edward's blade slicing into his chest, James thrusted up with his arm and smashed his rock into the side of Edward's arm with all his strength.

Upon impact, Edward lost his grip on the sword, its blade slipping beneath the water's surface.

James attempted to strike Edward once more with the large rock, but the impact of Edward's fist upon his jaw caused James to stumble and drop the rock into the current.

With nothing but the weight of their mutual fury, the two men threw punch after punch into their opponent, each strike landing with an appalling force. Finally, through the unspeakable state of exhaustion, James saw it.

His vision was blurred, and so he couldn't be sure at first glance. But as the brawl carried on, the small artifact swinging against Edward's chest became clearer, and clearer.

Cynthia's cross.

The sight of his daughter's gift, and the remembrance of Edward's abuse towards it sent James into a frenzied rage. James launched for his combatant's face, but when Edward effortlessly threw the physically inferior James back onto the riverbed, James could feel a hard steel press against him between the rocks.

The hilt of Edward's sword.

In one motion, Edward used one hand to grip James' white linen shirt with an inhuman, hateful strength, while another hand gripped a giant jagged rock.

As Edward brought James to the spot where his rock would conquer the backcountry rogue, James catapulted the end of Edward's sword directly into the soldier's heart.

The blue eyes of James Jack locked with the serpent green eyes of Edward Morrison. James could not look away as Edward's fearsome eyes leveled from those of a monster, to those of a man, to those of an empty shell.

James pulled the sword from Edward's chest, and as the titan fell backward into the sea of red, James tore his daughter's blessing off of the dead man's neck.

The bald eagles circled curiously, and as the sun beat down that summer afternoon, the remains of Edward Morrison floated down the river, floating atop a crimson cloud.

James waded across the river, and at long last, pulled himself onto the river's banks before collapsing onto his back. James dropped Edward's sword at his side, and fought to capture his breath.

With Pilgrim and the haversack bag both safely in tow, James Jack looked up towards the hidden stars and thanked each of them, for delivering him from the phantom of Shenandoah, for giving strength to the sickly, for giving help to the helpless.

Chapter 17: Beyond these Gates

Wind from the Neuse and the Trent rivers whispered through the streets of New Bern with a resounding sense of purpose. The fragrance of the salt mixed in the river's brackish waters, formed with the fumes of the turpentine and tar ascending from the city's docks.

As the aromas of the town glided towards the governor's palace, they became infused with another odor: burning wood, soot and ash.

Every incision of gold and iron, every chiseled tribute to the monarchy of Great Britain was now illuminated by the light of hundreds of torches, each brandished by a member of the patriot force now gathered at the main gate to the Governor's mansion, known to its advocates and detractors both as Tryon's Palace. Across a perfectly manicured lawn, there was nothing but the slow rotation of the two story windmill in the garden to offer any movement in the desolate grounds.

Where once there had been an army of British soldiers and enslaved laborers working to maintain the beauty of the Governor's home, now there was nothing but the moonlit darkness of a perfectly kept, but abandoned estate.

From the center window atop the second floor of the palace, one man kept a dutiful watch as the great mob of patriots grew more, and more powerful.

With two solemn candles lit on either side of his gaunt countenance, the highlighted lines across his furrowed brow showed that Josiah Martin was as close to collapsing as the black wrought-iron gates that separated the crowd of protestors and himself.

Josiah's ocean blue eyes focused closely on the particular features of as many of the protestors as the unsteady light could afford him.

Men, mostly. Some of the men gathered at his gate were quite old, with white hair like crowns of snow. Others in the crowd were so youthful, Josiah couldn't help but worry for their safety in the gritty gathering. Still among the crowd of rebels were women and freed African Americans, all mustered together by the imperfect, but cherished cause of freedom.

As the mob pulled and tore at the gates, Governor Martin pondered to himself.

How far had these people journeyed to assemble at his gate? What galvanized their resolve? Faith in the cause of independence or revulsion of the crown?

Josiah stood as stoic as a statue pondering these questions and more. The stiff-upper lip of the British aristocracy as steadfast as the brick foundations of the palace.

What crimes would the jury find I had committed in the execution of my office and role?

At last, the sight of the rebels became too great to bear, and Josiah Martin turned inward to see the remaining faces of his party in the large hall.

Across the great hall, the noise of hurried footsteps echoed. The stoic demeanor painted across Josiah's face began to crack at the sight of his wife, Elizabeth, and the feeling of her unrestrained hug. After a moment to collect herself, the woman stepped backwards from her husband. The moonlight through the window exhibited that her skin was pale and her expression one of severe concern. Her hands clutched the sides of her skirt as she began to speak.

"Josiah, please," she pleaded softly, her voice trembling, "you must come with us now. The children are ready."

Josiah's expression darted rapidly between a dutiful stoicism, and the sensitive fracturing of a distressed husband and father. Despite the tearful pleas of his wife, Josiah remained resolute. "Not yet, Elizabeth. I must see this through." Josiah's voice was steady despite the tremor of unease in his chest.

Elizabeth stepped forward, her eyes filled with tears, the sleeves of her green dress flailing as she began to yell.

"How did it come to this, Josiah? What happened, why have your men abandoned you?"

Josiah turned back, and positioned himself between the fading light of the two candles perched in the frame of the center window.

"We underestimated them, my love. The attack on Charlotte, it was done according to the laws of justice." Josiah's voice was quieter now, filled with the weight of resignation.

"I would have never expected the colonists to respond in such a manner. Least of all the residents of our great city."

Josiah narrowing his eyes as he looked out at the swelling mob. "You ask me why my men abandoned me?" Josiah looked down at the unguarded perimeter of the palace. "They did nothing but heed my commands."

"The men who truly abandoned me are the ones currently attempting to tear down my gates."

Josiah had once again resumed his steely and stoic surveillance of the estate.

Elizabeth reached for him, her hands trembling as she clutched at his sleeve. "Josiah, please. Come with us. We can leave now, while there's still time."

His shoulders sagged for a moment, but then, with a sorrowful glance into the eyes of frightened wife, Josiah answered plainly,

"I will join you soon, love. But you must go ahead. I cannot abandon my post, not yet." He pulled her into a brief embrace, then turned back to his station. With the encouragement of two soldiers, Elizabeth Martin was escorted to the place where her children waited.

After a few moments of quiet reflection, Josiah Martin became aware of the fact that he now stood alone as the final steward of British authority in the palace. Josiah turned away from his station by the center window, and began his journey down the hallway and towards the master bedroom, where for the last four years, he and Elizabeth had slept in regal comfort.

At the sight of the unmade bed and the remaining pieces of Elizabeth's drawer of makeup, Josiah was washed over with a profound sadness.

Nevertheless, he knelt beside his four-poster bed, and with a grunt, pulled a large chest out from underneath the feather mattress.

Josiah pulled the bronze lever on the front of the chest, and opened it with a deep reverence. With the same care one might give to the handling of a newborn child, Josiah removed the colorful fabric from the chest, and folded it gently in the palm of his hands.

As the roaring of the mob grew closer and closer, Josiah calmly rose from his knees, and turned out of his chambers, taking one final glance at his sanctuary, now forever loss.

The moonlight traced his shadow, his silhouette cast upon the walls. The Royal Governor marched the length of the hallway and down the mahogany grand staircase, until arriving at the palace's magnificent parlor.

Under the intense gaze of marble busts with formless eyes, Josiah Martin carefully removed one hand out from underneath the folded fabric, as he pushed open the cream-painted front door of Tryon Palace.

The protests from the patriots were deafening.

Josiah Martin stared stoically into the mass of patriots gathered beyond the gates. Their numbers were plentiful, and their fury was unmatched. Regardless of the threat, the royal governor stayed focused on his assignment.

With confidence he strode over to the palace's flagpole, a processed pole of locally sourced pinewood.

Under the watchful eyes of a starry heaven, Josiah Martin started the process of lowering the Flag of Great Britain down from its elevated position over the New Bern skyline.

To this sight, the mob of patriots cheered in jubilation.

Once the Union Jack had been lowered to the ground, Josiah Martin began the process of unfolding the colorful fabric he had tenderly borne from the chest in his former bed chamber.

After carefully pulling back the corners, Josiah Martin held in his hands a five by three foot flag adorned with numerous heraldic symbols meant to signify the monarch's various domains. Through the tidal wave of jeers and threats levied at Josiah from the crowd beyond the gates, he focused his efforts as he affixed the Royal Standard of King George III onto the pinewood flagpole.

In a final display of defiance against the patriot mob, Josiah heaved as he raised the red, purple and gold banner high into the night sky; the lions of England and Scotland, the harps of Ireland, and the white stallion of Hanover all fluttered over the land where the Trent and Neuse rivers intersect.

With the banner of his Lord raised high in the air, Josiah stoically turned his back to the mob, and entered back into the palace.

His pace was focused and brisk. Josiah Martin quickly found his way to the backdoor of the palace, and spoke just three cool words to the servant waiting for him.

"I am ready."

The dark green backdoor to Tryon Palace was left open as, side-by-side with his servant, Josiah Martin hurried down the five hundred foot field that sat between the grand house and the river. Running without torches, the two men relied on the bright shine of the moon to illuminate their path. As they drew nearer to the edge of the Trent River, Josiah began to hear the mob's dissents on the other side of the house grow more and more boisterous.

Without having the visual aid to confirm his suspicions, the fleeing governor felt sure in his heart that the patriots were now beyond the gates.

His pace was now a sprint.

At last, the panting and fatigued governor arrived at the two man row boat that was left pushed upon the river's shoreline.

"Quickly, my Lord!" The servant ushered Josiah into the row boat, offering him his hand for assistance. Once he was placed in the boat's back seat, the servant pushed the row boat off the marshy banks, and leapt inside, causing it to rock hazardously.

Before long, the steady arms of the servant were gliding the boat's oars through the shimmering waters of the Trent River. Josiah Martin looked onward in his seat. Facing the downward gaze of his servant, Josiah looked beyond him, as they sailed further and further from his palace home.

Josiah felt a stirring in his heart to share a eulogy for the conclusion of his chapter in New Bern, but the words could not find their way through the intense entanglement of hatred and despair.

Suddenly, the servant cautiously spoke, as if afraid to break his Lord's trance.

"Sir, we have arrived."

Josiah slowly shifted his blue eyes toward the servant, who pointed behind Josiah's back.

Josiah gripped the sides of the row boat, and as he turned, his blue pupils widened at the sight of a large British sloop-of-war ship, the HMS Cruizer.

With great care in his steps, the royal governor ascended the rope ladder placed along the ship's hull. Placing his buckled shoes in one square of the ladder's rope at a time, Josiah eventually reached the top of the ladder, where a multitude of hands waited to hoist him up onto the ship's deck.

The details of the ship, its long wooden planks, massive center beam, large white sails and refined captain's quarters all came to Josiah's senses secondarily; his primary focus being on his wife Elizabeth and on his young children, who all hurried to greet their husband and father.

"We are safe now," Josiah said with a defeated, but relieved inflection.

After welcoming the embrace of his young family, Josiah Martin turned to walk towards the port side of the HMS Cruizer. For one final moment in time, Josiah took his station watching over the grounds of Tryon Palace. From aboard the mighty vessel, Josiah watched as one particularly emboldened patriot climbed the length of the pinewood flagpole. Upon reaching its peak, the unknown assailant ran a torch under the king's standard. After letting it burn for several minutes, the rogue pulled a dagger, and cut the fabric down. The winds off the Neuse and Trent rivers tossed the burning banner as it fell into the grassy lawn below.

Josiah turned his eyes towards the captain of the Cruizer, and ordered him that now was the time to leave.

"It is time. We must sail for Fort Johnson on the Cape Fear, we will regroup once there." Josiah turned back to the overtaken acres of Tryon Palace, before concluding his thoughts.

"I will never abandon this colony. By God's right, it will fall back under the king's domain."

The HMS Cruizer began its slow retreat down the Trent, and into the Neuse river, where it carried the last of North Carolina's royal governors out to sea.

***

"Pull it open, lads!"

After hours of thrashing against the wrought-iron gates, finally the collective strength of the patriots forced the barrier to give way. The mob pulled open the gates, and together they stormed onto the lawn; from the views of the ravens perched upon the roof of the palace, it appeared as if an army of three hundred patriots had conquered the abandoned grounds of the front lawn.

With a monumental kick to the door knob, the cream-colored front door of the palace burst open.

The mob of patriots was ferocious, but rather unfocused. Some portions of the mob stormed up the grand mahogany staircase, flipping furniture, and destroying any homage to the monarchy. While others, under the disguise of many men, looked to loot the various treasures lining the walls and drawers of the palace.

"Wait, stop!" Screamed one patriot. "You fool, do not set fire here! This is our new home!"

With this sensible order, the arsonist extinguished his flame, and resumed his rampage of the home.

Naught in the palace was safe from the clutches of the patriots, whose grasps knew neither mercy nor bounds.

The mob went room to room, maundering as they went. Eventually they found themselves in the palace dining room, where fresh fruit, plates of vegetables and pastries still remained placed out on the table.

"Finally! Gentlemen, time to feast like kings!"

The patriots began to ravage all the food upon the large imported table.

"Raid the pantry, see what other goods the fleeing bastard left us!"

When a half dozen patriots moved on from the dining room and into the massive pantry in the adjacent room, they came upon a sight so bizarre it nearly stopped them in their tracks.

"What the -"

The patriot's statement of bewilderment was interrupted by the sound of silver goblets being dropped to the ground.

Slouched behind a large table heaped with half-eaten pastries and emptied goblets of wine, were the esquires—John Dunn and Benjamin Booth.

Thoroughly bloated and properly drunk from their gluttonous campaign, they appeared startled, but mostly just confused by the patriots presence.

"You guys here to peach to the Governor about that blackguard James Jack?"

Booth's words were barely discernible between the incessant slurring of his tongue.

"Well too bad! That's the rub... cause we, cause we, beat you to it."

Just as he'd done before Justice Brown weeks earlier in Salisbury, John Dunn nodded his head in an enthusiastic endorsement of his partner's words. Though this time, the nodding was much slower, and the smile lopsided.

With the drunkened esquires the final, pathetic trace of reverence for the British crown left in the colonial capital of New Bern, the mighty walls of Tryon Palace fell squarely into the hands of the American patriots. As the fire swept through Charlotte, the ashes of North Carolina were remade into the steel of a nation reborn.

Chapter 18: The Deliverance

The long stretch of road from the outskirts of Philadelphia appeared nothing like the relentless and untamed wilderness James had journeyed through the past several weeks. No dense looming forests, no soaring hillsides, raging fires or foaming rivers. Here, the sky felt weightless, warm and still like a pasture at dawn.

The city of Philadelphia rose before him like a great tribute to civilization—its buildings were taller and more meticulously crafted than any structure he had seen in the Carolina backcountry. Rows of three-story brick townhomes stood shoulder to shoulder along the thoroughfares, with their exteriors painted in deep reds with whitewashed trim and shuttered windows that blinked like watchful eyes. At the base of these townhomes were tidy gardens, much smaller in scale, but otherwise not terribly dissimilar from the ones Tom Jamison would grow alongside his cabin.

The streets were another distinctive feature, a testament to the city's thoughtful engineering. As Pilgrim strode over ground that was neither rutted trails nor oversized stone, she felt like a foreigner. The imported ballast stone, mixed with crushed oyster shell in the road's crevices, was a new sensation beneath the mare's tattered trotters.

As James listened to the clatter of Pilgrim's hooves echo against the paving with a musical quality, he heard them become mingled with the shouting of street vendors hawking everything from fresh oysters to tobacco. As James turned his head from left to right, he could see that the main roads of Philadelphia were lined with tall signboards creaking overhead—wooden images of hammers, globes, anchors, and wheat sheaves—each marking the locations of printers, shipwrights, bakers, tailors, and silversmiths.

Everywhere James looked there was movement. Carts and wagons groaned under the weight of imported goods: large barrels of molasses from the Indies, bolts of imported calico, and stacks of leather-bound volumes fresh from London. Ships offloaded at the wharves only blocks away, and legions of men in broadcloth coats and women in linen caps passed the slow-moving stride of Pilgrim with a speedy pace. James concentrated his ears on their speech: a muddled chorus of English, Dutch, German, French, and the thick brogue of Scots-Irish migrants.

Compared to the pine-sweet plains of the backcountry, Philadelphia felt impossibly grand, unnaturally ordered.

As James led Pilgrim farther into the city's churning heart, the bustling world of the city narrowed around them—stone, smoke, and unfamiliar stares. The streets had widened, but they felt tighter with every step Pilgrim put forward. Schools of people flowed past like a tide, parting only reluctantly for the battered pair who continued lethargically down the center of Market Street. The contrast was jarring, almost cruel. James in his sun-bleached and bloodied white linen shirt; the fabric worn to threadbare softness across the shoulders, and boots caked with mud from countless miles of fearful frontiers. The winds off the Delaware river lifted the layers of dust from a hundred unnamed places off of his skin. James' beard, now a scraggled and untrimmed goatee, sat unevenly beneath hollow cheeks. His body bore the stiffness of old injuries, of nights spent on cold earth and mornings waking to frost.

And then there was Pilgrim.

She limped beneath him, ribs showing through her thinning coat, hooves chipped from rough terrain and long stretches without care. One of her ears twitched against flies, slow and tired. Her breath came harder now, each exhale a labored plume in the morning air.

Around them, the city marched on in refinement. Men in polished shoes and powdered wigs, women in silk cloaks and lace gloves. No one offered a word to the wayward travelers, but their repulsed eyes said enough: a glance, a whisper, a wrinkle of the nose. Some stepped aside; others did not. James knew that, to many of them, he was a figment from the edge of a map that had no place here amid tea shops, brick chapels, and polished brass doorknockers.

And yet there he was.

James looked up at the towering brick buildings, the iron gates, the painted signs swaying in the breeze, and felt something settle inside him—not awe, not fear, but the hollowness of arrival. He had reached his destination, but there was no welcome in it. No arms to catch him, no warm fire waiting. Just the noise and the strangers, the weight of being seen but not known.

James felt a twisted sense of comfort in his own physical pain, but cringed greatly at the knowledge that Pilgrim hurt and ached as she did. Before any other stop was to be forged in the new city, James was going to make right his steed's suffering.

The scent hit James before the building came into view—iron and smoke—followed by the rhythmic clang of hammer on metal. It rang steady, like a bell keeping time with the heart of the city. The shop was tucked between two taller buildings, a low brick structure with soot-streaked windows and a forge that dispensed heat in rolling waves. The sign above the door had once been painted red, though most of the color had long since been eaten by sun and smoke. In its place hung the simple silhouette of a horseshoe, black against the pale morning sky.

James halted Pilgrim at the threshold, hand resting just behind her jaw, unsure if he should enter. But the decision was made for him. The hammering stopped, and a figure emerged from the glow of the furnace, equipped with broad-shoulders and a long leather-apron.

Oliver Helms looked at James and Pilgrim with a stunned expression.

"God above," he muttered, stepping forward. "That mare's been run through the devil's trenches, hasn't she?"

James nodded silently.

"She lame?"

"She's tired," James replied. "She hasn't had proper care since the mountains."

Oliver crouched near Pilgrim's front leg, examining her with a practiced hand. He murmured quiet words to her, almost like a prayer, and Pilgrim lowered her head. Trusting. Grateful. Or simply too tired to resist.

When Oliver rose again, there was sweat on his brow and something like compassion behind his eyes.

"I can fix her up," he said, brushing soot from his fingers. "She needs rest. Filing. Wrapping. I'll re-shoe her. Oats, if you've got coin."

James pulled the haversack bag forward, revealing something wedged in the grip of his worn leather belt: a blade.

It was Edward's sword—the brass of its hilt slightly dulled, but the edge inside as sharp as the day it spilled blood in the river. James removed it from his belt slowly, like a burden being laid down.

"I've no coin," James' said. "But I'll trade you this."

Oliver's eyes narrowed. "That's military steel."

"Aye," James remarked.

Oliver took the sword carefully, and ran his thumb along the hilt. "This'll do," he said. "You're not the first man to come in here trading war for rest."

He motioned toward the stables behind the shop. "Take her round back. There's water. I'll tend to her straightaway. Come back in a few hours."

James hesitated, his mind resisting the thought of separating from Pilgrim even for a moment.

"She's all I've got," he uttered meekly.

Oliver looked into the fatigued eyes of the sojourner. "Then she's in the right place."

James worked to ensure Pilgrim's comfort in the stables, before continuing his journey on foot, the haversack bag swinging against him with every step.

Within just a handful of blocks, James had arrived at a bathhouse that stood near the edge of Society Hill, just far enough from the noise of the main thoroughfare to feel like a hidden refuge. A carved wooden sign swayed above the door, the words

"Bathsheba's Bathhouse,"

etched in a gentle script, its curves softened by time and steam. A painted image of a woman at a spring adorned the signboard—locks of blonde hair cascading like water, arms open in welcome.

James stepped through the door into a hush that seemed to muffle the world outside. The scent of warm cedar, lavender, and something herbal—mint, perhaps—wrapped around him like the enticing waft of his father's smokehouse. The air was thick with moisture, rising like natural springs from the stone tubs and copper basins scattered throughout the dimly lit room. Lanterns flickered low, their flames made sleepy by steam.

James' placed his haversack gently on a worn bench, the leather base scratched and marked. He placed it where his eye could remain on it. The weight of it—of what it carried, of what it meant— remained at the base of his mind, like a loyal and unashamed hound remains with his master. Yet for a long-awaited moment, the journeyed satchel could rest. For now, James could rest.

He undressed slowly, peeling away the road-bitten layers of linen and leather like old bark. Each garment fell with a soft, sodden sound, as if exhausted from its task. His skin bore the tellings of the trail: bruises like ink blots across his ribs, cuts scabbed over with dust, a map of blisters winding from heel to knee. Yet still, James' moved his fractured form with care, as he prepared to enter the still waters.

The bath was a large stone basin set into the floor, fed by pipes that hummed faintly as warm water trickled in. A bucket sat beside it, carved from oak and worn smooth with use. Without ceremony, James stepped down into the tub.

The heat stole his breath.

He sank to his chest and let out a sound—half groan, half exhale—as the water embraced him. Every nerve quickly cried out, then quieted. His muscles, long locked in tension, unknotted one by one, like a fist opening from prayer. He leaned back, head against the lip of the tub, as he let the warmth seep deep into his bones. It was not the comfort of a bed, nor the pleasure of a fire. It was older than that. Elemental. A baptism of the weary.

James' took the wooden bucket and filled it slowly. The warm warter whirled in the bucket, and James' poured it over his head.

The water crashed down like absolution.

It soaked through the grime caked to his scalp, through the dried blood matted in his hair. Dirty blonde strands clung to his brow, heavy with road dust and memory. Again, he filled the bucket. Again, he let it fall. This time, he cupped his hands and scrubbed his face; cheeks, eyes, jaw, until the grit was gone and only skin remained. His breath came easier with each rinse, as if at last he was breaking from an unwelcome mold.

He washed until the water around him darkened, until the skin beneath the filth was pink and raw and clean. The ache in his joints dulled, not erased but soothed, and for the first time in weeks, maybe longer, James felt the shape of himself again—beneath the soldier, beneath the courier, beneath the man carrying burdens he was wholly unfit to bear.

James' stayed until the water began to cool, until the silence no longer felt foreign. When he rose, he did so slowly, almost ceremonially. After doing his best to clean his only surviving clothing, he begrudgingly stepped back into the stained trousers and cut shirt. After several minutes, James' shouldered the haversack bag, and left the bathhouse in silence, the scent of lavender and warm stone clinging faintly to his skin.

Outside, the city pulsed on—wagons creaked, vendors barked, church bells pealed in the far-off haze.

James turned back toward the farrier's shop, toward Pilgrim, toward the last piece of himself waiting to be made whole.

The farrier's shop stood just as he had left it—smoke curling up from the forge chimney, the rhythmic clink of ironwork ringing faintly from within. As James stepped around to the rear stable, the scent of hay and oil met him, warm and earthy.

There she was.

Pilgrim stood steady in a fresh stall, her legs wrapped in clean linen bandages, her coat brushed until it held a soft sheen that caught the slanting afternoon light. New shoes gleamed on her hooves, and her eyes—though still ringed with weariness—had lost their fearful edge. She looked up at James as he approached, ears flicking forward, and released a low nicker that bloomed like a welcome in his chest.

He pressed his forehead gently to hers and closed his eyes, one hand resting behind her ear.

"What a beautiful new coat," James spoke gently. "All you're missing is your wings, brave pegasus."

"I reckon she'll outlive us both," came a sudden voice from behind.

James turned to find Oliver Helms standing in the doorway, arms crossed, a small smile hidden beneath his beard. In his hands, he carried a folded bundle of clothes.

"Thought you might want these," he said, offering the bundle. "Found 'em tucked in a crate of old donations meant for the relief effort last winter. They've got more breath left in them than what you just walked in with."

James took the bundle carefully—worn but clean, a linen shirt, fresh coat and sturdy trousers; the soft, faded grays of second chances. He looked up, unsure how to repay such generosity.

"You've done enough already."

Oliver shrugged. "I've got no need for em'."

James dressed quickly behind the stable wall, then saddled Pilgrim once more. Pilgrim shifted beneath him with greater steadiness as he mounted. She was still healing, but James felt confident in the weight of every step she took.

Oliver raised a hand in farewell as James guided Pilgrim back into the street, the clatter of her new shoes a bright counterpoint to the city's drumbeat.

The ride through Philadelphia was short, but it felt like a procession.

As they neared Chestnut Street, the spire of the Pennsylvania State House rose into view, commanding and austere. Its brick walls bore the weight of a thousand words, all housed within those walls of red stone and white-trimmed dignity.

James slowed Pilgrim to a stop before the steps, the sound of hooves fading into the low whisper of men's voices from within. A few passersby paused to look, some curious, some indifferent. But James saw only the wide, sunlit steps before him.

He dismounted slowly, his dirty brown boots leaving a mark upon the clean cobblestone. He stood for a moment with one hand on Pilgrim's reins, the other on the haversack that held the words of his people. His coat hung straight now, his posture no longer bent by the road, and in James' deep blue eyes there was no uncertainty, only resolve.

He was ready.

And behind those doors, the words of the Mecklenburg Declaration would be sown amongst the Congress.

The heavy oak doors creaked open before James, their groan swallowed quickly by the cool hush inside. The scent of old wood and fresh ink clung to the air. Voices echoed from the main hall, their tone deliberate but restrained, like the conversation of men used to being heard.

James stepped into the wide corridor, his boots clicking softly against polished floorboards worn smooth by countless steps. The ceiling arched high overhead, and tall windows filtered in sunlight that struck the flagstone at sharp and vivid angles.

A cluster of men stood to his left, gathered around a long table strewn with parchment, quills, and tankards. Their coats were of fine materials: wool and silk, in shades of navy, pine, and gray. The men spoke in lowered tones over documents still damp with ink. James hesitated, uncertain where to begin, until his eyes fell on a figure seated at a smaller desk just to the right of the entrance.

The man was older than the others—perhaps the oldest in the room. He sat reclined, his legs stretched out in comfort, a pair of wire-rimmed spectacles perched low on his nose. His hair, once auburn, now silvered and tied loosely at the nape, and his stomach pressed comfortably against the buttons of his waistcoat. He looked more like a philosopher than a statesman—less rigid. The enigmatic man did not glance up, not at first. But he must have sensed the heaviness of James's gaze.

"You look as though you've traveled far," the man said, his voice low and amused, with the accent of Philadelphia's elite softened by years abroad.

"I have," James replied, stepping forward. "From Mecklenburg County, North Carolina."

The old man leaned forward then, peering up at him with keen eyes behind his spectacles. "From North Carolina? What brings you so far north, Mr...?"

"James Jack," he said. "I've come to deliver a document—on behalf of the people of Mecklenburg."

The man gave a thoughtful nod, then gestured toward the east corner of the hall, where three men stood in quiet conversation. "You'll want to speak with the North Carolina delegation. Caswell, Hewes, and Hooper. That corner, just there."

James followed the direction of his finger and nodded his head in thanks. The old man gave a knowing smile, and added, almost as an afterthought, "Give them my regards. And tell Caswell that Franklin says to keep his ink dry this time."

James paused mid-step, before continuing on to the three delegates.

James approached the three delegates, his boots growing quieter with each step. An unavoidable anxiety quickly filled James' chest. The arrival of the moment he had labored so long to produce was an overwhelming sensation, and James' did his best to appear routine in his delivery.

As James came within earshot of the men, he began to speak.

"Gentlemen, my name is James Jack. I bring with me the words of Mecklenburg."

All three men turned at once, their expressions shifting from curiosity to attention. Richard Caswell stepped forward first—tall and commanding, with a soldier's bearing and a statesman's eyes.

"The words of Mecklenburg?" he echoed.

James unslung the haversack, unfastened the flap, and gently withdrew the tightly rolled parchment within—sealed in wax and bound in leather cord. He held it out with both hands.

"We have drafted our own declaration," James said. "On the twentieth of May. It was signed by the members of our county militia. The Crown has abandoned us, and we see no future under its rule. This is the will of our people."

Caswell accepted the parchment with care, his eyes flickering over the wax seal before handing it to Joseph Hewes, who broke it open with precise hands. William Hooper leaned in over his shoulder, reading along in silence.

When they finished the first lines, they exchanged glances—serious, then surprised, then impressed.

"You carried this all the way from Mecklenburg?" Hooper asked.

"On horseback," James said. "With little food, no money, and a horse near broken by the road."

Caswell looked back down at the document, then at James. "Upon your delivery, what was it you hoped my colleagues and I could do for you, Mr. Jack?"

"Join us, sir," James professed boldly. "Have the declaration read before the remaining Congress, and make real our call for independence across the land!"

The men conferred quietly for a moment. James Jack watched on precariously. Then Caswell turned back.

"We'll read this through the night. What you've delivered... this is worthy of discussion."

James nodded, the weight of the journey shifting slightly off his shoulders.

"You'll stay in Philadelphia tonight," Hewes said. "City Tavern Inn, just down the street. We'll cover the cost—consider it the least we can do. Come back in the morning, Mr. Jack. We'll have our thoughts ready by then."

James offered a final nod of thanks, then turned, making his way back through the great hall. As he passed Franklin's desk again, the old man gave him one last look—approving, amused, and something deeper, the kind of look that lingers long in memory.

Outside, the day was waning, and the sun lit the bricks of the Pennsylvania State House like fire.

James mounted Pilgrim once more. She turned willingly down the street, her step lightened not just by new shoes, but by a rider who was now lessened with the enormous burden he had borne since before Salisbury. The question lingered in his mind as to how the delegates would ultimately proceed, but James was overcome with gratitude to have finally arrived at his deliverance.

As the sun began to set over the Philadelphia skyline, James Jack rode for the City Tavern Inn.

The City Tavern stood like a manor of light in the gathering dusk—its brick walls glowing in the lantern-haze, windows flickering with warmth and the soft clatter of utensils and voices within. James dismounted slowly, handing Pilgrim over to a stablehand with quiet instruction and a parting stroke along her neck. She turned into the stall without resistance this time. She knew she was safe.

Inside, the inn welcomed him with well-oiled wood, brass fixtures, and the low murmur of conversation in the dining hall below. Servants moved with quiet efficiency, their coats crisp, their hands gentle. A man in a fine waistcoat led James' up the stairs to the upper level suite—larger than anything James had stepped into since leaving home. The bed alone looked like a ship dressed in linen and down. A basin stood ready with clean water. A fire cracked in the hearth, its glow stretching long shadows across the rug.

He placed his haversack on the table near the window but did not sit. The room was warm, quiet, still—but stillness had a way of stirring memory.

He stepped out onto the small balcony that overlooked Walnut Street. Below, the city moved slowly in the soft bloom of lanternlight. Wagons rolled home over oyster-laid cobblestone, and the silhouettes of pedestrians drifted like shadows across the moonlit avenues. In the distance, the steeples and rooftops of Philadelphia stood outlined against a sky painted in ink and silver. Somewhere, a violin played in the corner of a tavern. Laughter floated faintly through the air.

James rested his hands on the balcony's wooden rail. He looked out across the city and thought, not of the day behind him, but of home. Of warm pine floors and the scent of pipe smoke curling through the rafters. Of his father behind the bar, telling stories with the cadence of scripture, as if each tale might save a soul. Of the rough laughter of familiar men and the closeness of a room where everyone knew his name.

He thought of Margaret and her special kiss. He thought of Cynthia, and the joy his mother Lilas brought to both her and his son, Patrick.

His heart yearned to be the mild-eyed manager of his father's homely tavern once again.

James' leaned forward, elbows on the rail, as he let the wind touch his face. It was cool and carried the smell of lamp oil, wet stone, and distant river. He closed his eyes and, without willing it, began to sing—not loud, not for anyone else. Just for the summer night. Just for himself.

A psalm, whose words remained embedded in James' memory.
"By the rivers of Babylon, there we sat down, yea, we wept, when we remem-
bered Zion.
We hanged our harps upon the willows in the midst thereof.

For there they that carried us away captive required of us a song;

And they that wasted us required of us mirth, saying,

Sing us one of the songs of Zion.

How shall we sing the Lord's song in a strange land?"

James repeated the lines of Psalm 127 several times, as his eyes focused on detailed rooftops and plentiful streets.

When he was finished, he did not move. He stood for a long time, his hands resting on the wooden rail, listening to nothing and everything.

Behind him, the fire crackled.

Below, the city turned over in its sleep.

And above, the stars of heaven watched on in perfect silence.

Chapter 19: Memorialize your King

A soft drizzle of rain had begun to freckle the window panes that decorated James' suite at the City Tavern Inn. When James rolled over on the feather-filled mattress, he became immediately disappointed at his perception of the evening's pace. For the first time in over a month, James had enjoyed a proper rest, and it was if it was over before he had the chance to relish the recess. As James' ears focused on the sounds beneath him, he listened on as the dining room filled with the indistinct mutter of early patrons and the gentle clink of silver on porcelain.

James pulled himself out from underneath the warm wool blankets and got dressed in the gray coat, shirt and trousers that Oliver had given to him the day before. After a brief foray onto the balcony, James breathed in the cool Philadelphia breeze, and descended the steps to enjoy a formal breakfast ahead of the day's monumental mission. As James descended the steps of the inn, his own mind descended further into doubt and speculation about the delegate's response to the declaration.

Perhaps they will want me present when they recite Abraham's words before the Congress, James mused internally.

Or perhaps they could not contain their glee, and have already enlisted the members of the Congress to the cause of independence.

What then, James pondered, *could be Charlotte's role in the war to come?*

What would my father have to say when he learns that his son had been the harbinger of liberty for all upon this vast new world?

James prayed reflectively, and his spirit quaked with the awareness that he was standing on the doorstep of his destiny.

After reaching the dining room of the inn, James collected himself and calmly walked into the gallery, not terribly unlike the one he oversaw back at Pat Jack's tavern.

James sat at a corner table, staring down at a breakfast that would have seemed heavenly to him just weeks prior: thick slices of salt-cured ham, scrambled eggs flecked with sage, warm molasses bread, and a generous wedge of soft cheese. A steaming bowl of barley porridge, laced with butter and dried cherries, steamed invitingly before him.

But he could not eat.

His stomach, now trained to survive on hardtack, wild mushrooms, creek water and silence, twisted at the richness. The scent of meat and cream made him nauseous. He took small, mechanical bites out of obligation rather than hunger, pushing the food around his plate like a man pretending at normalcy. The tavern's warmth pressed in on his gray coat, made heavier by the anticipation coiled in his chest.

How would they receive it?

The thought returned with every shallow breath.

The parchment had left his hands, but not his heart. The declaration—his burden and his banner—was now folded somewhere behind oak-paneled doors. Would it be read with fire, or buried with fear?

After finishing his meal, and watching the light morning rain give way to bright sunshine, James stepped outside to be rejoined with Pilgrim.

As James walked around the perimeter of the inn and towards the stables that housed Pilgrim, his mind was fixated on the light, but still distinguishable, difference in the haversack bag's weight. James chuckled at the thought that he had become so accustomed to the declaration's presence in the bag, that its absence was enough to create a physical observation.

Once James arrived at Pilgrim's stable, her eyes lit at the sight of him. Her hooves thudded gently as he brushed a hand down her neck. She had been fed, watered, and cleaned—and was ready to carry her master to his final stop on their grand journey.

Together they walked the short distance back to the Pennsylvania State House. The streets were quieter now, still slick with rain. Shopkeepers swept their thresholds, and a handful of children darted barefoot through puddles, laughing. James could do little else but keep his eyes straight ahead, and his mind focused on the task.

The morning air held the scent of the nearby Delaware River, mingled with the faint traces of bread baking in the markets and the ever-present musk of horse and sweat.

As he crested a small rise near Chestnut Street, the towering spire of the Philadelphia State House pierced the sky ahead. Its wooden steeple, still proud though weathered by wind and rain, rose above the bustling city like a sentinel. Just as Pilgrim's hooves struck the street's worn center stones, the deep, resonant clang of a bell rang out from within the building's steeple.

"Boom!"

It was not a crisp, singular note—it was heavy and deliberate, its power reverberating through the streets of the city, and through the heart now pounding within James.

The mightly bell struck again.

"Boom!"

He closed his eyes for a brief moment, inviting the vibration of the bell to root itself in his chest. The rising of the bell felt like a summoning, not just to the Congress, but to the memory of every hardship along the way. Every mile, every bruised bone, every vow whispered to the trees.

The bell struck a final time, as James prepared to answer its call.

James pulled the reins gently, bringing Pilgrim to a trot. Townsfolk turned to look, a few pausing their morning errands. The long and solemn notes played out like a heavenly herald. Under the shadows of a massive edifice, and the singing of the titan bell, the humble tavern owner secured Pilgrim to a nearby post and set about towards the delegates.

Pilgrim issued a soft nicker for James as he walked away from her, and positioned himself before the State House steps.

He began his climb.

The doors swung open with ease this time. No longer a stranger, but not yet a guest, James entered.

He had scarcely stepped inside the building when three figures emerged from the main hall—Caswell, Hewes, and Hooper—all walking with hurried purpose, their expressions unreadable. They surrounded him almost immediately, as though they had been waiting for the sound of his weathered frontier boots on the floor.

"Mr. Jack," Caswell said, extending a hand. "You are well met. We've reviewed the documents you carried from Charlotte."

"Gentlemen," James replied, steadying his breath. James could read their faces easily—respect, sympathy, and something else. Doubt.

"If you may, please follow us."

James followed the three men as they lead him away from the more visible sections of the hall, and into a room far more isolated. James could not yet determine what to gather from the men's hushed attitudes.

The room was sparsely adorned, yer everything within the four walls felt purposeful: the long wooden table with burnished legs, the dustless shine of a polished arm chair. James ran a hand along one of the chairs, grounding himself, as if the grain of the wood might pass its steadiness into his blood.

Joseph Hewes resumed the conversation.

"We wish first to thank you," Hewes spoke. "Your journey was no small feat. You've done your county proud. And you've done us proud."

"Thank you for your kind words," James responded.

Hewes continued.

"The spirit of your kin is commendable, and we celebrate their courage."

"But..." Hooper interjected gently, his voice marked with the kind of hesitation that only accompanies unwelcome truths.

James tensed as he looked upward at William Hooper. "But what?"

Richard Caswell's tone softened as he replied on Hooper's behalf.

"The Congress is... already at work on a formal petition to the King. An appeal for peace."

"The Olive Branch Petition, is what they are calling it," Hewes confirmed.

"A final attempt," Hooper added, "to avoid a war."

James could not believe the words that had just poured out impassively before him. Without meaning to, he stared for a moment, his eyes flicking from one face to the next.

"But sirs, the war has already begun. You know this," James persisted.

Caswell did not flinch. "A war with the armies of King George is not one that we could find victory. You know this, as well."

James instinctively shot back.

"I do not believe this to be true." James turned his head down in frustration, before raising it to speak in a tone more ablaze with anger.

"A petition? After everything that has happened?" James shook his head, his disbelief simmering into a fury. "The king will not listen, why not rally the colonies now, to fight!"

The three delegates shifted uncomfortably, and allowed for several seconds of agonizing silence.

Finally, Richard Caswell spoke. "We know the hearts of the men with whom we share the Congress with, Mr. Jack. The tide is not yet with us. The Mecklenburg Declaration... it would be dismissed outright. Or worse—seen as incendiary. Premature."

"Then take that chance, gentlemen. If it is true that the Congress still believes in reconciliation then make them see otherwise. "Tell them that war has already come," James said, his voice low but sharp. "Tell them that the king has sent his men to burn our homes, to trample our fields, to hang our neighbors. Ask them then, if they would still petition?"

James stepped forward, firmly gripping the back of a fine wooden chair. "What my kin-", James cut himself off and restarted. "What my countrymen have entrusted me to deliver is no mere request—it is a declaration. The men and women of Mecklenburg have already cast their lot. We are a free people now. We ask not for permission but for recognition, and for your support in our struggle!"

Richard Caswell stepped forward and spoke with a conflicted tone.

"And that support is freely given to you by all three of us, Mr. Jack, but we will not put forward a call for revolution as the Congress pens the final lines of their petition for peace."

James' stepped back, as if the distance might dull the sting of their cowardice, and for a moment he said nothing. But then the heat began to rise in him—the fire of the road and of lost nights in the wilderness. He thought of Morrison, of the burning woods, of the blood that stained the Susquehanna River. He thought of his mother and father, of Margaret and Cynthia and Patrick, and of the men who had risked everything to sign the paper now resting in these delegates' hands.

He looked them full in the eye and spoke with a clarity sharper than steel.

"Gentlemen, you may debate here about 'reconciliations' and memorialize your king, but bear it in mind, Mecklenburg owes no allegiance to, and is separated from the crown of Great Britain forever."

The words struck like a musket ball through fog—clean, final, and undeniable.

Caswell took a breath, but said nothing.

Hewes lowered his gaze.

Hooper simply nodded—one solemn movement, not of agreement, but of respect.

Caswell looked away, exhaling through his nose. "It is not that we disagree," he admitted. "But you must understand, Mr. Jack—there are many in this

Congress who do not yet have the will for independence. They still seek reconciliation, for the alternative is war unlike any we have known."

"Then let us hope they find their courage soon," James retorted. His voice did not shake, nor did he waver as he looked each of them in the eye.

Caswell reached into his pocket for a small purse of coins.

"Please, Mr. Jack, remain in Philadelphia and rest. You have no need to begin your return to Mecklenburg right away."

Still reeling in disappointment from the delegates, James now looked upon the purse with the same repulsion he felt for that morning's decadent breakfast.

With images of vast green hills, tall castles built of oak, sycamore and pine, the love of his family, and that uniquely blue Carolina sky, James faced the men.

"My cause here is done. I am going home."

James retrieved the Mecklenburg Declaration from the men in powdered wigs, and secured it within the fold of his storied haversack bag.

James turned without another word and walked back through the great hall. The moment had already passed, but the echo of it seemed to linger in the rafters above, like the last note of a hymn refusing to die.

Outside, the air was fresh with the scent of rain.

James descended the steps with his head high, the echo of his boots steady and unhurried. Pilgrim greeted him with a gentle nudge, and he untied her reins as if sealing a chapter closed.

He did not look back.

He did not need to.

For all the suffering of his long adventure, and for the courage he found in his own heart, James could not stir the same devotion in the conscious of the delegates.

The failure was devastating.

Yet as James looked upward into the clouds, somehow he felt confident that the journey had not been in vain. With the worthiness of the declaration's message now fully parted on him, James readied Pilgrim for their travel.

The wind was at his back, and though the Congress had not yet found their courage, James knew in his bones: they would soon.

The colonies would awaken. And when they did, they would find the courageous spirit of Mecklenburg there to lead them in liberty.

Chapter 20: An Abiding Cause

The sky was a pewter gray that morning, neither storming nor still—just heavy, like the weight James carried as he knelt down upon the dirt.

Dew clung to the grass like sweat, and the air smelled of ash and loam. The scent was bitter and raw. Smoke still lingered faintly in the wind, as if the fire that had consumed everything still whispered its threats.

The grave was simple. No headstone, only a wooden plank hammered into the soil, bearing his father's name carved by a careful hand: Patrick Jack. No dates. No epitaph. Just the truth of loss, sunk into the weeping earth like a great boulder.

James knelt there a long while, his father's tricorn hat pressed tightly against his chest, his head bowed in a silence that bore more than reverence—it bore confession.

His hand, calloused and stained from weeks on horseback, reached out to brush the edge of the plank. The carving was deep, it's etchings meant to be eternal.

"I should've carved it," James whispered softly.

A breeze stirred the long grass around the grave, the blades brushing James' coat like reaching fingers. He closed his eyes and remembered the last time he'd seen his father—standing by the courthouse, arms folded, that familiar look of knowing stubbornness drawn across his face.

James could not place the exact words his father had said to him, but the understanding that they were surely filled with a comforting kindness and humor, gripped James' heart in an unforgiving squeeze.

James remained knelt before the simple grave, his fist clinched tighter and tighter as he cried to himself softly, his mind wracked with desperation as he sought to fill his mind with the image, sound and touch of his departed hero.

When James set off from Charlotte, he thought surely he'd return with victory, with pride, with evidence that their gamble in the courthouse was worth every jeopardy.

Instead, James' had returned to see his home in ashes, his family broken, and his people scattered.

His lips moved in prayer, but the words trembled between a praise and plea.

"Forgive me, father. I wasn't here. I thought if I rode fast enough, if I delivered those words... maybe I'd come home to a place still standing. To you, still standing."

He swallowed hard, and looked down at the dirt, his fists clenched in his lap.

"I should've been here. I should've stood beside you when the redcoats came. I should've died here, in fire or in fight—not out there in clean halls and city streets. I rode to save someone I thought still lived. And I was too late."

The guilt that James felt disoriented the caliber of his own personal sufferings.

The words of tearful prayer scraped his throat. His breath was caught between irregular gasps.

He bowed his head until his forehead touched the earth.

"I love you," James meekly whispered.

In the silence that followed, a merciful release washed over James.

He saw again the warm glow of candles against the tavern walls, the ring of laughter echoing through the rafters. His father's boots creaked on the floorboards as he moved behind the bar, slapping shoulders and filling mugs. Despite his misery, James could not help but produce a soft chuckle at his father's many stories. There was always one ready on Patrick Jack's lips—some half-truth about the Regulators, or that time in the woods with the bear that "wasn't quite a bear, but close enough." The men of the tavern could not get enough of his tales.

James wiped his eyes, his shoulders rising slowly with a breath long held and now finally loosed.

No one had forced Patrick to remain in the tavern when the redcoats had come. James knew in his heart his father chose his end, just as he had every other chapter of his life.

And James knew deep down, that his father was glad with his journey. James opened his eyes, and placed his right hand upon the wooden marker at the grave.

James knew there was one more way he could make his father proud.

He stood, and walked the familiar path back towards the grounds of his home.

James walked across the scorched field, and before long, the charred bones of the tavern came into view.

The blazed earth crackled beneath his boots as James crossed the field. Each step felt heavier than the last, as if heat was still trapped beneath the blackened grass.

What remained of the tavern looked less like a building and more like the carcass of a creature devoured by flame. Beams collapsed inward like broken ribs. Stone and char framed the hollow shell of what once a lively gallery. Only the steps—just three of them—stood intact, jutting out from the soot like the last teeth of a burned-out mouth.

He stopped before them. For a moment, he saw it as it had been—painted shutters flung open to the breeze, the clatter of mugs and spoons, the clamor of men arguing over politics and pies. The warmth of hearthfire, of bodies packed tight on cold nights.

He heard his father's voice again: "James, you've got to watch the flame. Not just light it."

He'd always thought his father meant the fire in the hearth.

But now, James thought otherwise.

A soft murmur broke the stillness, and James looked up.

They were there.

At first, he saw only a handful—men in familiar militia coats, faces drawn, arms folded. But then more shapes emerged from between the trees, from behind stone fences, from the paths leading in from the west road. Dozens.

Maybe a hundred or more. The crowd swelled like a tide coming in on a ruined shore.

Some wore black. Others came in work shirts, sleeves rolled up, faces still smudged with soot. A few held children in their arms. James saw farmers, housewives, boys too young to hold muskets, and women who had lost sons and husbands but stood as straight as pine.

James' watched the members of his great extended family crowd the grounds around him.

He saw Thomas McKee, who'd lost three hogs in the surprise ambush on the British raiders, but smiled every time he retold it like a comic parable. He saw Ruth Tabb, who had pulled five neighbors into her cellar during the raid and only came out when the smoke thinned. There were two boys whispering behind a wagon wheel—one of them pretending to hold a sword, the other mimicking a horse.

And he saw his mother, wrapped in a shawl too thin for the weather, alongside his wife and children, who he had been reunited with the night before under the shelter of John Haigler. With Pilgrim secured in the lush fields of Haigler's lawn, James moved for the first time in weeks, alone.

A hush moved through the crowd as James stepped forward.

He didn't feel ready. He felt cracked and hollow. He knew not what support he could offer these people—his people—when he had failed to bring the power of the Congress behind their cause.

But still, they parted for him.

The path opened without a word, and in spite of the deathly silence, James could feel their loving embrace.

James walked forward, slowly, deliberately. He could feel every eye on him, every breath drawn back in anticipation. No one spoke. Even the cardinals had stilled in the trees.

At the steps, he paused. His fingers brushed the edge of the lowest one, worn smooth from years of boots, spills, stomps, and dances. He remembered standing on these very stones watching out over a sable sky on the night they created the declaration.

He never imagined he'd stand here like this.

James climbed the steps.

Just three. But they felt as towering as mountains.

From the top, he turned to face them—not as a rider, not as a messenger, but as a man laid bare.

The hush deepened. In the back, someone sniffled. A baby fussed and was quickly quieted. The air hung dense with breath and memory.

He took in the faces. Worn, smudged, scarred. He found no judgment there—only weariness. And the same question reflected again and again:

Was it worth it?

He drew in a long breath.

And he began—not with flourish, but with a truth.

"I come back to you," he began, voice low but steady, "not as a hero. Not as a savior. I come as your kin."

A breeze fluttered, and somewhere in the crowd, a baby let out a soft cry. No one moved. No one looked away.

"I come with dust in my lungs and smoke on my coat. I come with blood on my hands—not from battles fought, but from leaving them behind. I left this place to carry our voices. But I did not forget the sound of home."

He looked out across the people—faces he had known since childhood, others he had only passed in the market or seen from the saddle.

"I rode north not to seek glory, but to carry your truth. I rode with no flag, no escort. Only memory. I slept beside frozen creeks, I broke bread in solitude. I carried the call of Mecklenburg in my mouth like fire. I carried you."

He paused, wanting to deliver well his sermon. "When I arrived in Philadelphia, I did not walk into that hall with parchment. I walked in carrying the resolve of my countrymen: their fortitude, their grit, and their dreams."

A low murmur moved through the crowd—like the shifting of soil over roots.

"I stood before men who wore powdered wigs and silk stockings, who spoke of 'timing' and 'deliberation.' And I told them what we already knew: that the crown had abandoned us. That we owed no loyalty to a tyrant."

A few heads nodded in the crowd.

He lifted his voice, the weight behind it growing sharper.

"And yes, they refused our call to arms. They told me to wait. To be patient. To let the politicians of the Congress take their time with words. But I could not wait. We could not wait. The redcoats did not wait when they stifled our churches and bled our sons."

He stepped down one of the steps, closer to them.

"I did not leave that hall in shame. I left it in truth. I stood tall and declared before the delegates, *'Gentlemen, you may memorialize your king—but Mecklenburg owes no allegiance to the Crown of Great Britain, and is forever a free people!'"*

A cheer burst forth from the battered crowd, raw and surprised. Some clapped. A woman near the front wiped her eyes and held her child tighter.

James's voice softened, but it did not falter.

"I know what we have lost."

He looked to the horizon, his blues eyes damp but bright.

"I also know what we have gained; a crucible, in whose flames we have each found our lion-hearts."

"I heard a story of that night, where in the hills of the Waxhaws, Jackson's boy, not yet old enough to hold a shaving razor, stood firm against a British blade. That boy was Andrew. You know his name, and one day, I have no doubt the world will too."

A hush again.

"My own father, Patrick, glances joyfully down upon us from God's assembly. We are all bound in Providence."

James' turned his gaze to two boys sitting on a barrel—still whispering, pretending to ride invisible horses, while one of them raised a stick like a sword.

"When the redcoats came, we did not waver. We did not hide. We honored the resistance of our ancestors and gave the first of a thousand worthy fights in the pursuit of liberty."

He took another step down. Only one left now.

"Until Moses parts a second sea, we will remain in our struggle. Until Job curses the heavens, we will be steadfast in our faith. Until the roots of Jesse wither, we will remain planted in this ground. To our children's children, this is yours to inherit. "

The silence was no longer hollow. It was reverent.

James looked around once more, eyes locking with face after face. "The world may never know our names. But they will know our defiance. Because in the fire of our trials, and in the depth of our tribulations, we have found truly, an abiding cause."

James stepped down the last stair, and walked into the crowd.

It was not drunken courage or an unprincipled contagion that brought the crowd to cheer for the homeward hero, it was a battle-hardened and trial-tested resolve that resurrected their spirits.

Through the crowds James saw his mother moving toward him. She looked older—frailer than he remembered—but her eyes were the same. Soft, and storm-strong. She said nothing. Just reached for his hand and squeezed.

"You brought him back with you," she said quietly. "Your father. You brought him back in your voice."

James blinked hard. "I only wish he could've heard it."

She looked toward the sky. "Oh, he did."

They stood together alongside Margaret, Cynthia and Patrick. Together they held one another closely, and drank freely from their united fountain of healing and love.

James looked out over the land. It was still wounded. Still smoldering in places. But it was theirs.

And they would rebuild.

Not just the tavern. Not just the homes. But their spirit.

The kindling had caught, and somewhere beneath the ash, the flame had survived.

He turned toward the road, the long dirt path winding eastward. Tomorrow, he would help to clear the wreckage. He'd help lay new beams. He'd teach the boys how to load a musket, and show the girls how to tend wounds and wield words. Tankards would once again be raised—not just in memory of the road traveled, but in promise of all that remained.

But today... today, James walked the hills of Mecklenburg once more, not as a messenger, nor as a soldier—but as a proud and grateful son of Charlotte.

Epilogue I
Halifax, North Carolina
April 12th, 1776

The town of Halifax stirred early—wagon wheels creaked over muddy roads, and horses stamped their hooves outside the meeting hall. It was a sunny April morning, and history was beginning to rustle beneath the redbud trees.

Robert Irwin dismounted his steed near the edge of town, his boots sinking into the soft ground as he landed. He patted the horse's flank, then reached inside his coat pocket and curled his fingers around the small wooden cross tucked safely therein.

Cynthia's cross.

James had given the cross to his friend before he set off on his travel to join the 4th North Carolina Provincial Congress. James had pressing it into his friend's hand with a whisper: "For the next rider."

Robert walked the rest of the way through Halifax with quiet purpose, passing groups of men gathered under awnings and balconies, speaking in low tones that buzzed with anticipation. There was no need to ask why he had come. Every man here bore the same expression—with equal parts determination and weariness.

They came from every corner of the colony: farmers from Rowan, merchants from New Bern, blacksmiths from the Piedmont, surveyors from the Cape Fear. They brought with them not just votes and voices—but scars, stories, and the heavy air of change long in the making.

And at the center of it all stood the hall, its windows thrown open, its doors wide as if to welcome the birth of something truly bold.

Inside, the Fourth Provincial Congress had already begun its session.

Robert slipped into the chamber quietly, taking his seat among the delegates. The air was warm with breath and candle smoke, and the oak beams above held echoes of voices still lingering from days before. He recognized many of the men: Richard Caswell, sharp-eyed and steady, Joseph Hewes, fresh from his travels in Philadelphia, and William Hooper, whose pen had drafted a thousand letters and whose patience had been tested by twice as many delays.

Statesmen and planters now prepared to join in the great backcountry-led conspiracy.

Caswell stood.

"Gentlemen, we gather to determine whether this colony shall remain one with Great Britain, or if we shall charter our own course forward."

The silence that followed was no silence at all, but instead, a pause matted with breath, thought, and the rolling thunder of distant consequence.

Robert's eyes drifted to the window. Outside, beyond the muddy streets and the hum of conversation, was a North Carolina that was ready for war.

"In May of last year, a legion of patriots stormed the gates at Tryon Palace. Its gilded walls and soaring ceilings now belonging to our provincial government."

Caswell paused before continuing.

"Then came our victory at Moore's Creek Bridge."

Robert had not fought there, but he had heard the stories a dozen times over: how the loyalists charged the plank-bridge in the early morning fog, only to be met by a tangle of sabers and musket fire from the patriot lines. A swift, staggering victory. And in its wake, the final unraveling of British control.

"In the wake of our triumph, Governor Josiah Martin fled once more upon his ship, unable to raise his troops in Wilmington, and now forever stranded off our shore."

In response to this summary, the room erupted into cheers and jubilation.

And as Robert sat among the rows of men, he could tell clearly that the question no longer lingered in shadowed corners or whispered behind the cover of towering oaks. It was spoken, written, and read aloud in the chamber:

"That the delegates for this colony, in the Continental Congress, be empowered to concur with the delegates of the other colonies in declaring independence..."

Robert's chest tightened. He reached again for the cross.

He thought of James.

Of the night they'd sat beneath the stars, firelight licking their boots, James still raw from what he'd seen in Philadelphia. "They don't know what we've already decided," he had said. "The rest of them are just catching up."

And now, on that pleasant morning in the season of bloom, they were.

Caswell read the resolve a second time.

"That they use their utmost endeavors to obtain an equal and just peace..."

A few whispers ran through the chamber.

Hooper leaned forward, his voice smooth but firm. "This is not an act of rash rebellion. It is a formal answer to a long tyranny. We are not separating from the king—we are acknowledging that he abandoned us first."

Another delegate stood, Thomas Eaton of Bute County. "Let us not forget that our people already shed blood for this cause. This is not a question of if we fight for freedom. Only whether we do so as free men."

A long pause. Then Caswell nodded—once, firmly.

The vote was taken. Voices rang out, clear and full.

Aye. Aye. Aye.

Not a single dissent.

It was done.

North Carolina had spoken before any other colony. And with that declaration—the Halifax Resolves—the path to full independence opened like a sun breaking through morning fog.

Robert sat again, the cross still warm in his hand. While seated in the wooden chair, a soft current of hard-fought peace wrapped around him. He smiled lightly.

Later that day, he stood by the banks of the Roanoke River as the sun slipped west. The water shimmered in the wind. Spring birds called from the trees. A few of the other delegates had gathered to stretch their legs or smoke their pipes. He stayed a step apart, watching the current.

Robert had no need for further discussion. He stood dutifully and looked ahead.

The river, like the people, like the wind, was rushing onward. Unstoppable.

And somewhere back in Mecklenburg, perhaps atop a mighty green hill, or walking the fields beyond the old tavern steps, Robert was certain James Jack could feel that wind too.

Epilogue II
Elbert County, Georgia
September 13th, 1820

The road to the Jack homestead wound gently through late-summer fields, where the corn had already been harvested and the leaves along the riverbank whispered of coming autumn. Dust clung to the cuffs of Levi Harper's trousers as he dismounted, tying his mare to the split-rail fence before approaching the modest house nestled in the gentle shade of pecan trees.

He had never been this far south before.

Georgia's sun felt different here—older somehow, as if it burned slower in reverence for the lives it warmed. The air smelled of hickory and tobacco and earth turned many times by calloused hands.

A man stood on the porch, broad-shouldered and near Levi's own age, wiping his hands on a cloth. His shirt was rolled to the elbows, and he wore the look of someone who didn't take kindly to interruptions—but carried decency in his bearing.

"You're the writer," the man said, not unkindly.

"I am," Levi replied. "Levi Harper, *Carolina Gazette.* I sent word ahead—"

"You did." The man stepped aside and nodded toward the door. "He's waiting."

Levi crossed the porch, boots tapping softly on the weathered wood. "You're his son?"

"Patrick Jack," the man said, offering a firm handshake. "Named for my grandfather. He's been expectin' you since morning."

Inside, the house was quiet, the kind of quiet built by time rather than silence. The scent of old paper and pine lingered faintly beneath the rafters.

James Jack sat in an old rocking chair by the window, where the light could fall across his lap and catch the silver of his hair. His frame, once formidable, had softened with age—shoulders bent slightly forward, hands resting on the arms of the chair. A thin wool blanket covered his knees, though the afternoon was still warm.

He turned slowly as Levi entered, eyes sharp despite the years. They were pale blue—faded, but not dulled.

"Mr. Jack," Levi said, bowing his head. "It's an honor."

James gave a small nod. "Come in, son. Sit where the light's good. You've come a ways."

"I have. I wanted to meet the man behind the legend."

In response to this comment, the old soldier's lips curved into a humble smile.

Levi settled into the chair across from him, pulling a folded page from his satchel. "I was recently in conversation with some men up in the Carolinas.

Your name—your story—was on the lips of every patriot from Hillsborough to Charleston. They called you a hero."

James' gaze drifted toward the window. The humble man of seven and a half decades was at a loss for words.

He looked back towards the young journalist.

"I answered the call of my young country."

Levi leaned forward, eager to hear more from the seasoned patriot. "It's said you refused promotion until the war was won. That you led men into battle, but never once sought to rise above them."

James nodded once. "Aye."

"Why?"

He took a breath, slow and shallow. "I only ever wanted to see my people live in freedom from the crown."

The wind outside stirred the trees, and the soft creak of a rocking chair echoed from the back porch. Somewhere, a bird called.

Levi looked around the room—bare, simple, honest. No medals. No portraits. Only a small bookshelf, a rifle mounted above the mantle, and what looked like a hand-carved wooden cross resting in the windowsill, smoothed from years of handling.

Levi swallowed the lump in his throat. He'd expected pride, perhaps even grandeur. He hadn't expected grace.

He stood slowly, knowing not to press further. "Thank you, Mr. Jack. For your time. And for your service."

James gave a nod—smaller this time, but no less certain. His voice, though worn, held firm.

"I served in the revolution from its commencement to its close."

Levi smiled, placing a hand briefly over his heart.

"Aye," he said with reverence, "that you did."

Levi shook James' elderly hand, and exited quietly from the home of the humble hero.

In the hush of that simple wooden house, Levi looked back one last time to see the old man sitting by the window, rocking slowly—and enjoying a quiet sunset over the endless American frontier.

Afterword

I want to begin this afterword by expressing my deep gratitude for the opportunity to write this book. The past three years have been an unending adventure of discovery. As a first-time novelist, I was fortunate to build my debut story upon the rich, palpable, and exciting history of Charlotte's revolutionary past.

In this section, I'd like to share a bit about my process for developing the story — particularly the balance I sought to strike between historical accuracy and creative fiction.

First and foremost, I want to reiterate to the reader that *The Legend of James Jack* is a work of historical fiction. Creative liberties were taken throughout, and I'd like to highlight several of the major ones here.

If we accept the account published in the April 30, 1819 issue of the *Raleigh Register and North Carolina Gazette*, written by John McKnitt Alexander, to be historically accurate, then the first two chapters of this novel unfold largely as history tells it. An express rider (unnamed in traditional tellings) from Massachusetts arrives in Charlotte on the evening of May 19, 1775. According to most accounts, he stumbled upon a militia meeting already in progress. In my version of the story, the rider first stops at Pat Jack's tavern — a creative choice meant to introduce that setting.

From there, the Mecklenburg Declaration is written through the night and into the early hours of May 20th. Historical tradition holds that James Jack volunteered to carry the document to the Continental Congress in Philadelphia. From that point onward, however, many of the novel's details become increasingly fictionalized.

For example, the real-life James Jack was approximately 43 years old at the time of his journey, whereas in my telling, he is roughly fifteen years younger. It is also unlikely that he rode a single horse the entire way, and the character of Pilgrim is entirely fictional. The inclusion of Tom Jamison and John Haigler were personal tributes to my own family history and are not meant to represent actual historical figures.

Creative liberty was also taken with the characterization of James Jack himself. While he lived a well-documented and respected life, much about his personality remains unknown to historians. As such, most of the traits, motivations, and interactions attributed to James — and many of the other characters — should be considered fictional.

Traditionally, the story of James Jack recounts that he "rode the 550 miles to Philadelphia and delivered the declaration to the delegates, who deemed it premature." Later versions mention that he "slipped past British regulars, spies, and thieves," but little detail is provided. That absence of detail is precisely what inspired me to write this novel. By drawing upon real people, places, and events, I aimed to build upon the heroic framework of the traditional account and expand it into a complete, emotionally driven journey.

Some characters — such as the "esquires" — were loosely based on real loyalists from Salisbury who, according to some accounts, had a confrontation with James Jack. However, there is no evidence that either man traveled to New Bern.

Speaking of New Bern (the beautiful town I currently call home), it's worth noting that Tryon Palace, its fall to patriot forces in the spring of 1775, and the escape of North Carolina's final royal governor, Josiah Martin, are all based in fact. However, the character of Edward Morrison and the British soldiers featured in the book are fictional creations. While Tryon Palace did fall into patriot hands in May 1775, it is not linked to any battle in Charlotte. The actual Battle of Charlotte occurred in 1780 — five years later — and did indeed involve the destruction of Pat Jack's tavern. As for Patrick Jack's death, the historical record is less clear. British soldiers are said to have "removed" him from his home and business, and the shock of that loss is believed to have caused his death sometime afterward. My depiction of his death — along with other dramatic elements like the livestock stampede — are fictional.

Other real-world details include the towns of Bruce's Crossroads and Bloomsbury, both of which existed in North Carolina at the time. James' encounters with smugglers, soldiers, and thieves, however, are entirely fictional.

If you would like to learn more about which elements of the story were historically accurate, which were inspired by real events, and which were purely fictional, please visit the book's website: www.thelegendofjames-jack.com

Once again, thank you for allowing me the privilege of joining the long line of storytellers who have sought to preserve and share the legacy of James Jack and the Mecklenburg Declaration. It's been one hell of a ride.

Acknowledgements

This book would not have been possible without the support, guidance, and encouragement of so many people, and I am deeply grateful to each of them.

First and foremost, I thank God for granting me the life, perspective, and passion to complete this project. Every step of this three-year long journey has been guided by His hand, and I am humbled daily by his mercies.

To my family, who have endured countless conversations about history, plot details, and revisions—your patience, enthusiasm, and unwavering belief in me have been the foundation upon which this novel was built. The endless phone calls, creative suggestions, and general encouragement has been invaluable.

To my wife, Erin, who has encouraged my fondness of history in all of our many adventures together, your unconditional love has uplifted me through the sleepless nights that becoming a debut author often entail. Your belief in this story, but more importantly in me, has brought my life daily joys beyond imagination.

To the lifetime of mentors at Philadelphia Presbyterian Church, living and deceased, kin and otherwise, your dedication to preserving our shared heritage has inspired me in more ways than I can begin to adequately express. Your faithful stewardship ensured I always found a home within our sanctuary, and for this I am forever grateful.

To local author, Scott Syfert, whose meticulous research and dedication to the Mecklenburg Declaration of Independence laid the foundation for so much of this book, I am also thankful. His work, *The First American Declaration of Independence?*, was a crucial resource, and I am indebted to his scholarship.

I would also like to extend a heartfelt thanks to my friend, Lonnie Hastings, for his partnership in marketing this novel. Your expertise, creativity, and camaraderie has been a welcomed company throughout this process.

Lastly, to the readers of this novel—thank you. By picking up this book, you've afforded me the privilege of sharing the story of a heritage that I treasure deeply. The rolling hills of Mecklenburg (and Union) county is the place I was raised, the Presbyterian faith what has steadied me my entire life. The strength, humor, love and devotion of the Scots-Irish Presbyterian has been a constant in my life, and I hope that in the pages of this novel you've found a small piece of that essence that resonates with you. I am grateful for the opportunity to add one small chapter to the legend and tradition of Charlotte's greatest hero.

About the author

Zachary Allen was born in Charlotte, North Carolina, and raised in the neighboring town of Indian Trail. His love for local history began with his upbringing in a two-and-a-half-century-old Presbyterian church, where he became the seventh generation of his family to attend. He later moved across the state to attend East Carolina University, earning a Bachelor's in Political Science with a minor in History—along with a deep appreciation for the landscapes and heritage of Eastern North Carolina.

As an eighth-grade history teacher, Zachary enjoys bringing the past to life for his students, blending education with storytelling. When he's not sharing his passion for American and North Carolinian history, he enjoys surf-fishing along the coast and day-tripping with his wife, Erin. He also spends countless hours lost in the rich and exciting worlds of history—both real and imagined.

To stay updated on Zachary's upcoming books, visit:

www.allenhistoricalpress.com